Has the Death Merchant's time run out at last?

Camellion thought of turning back, of scratching the kill-probe. Certainly, to continue was to increase his chances of getting his head blown off. But he couldn't keep running and dodging for the remainder of his life.

And so he moved from tree to tree, stopped, waited, looked around, and moved again. Much closer now, the house became three dimensional; massive, virulent, deadly. It was alive! A cold-blooded enemy, waiting to devour him!

The four guards spotted Camellion at the same time he sighted them. He had hoped to cut them down before they could fire a warning shot. If he could, he might then be able to smear the jokers in the jeeps before they could swing into action and throw lead in his direction.

No such luck. . . .

Come on, Brother Death, Camellion thought, *let's go to work!*

The Death Merchant Series:

#32 in the incredible adventures of the

DEATH MERCHANT
DEADLY MANHUNT
by Joseph Rosenberger

PINNACLE BOOKS   LOS ANGELES

DEATH MERCHANT #32:
DEADLY MANHUNT

Copyright © 1979 by Joseph Rosenberger

An original Pinnacle Books edition, published for the first time anywhere.

First printing, February 1979

ISBN: 0-523-40475-1

Cover illustration by Dean Cate

Printed in the United States of America

PINNACLE BOOKS, INC.
2029 Century Park East
Los Angeles, California 90067

This book is dedicated to

Donald Hamel, Esq.
Michiana Shores
Michigan City, Ind.

Aggression is primarily not a reaction to outside stimuli, but a built-in inner excitation that seeks for release and will find expression regardless of how adequate the outer stimulus is: it is the spontaneity of the instinct that makes it so dangerous.
—K. Lorenz, 1966

Man is a killer—with six thousand years of excuses behind him!
—Richard J. Camellion

Chapter One

That parked car! It's a trap!

Richard Camellion was not surprised. He had expected trouble ever since he had returned to the United States, several days earlier. While still in Seoul, South Korea, he had arranged to have trusted CIA agents have a small Lear jet waiting for him in Los Angeles. With one of the company men he had flown from L.A. to Valle Hermoso, Mexico, a small town only 37 miles southwest of Brownsville, Texas. The spook had taken off with the jet, to take the plane back to L.A. Armed with two 9mm Browning autoloaders, Camellion had taken the Jeepster—also supplied by the CIA—to the weatherworn ranch of Juan Sontoya, the elder brother of Jesus Sontoya. For nine years, Jesus Sontoya had taken care of Camellion's ranch in the Big Thicket region of Texas—until he had been murdered!

Jesus Sontoya had been found hanged with piano wire, dangling from a beam in Camellion's living room.

His eyes on the car parked half a mile ahead, the Death Merchant recalled the words of Juan Sontoya: *"Yo acostumbro, Senor Camellion, llamar al pan pan y al vino vino.* Whoever it was that killed Jesus did it to convey a message to you. His arms and legs were broken before he was hanged. It was not the work of thieves. Your house was left in perfect order. *Amigo,* someone has marked you for death."

"Senor Sontoya, I too am used to calling a spade a spade," Camellion had said. "I know I'm the real target. Whoever killed Jesus wants me to know I've been tagged in the game of death. I'll tell you something else, *compañero.* The man, or men, who killed him will answer to me. I'll find out who did it and I'll be the judge, jury and executioner. That's a promise."

Juan Sontoya had only shaken his head and muttered, *"Tu le andas buscando los pies al gato y te va a pesar. . . ."*

1

The words burning in his mind, Camellion permitted a trace of a smile to play along the corners of his mouth. *Yes, Juan. I'm looking for trouble. But I definitely won't be sorry.*

Keeping one hand on the steering wheel, the Death Merchant pulled one of the Browning automatics from its shoulder holster and placed it next to him on the seat. With his eyes on the station wagon and the woman standing on the road next to the blue and white Ford, only a quarter of a mile in front of him, he switched off the air conditioning system, then rolled down the window on the right side and picked up the Browning.

He had to give them credit for cleverness, whoever they were. The spot up ahead was ideal for an ambush. On either side of the concrete ribbon of road was desert scrub land, with tall, stately Saguaro cacti, a wasteland of heat baking in the midafternoon sun. The road itself stretched out as straight as an arrow, but turned sharply to the left several hundred feet ahead of the station wagon. A hundred feet to the left, directly across from the station wagon, was a chopped up mass of hills covered with sand and broken shale.

He slowed the Jeepster slightly, the strangeness of the trap digging at one side of his mind. How had they known he would go to Valle Hermoso? How had they known *when* he would go to Valle Hermoso and *when* he would be on the road to Brownsville?

It was the woman standing by the car who had given away the show, who had tipped Camellion to the danger. Cars do break down in the desert. Women do get out and try to flag down help. *But they don't do it with a baby in their arms! With a blanket around the baby! Not in 112 degree heat!* Even a dumb mother would keep an infant inside the car, and if the car wasn't air conditioned, she wouldn't take the baby from inside the vehicle wrapped in a heavy blanket. No way. Nor would she stand there in the hot sun wearing only shorts and a halter.

Camellion was now a few hundred feet from the rear of the Ford station wagon. He slowed a bit more, giving the impression he was about to stop by the side of the woman, who was waving one hand, signalling him to "help" her.

Within the next five seconds, Camellion sized up the

2

woman and the car. In her mid-twenties, the woman wore large sun glasses and a straw hat, long blond hair hanging from underneath the hat. From the way she held the blanket, he was positive that it was either wrapped around a doll—*or a submachine gun. We'll know very soon.*

There wasn't any way he could be certain, but hadn't he caught a glimpse of figures moving in the rear seat? It was all very simple and very deadly. He was supposed to stop and help the woman. She and the others would then blast him. And unless they were rank amateurs, they would have a backup—*in the hills. To catch me in a crossfire. Or to head me off, should the doll and her people fail to do the job.*

Seventy or so feet from the rear of the station wagon, Camellion thumbed off the safety of the Browning, raised the hand gun and turned the steering wheel to the left, swinging the Jeepster off the road. As the vehicle started to leave the concrete, he fired through the open window, the sharp cracks of the Browning stabbing holes in the stillness of the hot desert.

His first bullet tore through the top end of the white blanket, several inches where the top of the baby's head would have been, if there had been a baby in the blanket. The woman instantly proved there wasn't, that Camellion had been right. Her surprise turned to fear. She dropped the blanket to the ground, one section falling open to reveal an Ingram Model 10 submachine gun.

The woman didn't dare try to get back inside the car. Camellion's five other slugs were stabbing through the rear window and into the left side of the station wagon. In desperation, the woman dropped flat and tried to crawl to the front of the car while glass shattered and full metal jacketed slugs cut through metal.

The Death Merchant didn't have time to see the results of his sudden attack. He couldn't steer with only one hand, not on the rough and uneven terrain. He dropped the Browning on the seat, grabbed the steering wheel with his right hand and, pushing down on the gas, headed the Jeepster toward a long hollow between two high mounds of rock 150 feet to the northwest. There was a flash of light several hundred feet to the north, as if the rays of the sun had momentarily struck a mirror. The Death Merchant, realizing that the sun had flashed from some

3

part of a weapon, began to swerve the Jeepster. Several weapons—*they sounded like CAR-15 carbines!*—began firing, the projectiles thudding into the Jeepster. High velocity 5.56mm projectiles stabbed holes in the right rear window and, continuing on their way, filled the left rear window with spiderwebs of cracks. Other slugs, hitting hard outside steel, ricocheted with screaming whines. Several bullets, burning the hot air on their deadly route through the right front window, came dangerously close to the Death Merchant. One barely missed his hand as it first struck the steering wheel, then glanced off to smash through the inside of the front glass, a foot and a half to his right. The second long bullet, coming in from the right, clipped the edge of the front brim of Camellion's Western styled Moose River hat and took its leave through the left front window. It was only by pure luck, compounded with the bouncing up and down of the Jeepster, that Camellion escaped being hit.

Camellion fought the wheel. Engine roaring, tires crunching over small rocks, the Jeepster headed for the two rocky hills.

There were slight ripping sounds as slugs, angling downward, tore through the vinyl roof and thudded into the front and rear seats. Several narrowly missed Camellion, the closest cutting through the brim of his hat, missing his right shoulder by less than half an inch.

The glass in the rear window dissolved and so did part of the front windshield, from slugs fired by the would-be assassins who had been in the car by the road. More slugs zipped through the roof from the CAR-15s being triggered from the summit of a hill to the north.

Worried because he had only the two Brownings, Camellion drove the Jeepster between the two hills, slammed on the brakes, picked up the Browning on the seat, then jumped out of the vehicle, pulling the second autoloader the instant his feet were on the hard ground.

A quick glance around revealed that there was less than six feet of space between the vehicle and the side of the hill on the right side and less than five feet on the left side. Neither jagged hill was higher than twenty-five feet, the sides sloping sharply. Both inner sides were also riddled with cave openings, the result of enormous gas bubbles, hundreds of millions of years ago when the formation solidified at the bottom of the sea and later rose to the surface. The Death Merchant had been in such caves before and knew that they were usually confined to the surface and were never very long; furthermore, they usually had more than one opening.

Camellion didn't waste time. Since the killers from the station wagon had to be closer to the Jeepster than the riflemen on the hill, Camellion ran to the right of the vehicle and took a position by the corner of the hill, getting down behind a slab of limestone that jutted upward from the ground.

I've boxed myself in, but it's the only thing I can do at this time. He looked around from the side of the rock and there they were: the woman from the station wagon and three men, the woman carrying the short Ingram, the men armed with Armalite-18 rifles. All four—perhaps a hundred feet to the southeast of the Jeepster—were advancing slowly.

Stupid amateurs! Camellion moved from the side of the rock, raised the twin Brownings and snap-fired, pulled the triggers so fast the cracks of the shots sounded almost as one. The woman screamed and jerked violently from the impact of a 9mm bullet that smashed between her breasts. She dropped the machine gun, spun to her left and fell to the ground. Simultaneously, two of the men cried out in agony as 100-grain projectiles popped into their chests and ended their lives.

The fourth man was quick-thinking. If he had tried to fire at the Death Merchant, the few seconds lag time would have been against him. But the man didn't attempt the impossible. Instead, before Camellion could put a bullet into his body, the man flung himself behind a small hill. Camellion shook his head. From this end it was a Mexican standoff.

He ran to the other end of the narrow space and crouched down behind a tombstone-shaped rock. He took off his hat and, holding it between thumb and forefinger, held it out from the side of the rock so that part of the brim and part of the crown were exposed. Camellion wasn't surprised when CAR-15s roared to the north and streams of 5.56mm slugs pulverized the half of the hat that was exposed, the swaged projectiles stopping when they cut into the grill of the Jeepster. All of it was bad news for the Death Merchant because the projectiles had come straight in on the horizontal, which meant that the rest of the attackers had come down from the hilltop and were trying to close in on his position.

Knowing how the last man on Earth must have felt when he heard a knock at the door, Camellion analyzed the situation. While a man always needed a certain amount of luck in any fire-fight, whether or not he would live depended mostly on experience and his ability to think of techniques in the field; and one had to be willing to gamble, as Camellion was now. There is never an easy way.

Still on the right side of the Jeepster, Camellion hurried to the center of the hill and moved into the mouth of the largest cave. Reloading one Browning, he heard more CAR carbine shots and presumed that the men who had been on the hill were trying to get him to return their fire, in an attempt to pinpoint his position. There was also the lone man to the south to contend with. There wasn't any way of knowing what he might do. Either he would retreat to the station wagon or stay put to await developments. He could be crazy-brave and advance, Camellion thought. *I just hope I haven't picked a tunnel that doesn't have more than one opening.*

Camellion pulled a penlight from one inside pocket of his featherweight pants and flashed the tiny beam around the low tunnel, all the while hoping that a startled scorpion or tarantula wouldn't drop on him. Bare, gray rock stared back at him. A tiny Dubaro lizard scampered frantically to escape the light. Ahead, the tunnel dwindled off into inky blackness.

Browning in one hand, pistol in the other, the Death Merchant moved ahead, the beam poking into the darkness. His finely honed sense of distance and direction told him he was moving to the southeast, away from the men who had been on the hill, but toward the lone killer who had been in the station wagon.

He estimated that he had moved 150 feet when, suddenly, far ahead, he saw the faint glow of another light— a light that moved back and forth, so it couldn't be sunlight from another tunnel opening. This light came from a flashlight, the glow indicating that it was coming from where the tunnel turned sharply to the east. No doubt about it, someone was coming from the opposite direction.

Camellion did some trigger-quick thinking. The men to the north wouldn't have had time to run to the south and go into another entrance. The light ahead had to be car-

6

ried by the single survivor of the group who had been in the station wagon; and since the man had had the foresight to bring a flashlight, he must be familiar with the area. How else could he know about the tunnels that riddled the hills?

It's going to be a turkey shoot! Camellion switched off the penlight, shoved it into his pocket and walked over to the rock wall on the left side. He lay down flat on the dirty floor and pulled the other Browning. He didn't have long to wait. Presently, the glow ahead turned toward him, and the yellow glow became an "eye" that moved back and forth, from side to side, as the man swung the flashlight from wall to wall.

The Death Merchant pulled the triggers of both Brownings twice when the man was less than 70 feet away, the four shots sounding twice as loud—ear-shattering—within the confines of the tunnel. The doomed man didn't utter a sound. Killed instantly, he dropped the flashlight and the rifle . . . sighed, died, and sagged forward to the rocky floor.

Camellion jumped up, sprinted to the man lying face down, and rolled him over. Sightless eyes stared back at him. Camellion studied the man. In life, he had been about thirty. Cleanshaven, he had wavy black hair and a chin with a deep cleft in the center.

Searching the corpse, Camellion found a .45 Colt automatic, a spare magazine of 5.56mm cartridges and a billfold. The driver's license identified the man as Cecil Bradlough, of Ocameron, a small town only twenty miles from the Mexican border. *Hmmmm, local Texas talent.*

He picked up the rifle and inspected it. The clip contained nineteen cartridges. The 20th round was in the firing chamber. A fine weapon, having a gas piston rather than a direct gas blowback system, the AR-18 was similar to the German Gewehr 43 and the Soviet Model 40 Tokarev rifle. Camellion decided that whoever was trying to kill him certainly wasn't stingy about weaponry.

Camellion picked up the flashlight and hurried down the passage through which the dead man had come. Another twisting 200 feet and he saw daylight—sunlight—in the distance. He switched off the flashlight, threw it to the ground and darted forward, stopping within six feet of the entrance. He switched off the safety of the AR-18, pushed the selector to full automatic and moved to the right side of the entrance, which was shaped like an upside down V. He paused and listened. Not a sound, except the low, eerie sound of the wind blowing through the mouth of the tunnel. He looked out around the side of the wall, looked in both directions and ahead, toward the other hill. Nothing, nothing but desert and barren rock.

The shots inside the cave would have sounded muffled from the outside; yet the other men had to have heard them and guessed that he had made contact with the gunsels from the station wagon. *But they won't know who walked away, now will they?* Now the question was whether they would wait, approach the Jeepster, or come around this side of the hill, or over it. There was another alternative. They might come through the other tunnel entrance.

Camellion looked at the hill across from him—sixty feet to the east. It was a risk. But life itself is a risk. He left the cave, dashed across the sixty foot space and began to race up the side of the hill, his suede Wallabees digging into sand and rocks. Within a few minutes he had reached the top and was throwing himself down on the other side, just over the ridge. He looked around in the bright sunlight. Nothing. No sign of life. He put on his dark sunglasses and studied the area. From this hilltop position he could see very clearly the Ford station wagon on the road. At the moment, another car was passing, but it didn't stop. No driver in his right mind would, not on this highway. There was always too much danger of being robbed, either by Mexicanos or by *basura gringos* from Texas. The car roared by and was gone.

Camellion also had a full view of the east slope of the hill he had just left, as well as its summit. To the north were more hills and scattered slabs of sandstone.

He looked at his wristwatch—3:34 P.M. Several minutes later he saw the first man creeping in from the north, coming around the bottom of the hill to the west. Camellion snuggled down and waited. A few moments more and he saw the heads and torsos of two more of the enemy. Both were together and both were coming up the west incline of the hill across from him. If they studied the hilltop on which he lay, they would soon discover his position toward the center of the ridge. He looked down at the first man, who was advancing very slowly. Then a fourth man came around from the north end of the hill and hurried up to the first man Camellion had spotted. All four men carried Colt CAR-15 submachine guns.

Camellion realized that he couldn't afford to wait; to do so would be analogous to a drowning man grasping at shadows. He was rearing up to fire when a fifth man came around from the north end of the hill. But it was too late for the Death Merchant to wait for the man to catch up with the other two. He had time only to glance at the fifth man and see that he was young, had a shaggy mustache, was dressed in khaki slacks and shirt and wore an open weave tropic cap to match.

In another split second, Camellion was standing erect and dropping the barrel of the AR-18 toward the two men on the other hill, who had started to drop down, freezing momentarily when they saw him. By then, a stream of 5.56mm projectiles was leaving Camellion's rifle, at a muzzle velocity of 3200 feet per second, and the two men on the hill were riddled before they could even raise their CAR submachine guns.

The three men on the ground, by the side of the hill, had only seconds to raise their sub-guns and fire. The squat, cob-nosed man halfway succeeded. He was raising his CAR-15 and pulling the trigger at the same time that Camellion, who had jumped six feet to the left, to a new position, swung the automatic rifle down and raked the side of the hill with the remainder of the clip. Cob-nose's slugs missed the Death Merchant by a good six feet, only he never knew it. Stone dead, the skin of his chest hanging bloodily over his ribs, he was being pitched backward by the force of Camellion's four slugs . . . tripping over the second man who had come around the hillside and who was trying to raise his submachine gun. He failed. His face and neck vanished in a spray of flesh, blood and chips of bone and he sagged like a wet sack of sawdust.

The third man, however, was luckier and much faster than his two companions. He didn't give Camellion any precious lag time by trying to snap up his CAR-15 and trigger off even a short burst. Like a highly trained acrobat, he threw himself back a split second before Camellion's three projectiles burned the air where he had stood. The Death Merchant dropped the muzzle and fired almost at the same time. Too late. Hitting the ground on his back, the man somersaulted backward, jumped up and disappeared around the end of the hill.

Camellion was so disgusted that he cursed in Russian—
"*Sookynsyn!*"[1] He didn't linger to stare after the man, who
had amazed him with his speed and agility. He quickly reloaded the AR-18 and ran down the east side of the hill,
determined to kill the last survivor of the hit force that
had tried to kill him and so far had failed.

He darted to the north end of the hill, dropped down
behind a slab of sandstone and looked out to his left, toward the end side of the hill to the west. The lone gunman
was not there. Camellion looked around the other side of
the rock, his keen eyes grabbing the other hills. He quickly
eliminated the three mounds to his right.

*Jumping Boy didn't have time to get to one of them. I
would have seen him. He has to be behind the big hill to
the left.*

For several moments he studied the long rocky rise
which was a hundred feet north of the two hills between
which the Jeepster was parked. There was only one tiny
flaw: there wasn't any cover. To reach the south side of
the long rise, Camellion would have to race 150 feet, in an
area that was wide open. If his opponent was concealed
in the rocks—*he could put me to sleep with one burst!*

Camellion debated what to do. He could ignore the odds
and zig-zag to the hill to the north, a course of action
that could be tantamount to suicide. He could sit there
and wait, in which case the enemy might try to sneak
around him. He had a third choice: to return to the station wagon on the road and continue the drive to the
U.S.-Mexican border, six miles to the north. He wasn't
concerned about the bullet holes he had put in the wagon.
He would park the Ford in some wash close to the border,
wait until nightfall and cross over into the U.S. on foot.
Dodging the Mexican Federales and the U.S. Border Pa-
trol would be as simple as walking a straight line. But,
damn it, he would lose considerable time. It was more
than five hours before darkness. Of course, there was his
own Jeepster. But it too was decorated with bullet holes,
more so than the Ford.

A low whine to the north prevented him, momentarily,
from getting up and racing back to the station wagon, a
whirring sound that grew rapidly in volume until it was
practically a roar.

[1] "Son-of-a-bitch!"

The rotor of a helicopter! The Death Merchant's face became one big scowl of disgust. The young gunman was escaping in an egg beater parked behind the long hill to the north.

All Camellion could do was wait and watch. The chopper, a two-man red and white Bell L-17, lifted off the ground, becoming visible once it had cleared the top of the hill. He didn't try to fire at the whirlybird. For one thing, he didn't want to reveal his position. The craft could be coming after him. For another, he couldn't fire at the craft. As the helicopter rose, the man sitting next to the pilot began spraying the area with machine gun slugs, no doubt in an effort to cover the escape.

Camellion snuggled down against the rock and listened to ricocheting slugs, several of the 5.56mm projectiles striking the top and the opposite side of the large slab of sandstone; yet he could tell, from the way the gunman was spraying the area, that the man did not know his position.

It was all over within minutes. The firing stopped and the helicopter shot upward, on a slant, toward the north. In a very short while it was gone, the sound of its rotor fading in the distance.

Knowing he was on a countdown to his own doomsday, Camellion felt cheated. As the CIA would say, "U.I's"[2] were trying their best to put him to sleep forever, and apparently they were well organized. Too, *they apparently have some way of knowing my every move, of knowing where I'll be and what I'll do next*. How they knew was what bothered him. A bumper beeper? A hidden transmitter concealed somewhere on the Jeepster? No dice. He had inspected the entire vehicle. Even so, how had the enemy known that he would be in Valle Hermoso? A lucky guess? Not very likely.

Camellion got to his feet and started running to the station wagon, wondering if the U.Is knew that he would—after crossing the border—stop first at his ranch, then visit CIA headquarters in Langley, Virginia. . . .

[2] Unidentified individuals.

11

Chapter Two

If plants held conventions, delegates would feel at home in the Big Thicket region of Texas. A biological crossroads of North America, the area is overlapped by Appalachian and southern forests, flora and fauna of the West, and varieties indigenous to Mexico's subtropics. Swamps and bogs, forests and savannas, sand hills and floodplains lie in close proximity, each supporting a complex ecological system of plants and animals.

The Big Thicket was originally the home of the panther[1], the bear, the wolf, and the ivory-billed woodpecker; later it became the denning-up ground of antislavery jayhawkers, moonshiners, and an assortment of thugs and misanthropes, along with more settled and peaceable folk with a taste for pioneering; but civilization has cut into the wedge of jungle that once covered three million acres. Railroads cross it, oil wells puncture it, and loggers have cut a lot out of it. Yet thousands of acres of wild country still remain—one of the last haunts of the red wolf and, just maybe, the ivory-billed woodpecker.

The Death Merchant had his ranch, named *Memento Mori*[2], in the northern part of the Thicket, situated between Votaw and Bragg, two little towns on the Atchison, Topeka & Santa Fe railroad.

And that's how Camellion came into the Big Thicket— riding the rails on the A.T.S.F. and getting out of the freight car at 12:30 A.M., when the train slowed to head into Votaw. Three hours later, he was lying in a clump of birch trees, staring at the stone house and the out-buildings of Memento Mori, his keen eyes, now accustomed to the darkness, scrutinizing each structure.

[1] Mountain lion, catamount, and cougar are other names.
[2] From the Latin: translated: "Remember Death."

After Jacob Big Kettle, an Indian friend of Camellion's, had discovered the corpse of Jesús Sontoya, the police from Votaw had carefully checked out the house and barn and, according to the CIA report, had discovered nothing unusual. Every piece of furniture was in place. Drawers had not been ransacked; there was no damage of any kind. The police had then sealed the front and the rear doors and the windows.

Camellion wasn't concerned about the animals. Jacob Big Kettle and his two sons would feed them daily and do the other necessary chores.

Lying there on his stomach, Camellion did not permit his win-conditioned mentality to let him entertain any illusions of safety. In itself, the concept of total victory is never a dangerous illusion, unless one puts the cart a mile in front of the horse . . . unless one sees the end result without considering the means to achieve that result. The Death Merchant didn't know how he would eventually overcome the main enemy. He was only supremely confident that he would. He was, however, positive that the enemy was very dangerous, superbly organized, and had some strange means of keeping track of him.

Did they know he was here at the ranch? Could they be waiting for him? *I'll soon know, won't I?*

A fully loaded Browning in his right hand, Camellion got to his feet and, leaving the deep shadows of the trees, raced to the rear of the house.

A total pessimist, he had built the house for just such an emergency as this. Because of this, he crept along the side of the wall until he came to the place where a wire clothesline was looped over a metal hook embedded in the stone. Quickly he removed the loop of wire and twisted the hook to the left. Without a sound, a section of the stone wall swung inward, leaving an opening so narrow that Camellion had to go in sideways. Once inside, he pressed a button mounted on a two-by-four. The stone door silently swung shut.

With the aid of a penlight, he made his way to the end of the narrow passage and pulled back on a small lever. The back stones of the rear wall of an enormous fireplace swung outward, and Camellion stepped into the dark living room.

Carefully, he played the small beam over the room. Everything was in order. His collection of knives and swords and medieval weapons had not been touched; neither had his collection of antique firearms. Every figurine in his collection of German porcelain was in place. At least the people wanting to kill him weren't thieves.

He paused at the mouth of the hall and did some thinking. It required nerve to set up an ambush for a target on a highway. On this basis, he wondered if the enemy might have returned to the ranch after they had murdered Jesus and after the police had sealed the house.

He went over to one wall, took down a long halberd, then went down the hall. The bedroom door was partially open. Using the halberd as a spear, he flung it against the door, at the same time turning and dropping flat to the rug. The tip of the halberd hit the door. The door opened wide. There was no explosion. Camellion got up and walked into the bedroom. Nothing was amiss. He proceeded to check out the other rooms of the house. All was normal. He retraced his steps, left the house by way of the secret stone door in the back wall, and made his way to the barn. Once more he used a hidden door in the heavy wood to let himself inside the building, which was strangely silent. He soon saw why. The stalls were empty. Cygni and Groombridge, his two stallions, were gone. So was Indi, the mare. So were the six Holsteins. No doubt Jacob Big Kettle had taken the animals to his own place, to save time feeding them.

Camellion went to Indi's stall, picked up a shovel and pried up a tiny square of the concrete floor. Beneath the square was a button set in a small black box, a wire running from the box. He pushed the button three times. He counted to five and pushed the button again, this time keeping his finger on it to the count of nine. He replaced the small block of concrete as a part of the concrete floor, in one corner of the stall, swung slowly upward, the rise causing a clump of dried manure to slide off.

Camellion went to the dark opening and descended the steel ladder. He stopped when he was three feet down, reached up and out, grasped the handle on the underneath side of the larger concrete block and pulled the block downward, closing the opening. He then climbed down the rest of the way and, reaching the stone floor, reached out to his left and flipped a light switch, flooding the low tunnel with dim light.

He was one hundred percent certain that the enemy had

not found his laboratory and arsenal. If they had, there would have been only a large hole in the ground.

Camellion reached the end of the thirty foot tunnel and stopped before a door which resembled the steel door of a large safe, in that it was fitted with two Master 1500 series combination locks. He worked the dials, pulled open the door, stepped inside the passage and turned on the single bulb hanging from the low ceiling whose walls, floor and ceiling were composed of armor plate. Except for a small table and a chair in the center of the room, and two units of metal storage shelves against one wall, the room was empty. There were three shoeboxes on the middle shelf of one unit. Two of the boxes contained $100,000 each in hundred dollar bills. The third box, a small bottle of colored water (calculated to drive any invader crazy. Why would Camellion keep a bottle of colored water in such a well-protected room?).

Any thief would have stopped searching once he reached The Room, in the belief that he had reached Camellion's treasure trove. The Death Merchant had planned it that way. But there was more, much more. . . .

Camellion picked up the chair, carried it to one corner of the steel room, stepped up on it, put one hand up to the ceiling and pressed one of the rivet heads. One of the steel plates in the forward wall quietly opened, revealing a short, narrow passage, at the end of which was another steel door that looked like the door of a safe. This door, painted a deep blue, contained four dials. It was this door that held certain death for anyone not knowing the proper combinations, for anyone who might try to open it, either by cutting, by "peeling," or by using explosives. Not that the door couldn't be opened by any one of these methods, but any tampering would automatically trigger a generator that would flood the area with microwaves of 250,000 megacycles. The microwave generator was the first Failsafe device that protected the room beyond the *second* door, this second door fifteen feet beyond the blue door.

His fingers played over the ivory buttons of the C-6 coded lock—9-4-3-10-9-9-9-1-7-5-0. A tiny bulb in the center of the inset glowed red, an indication that the door was unlocked. Thinking of Damon and Pythias, he pushed open the door and walked into the lab whose mercury arc lamps had been automatically turned on by the coded lock. He felt that his two pet pigs were safe. Their wallow, in back of the house, was bone dry. Jacob no doubt had taken them to his place, along with the other animals.

Camellion walked to the second failsafe mechanism and, pulling the switch downward, deactivated the 860 pounds of cyclotrimethylenetrinitramine. Better known as Cyclonite and/or RDX, the explosive was the most powerful of all military explosives. Camellion had chosen it, not only because of its tremendous power but because of its stability. RDX was not adversely affected by moisture and could not be detonated by shock.

The Death Merchant relaxed. In this room he was safe. To reach him here an enemy would have to use a small A-bomb. He walked across the room and opened the refrigerator. He took out a bottle of coconut milk, filled a glass, returned the bottle to the refrigerator and sat down at his desk. He didn't like the loss of time; yet he knew he did not have a choice. Only one passenger train came into Votaw, at 2:15 in the afternoon. The next freight would come through at 7:30 A.M. Even if he had the time to catch the 7:30 freight, he couldn't leave in the daylight, not knowing who might be watching. He would have to spend the day and part of the next night here, in the lab, and leave during the early hours of the next morning. He could use the same A.T.S.F. 12:30 A.M. freight he had used to come into Votaw—only this time he would be in disguise and properly armed, with Auto Mags.

I'll be in CIA headquarters within the next two days. Grojean won't like it, but I couldn't care less. . . .

Chapter Three

Courtland Juarez Grojean, the CIA's Deputy Director of Operations, had trained himself never to let his emotions reveal themselves in facial expressions. If he hadn't, his face would have resembled the wrinkled skin of a prune as he watched Richard Camellion, who was sitting in an upholstered arm chair across from the desk. To the Death Merchant's left sat Clark Wyland. To Camellion's right, leaning against the wall, was Simon Tuskin.

Grojean leaned back, turned his swivel chair slightly and looked at a large photograph of President Carter hanging on a wall.

"As I indicated earlier, we were limited in our investigation," he said in a calm voice. "We had to rely on reports given by the Votaw Police Department. We can only say that your handyman was murdered by persons unknown."

Camellion remained silent. Clark Wyland quickly added, "In fact, we didn't know your man had been murdered until one of our people in Texas heard about the hit on a local newscast; and you know we couldn't come out in the open."

Camellion turned and looked at Wyland, who was a muscular man in his fifties, with broad shoulders and a square, powerful head. He had been Grojean's assistant for five-and-a-half years.

"I didn't expect the company to send men to my ranch in cars marked 'Central Intelligence Agency,'" drawled Camellion. "I know the Agency couldn't make an investigation. I didn't expect one. I do expect some help in finding out who killed Sontoya, and who it is that's trying to kill me. When I find out who, I'll know why."

"We *have* helped," Grojean said. He continued to gaze at the photograph of President Carter and to tap his fingers rhythmically together, his elbows on the arms of the swivel chair. "We had a plane waiting for you in California. We sent a Q-man with you to Mexico. We had a Jeepster waiting in Valle Hermoso. Other than making our computers available to you, there's little else we can do. We certainly can't risk compromising our underworld pipelines, and I disagree totally with you that a leak came from Covert Operations."

"It's the only way the main enemy could have found out that I'm the Death Merchant, or have guessed it," Camellion said. "Whoever killed Sontoya left him as a direct promise to me. Whoever it was that did the job, or planned it, is all wrapped in what I believe to be a personal vendetta."

"You don't have any hard evidence," Grojean countered. "You're basing your premise on pure hypothesis."

"All men have enemies." Simon Tuskin shrugged matter-of-factly. "Sontoya could have been killed by a personal enemy, by someone who's not the least interested in you."

Camellion twisted his mouth into a half-smile. "And I suppose that the ambush set for me on the highway was pure chance?"

"Yes, the attack could have been coincidental." Tuskin's bubble of self-assurance burst abruptly. Doing his best to sound sincere, he said, "It might be that you just happened to be the first motorist to come along. That is rather dangerous territory below the U.S. border. Those bandits could have been out to rob and kill *anybody*."

Camellion grinned provocatively. "Some coincidence!"

"That was just a case of bad luck," Wyland muttered, scratching his left cheek.

"Luck didn't have anything to do with it," Camellion said, his voice as firm as a boulder. "Off the top, I should say that the odds of the attack against me being coincidental with the murder of Jesus are 100-trillion to 5. Someone is out to ice me forever and the motive is revenge. To me, this indicates a past mission I was on, probably for the company. I've done very little private work."

"I see we're back on that trip again!" Grojean's voice was tainted with annoyance. "I for one don't buy it! The idea that someone in the Agency leaked your identity is absurd. There are only eight people who know you're the Death Merchant. *You* know who they are. Now are you going to tell me that one of them is going around blabbing secrets? Ridiculous!"

Before Camellion could speak, Grojean added, "I'll tell

18

you again: we don't have any kind of device, electronic or otherwise, that can pinpoint a target at a distance. I wish to God we had. If we had such a mechanism or method—I'm leaving out hidden transmitters—we'd have the jump on the KGB and other commie intelligence agencies."

"I think your logic is deficient," Clark Wyland said, with an assurance he didn't entirely feel. But Camellion always made him nervous, as if disaster were about to happen. "What you have done is build the framework of an idea around a core of false assumptions. For example, the attackers ambushed you after you left the ranch outside Valle Hermoso and were on your way to Texas. On those facts you assume that the attackers had advance knowledge and knew that you would take that particular road." He crossed his legs and smiled. "Personally, I don't find anything mysterious about the attack. After all, Route 98 was the only road you *could* take. It was the only road moving north from Valle Hermoso. I'll tell you what you've done. You've let circumstantial evidence blossom into an airtight case that's riddled with coincidences."

Camellion's expression was one of amusement and delight.

"Suppose you tell me how they knew I'd be in Valle Hermoso? Have you thought of that?"

"They didn't know," Wyland replied promptly. "That's another one of your false assumptions."

"The Mexicans who attacked you were nothing more than common bandits." Grojean spoke cheerfully because he liked to preserve a light-hearted front and set great store by his reputation for inspiring optimism. "You just happened to come along at the right time, or maybe I should say the wrong time!"

"Oh, *bandits!*" Camellion said with mock solemnity. "Bandits who used Ingram submachine guns and CAR-15 automatic rifles! And a helicopter! I don't think bandits with that kind of equipment would take the trouble to stick up tourists. And they weren't Mexicans. They were *Americans.*" He looked Grojean in the eye, then glanced at a nervous Wyland and Tuskin. "I don't think either that any secrets came from Vallie West or from any of the former directors of Operations. The leak is from someone who has—or has had—access to Operations files. I think it's someone who took a little of this and a bit of that, mixed them all together and came up with the right answer, that I'm the Death Merchant."

Simon Tuskin made an angry face. Not only was he the overseer of day-to-day Q-Operations[1], but he was also the keeper of the ultra-secret Q-O files.

An imposing-looking man of 48, Tuskin had a manner that was generally amiable, even when issuing directives, but if his orders weren't promptly obeyed, he could emit a bellow that inspired instant compliance. By temperament and personality, he was ideally suited for his job. First of all, he was totally committed to *It's either them or us!*, the realistic philosophy of the CIA regarding the KGB and other communist intelligence organizations. Secondly, he had an uncomplicated view of life, firmly believing that the world was one vast jungle whose inhabitants were murderous savages. In this latter respect, Tuskin was similar to Grojean and Camellion, but dissimilar to Wyland, who believed in the essential goodness of mankind.

Tuskin spoke with angry assurance. "You're way off target, Camellion. Very very few people in Operations have access to the files." He walked in front of the Death Merchant and dropped into a chair by Grojean's desk, then stared at Camellion with coin-slots of eyes which he screwed up even tighter. "There are only seven—other than myself—who can get to the files. Damn it, you might as well accuse me or Clark or the Chief. As for Q-people who have quit or have been retired, we know exactly where they are and what they are doing. I personally would vouch for everyone of them."

"And so would I," interjected Clark Wyland.

"Tell me, Camellion," began Courtland Grojean. "Do you seriously believe that some of our agents probed the files and blew the whistle on you?" He fell back on the cool method that always stood him in good stead. "Be practical. You don't have the slightest bit of hard evidence, except in your own imagination."

Camellion did not intend to banter back and forth with these men. They blew a great wind, but nothing came out of the horn. Camellion knew why: they were in a bind. They wanted to help but couldn't—didn't dare—reveal

1 Q-Operations is merely a pseudonym for the Covert Action Staff. Sometimes this highly secret department is referred to as "C.A."

company secrets. There was also the danger that whatever he might do might somehow involve the Agency and make headlines. The CIA had already had more than enough publicity about its "dirty tricks."

"On the other hand, you can't deny that the files might prove that my intuition is correct," Camellion said easily, looking at Grojean. "Now and then even the best grown apple becomes rotten. Your people, active or retired, don't have halos around their heads."

For a moment, Grojean stared at Camellion, and for the first time Camellion detected the man's true feelings. It wasn't difficult to pinpoint Grojean's dilemma: he wanted to help but couldn't. He didn't dare risk involving the Agency; yet if he didn't lend a hand, the Agency might still become enmeshed in a scandal. For if the CIA often winked at state and federal laws—out of necessity, the Death Merchant usually ignored them completely. How would it look if the infamous Death Merchant were ever linked to the Central Intelligence Agency? The Liberals and the Left would scream "Foul!" the world over. The fair-minded American public wouldn't like it either, and it would be useless to try to explain that one does not fight Communism by playing the rules. That's the great flaw of Goodness: it takes time out to sleep content in its shell of righteousness, while Evil works steadily around the clock.

"Listen, Camellion. . . ." Grojean prepared to deliver a discreet warning. "If someone has discovered who you really are and is trying to neutralize you, I expect you to do what you have to do, but under no conditions must your connection with the company be revealed. You know why."

Camellion smiled indulgently. "Get to the point."

"If you get into trouble with the police, especially with the F.B.I., don't count on us for help!"

"Have I ever . . . in the past?" Camellion stood up. "Besides, who would believe me? What about the Operations files?"

Clark Wyland and Simon Tuskin, looking worried, locked eyes. Courtland Grojean's expression became chastened and pensive. "Camellion, we can't allow you to examine our computerized files," he said in a sternly official manner, holding up one hand, palm out, as he spoke. "I said, *you*. I didn't say *we* wouldn't use the files to help."

"What the devil are we supposed to look for?" Simon Tuskin said in exasperation. He looked from Grojean to the Death Merchant. "The computers contain a million bits of facts. We can have any information about any agent within minutes, but we must know what programming to use."

"We can't reveal our operatives in the field," Wyland said, a high note of incredibility in his scratchy voice. His angry eyes grabbed Camellion. "Even if you were authorized with a top clearing, we can't have you running around —God only knows where!—with that kind of information. God damn it! It might even be the KGB trying to make you inactive!"

"No, not the Ruskies," Camellion said. "The KGB would want me alive. The KGB would want answers to a lot of questions. As far as Q-men in the field are concerned, I—"

"We won't give him names or where the agents are stationed," Grojean cut in amiably, speaking to Wyland but smiling at Camellion. He had gotten up from his swivel chair and was sitting on the outside corner of his desk. "Which means, Camellion, I don't see how the files can help you. For example, we'll be able to tell you where agent X was born, the brand of toothpaste he uses, and give you other data about the man's personal life. But all the information will be irrelevant for the purpose you have in mind. None of it will prove or disprove that Agent X is a traitor."

"At the moment, I'm not interested in active operators," Camellion said curtly, his face preserving a mask-like rigidity as he spoke. "All I have to go on is a hunch, and that hunch says to check out the agents who are inactive, who have either resigned or have retired."

Grojean appeared to be genuinely perplexed. "Where do you suggest we begin?"

"With former agents who have been made inactive within the last five years," Camellion replied. "I know that when a man retires or resigns, you don't give him a gold watch and forget about him. You make weekly checks. If anything's amiss, you instigate an immediate investigation. I want to know who those agents are, where they're living and what they are doing. That won't tell us much, but it's a start."

"We can have that information for you within minutes," Tuskin said enthusiastically. "I don't think we'll find anything worthwhile." He glanced toward one of the phones on Grojean's desk. "I'll have one of the boys in Operations Files run a printout."

"No, Tuskin. I would prefer that you do it," Camellion said. "I don't want any of your assistants in on this."

Tuskin hesitated, his surprised expression turning to resistance, making it plain that he was averse to taking orders from Camellion, whom he considered a ruthless mercenary. His eyes narrowed and his lips parted. Just as it seemed that he was about to speak, Grojean drew attention to himself by loudly clearing his throat.

"Yes, Simon, you do the printout," he said placatingly to Tuskin. He smiled, first at Tuskin, then at the Death Merchant. "We must remember that our good friend here believes in 100 proof security."

"Is there any other kind?" Camellion asked.

"No, I don't suppose there is," admitted Grojean. He glanced at the tight-lipped Tuskin, who didn't even bother to excuse himself as he left the room.

Grojean looked at Camellion. "How about a drink?" He turned, walked to one side of the room and pressed a button in the molding. "By the way, how did you get here from Texas?"

"Where are you staying?" Clark Wyland asked.

The Death Merchant sat down and watched a section of one wall open, to reveal a small refrigerator and a well-stocked liquor cabinet.

"Any kind of fruit juice will do," Camellion said and shifted his attention to Clark Wyland, who was studying him with curious eyes, in an effort to see beyond the expert job of makeup Camellion had applied to his face . . . an ordinary, nondescript face, the face of a man in his late fifties. The hair, only a monk's fringe, was gray-brown, the nostrils wide, the mouth thin. The lips were as pale and as bloodless as the wan skin. He wore a tan suit of summer weight, with Tattersal shirt and tie to match.

"I'm here and that's all that matters," Camellion said. "I've a hotel room in Richmond. I drove in a rented car from Richmond to here."

"A long drive," Wyland said thoughtfully, "and it will be a long drive back."

Camellion did not comment. Wyland did not press for more information, knowing that he wouldn't get it. He also knew why the Death Merchant had made the drive from Richmond to CIA main headquarters. *He was hoping for another ambush!* thought Wyland. *And he hopes they'll try to ambush him on the way back to Richmond.* Yet Wyland was equally positive that the man called the Death Merchant was not courting disaster simply because he loved excitement or enjoyed killing. There was another factor involved. Camellion fought for some strange purity that could not be defined, for some eerie reason that only he understood.

Simon Tuskin put down the long, thin sheets while Camellion, Wyland and Grojean gathered around the table.

"There were less than forty agents who left the agency within the last five year period," Tuskin said compliantly. "Sixteen were retired. The others quit for a variety of reasons, mostly for better paying positions in private enterprise, work of a security nature."

Wyland said to the Death Merchant, "We'll give you a hand if you'll tell us the specific data we're to look for."

Camellion shrugged. "I wish I could tell you. But I really don't know myself. If something doesn't ring true— well, let's see."

He picked up one of the printouts. An hour and a half later, he was still scanning the data, the case histories of the IAA's[2] as well as the follow-up information. There was nothing to spark the fire of suspicion. Some of the IAAs were living on their pensions; others were either working for themselves, in this or that type of business, or were employed by private industry. Four held positions with the U.S. Government. One man had become a Brother in a Roman Catholic order. Two of the IAAs were women; one had resigned to get married. Now the mother of two children, she was living in Allentown, Pennsylvania. Her husband was an ophthalmologist.

The second woman, married to a real estate developer, lived in Los Angeles, California.

Oblivious to the other three men, Camellion continued to study the printouts. At length he came to the name Hugh Bernell Boden . . . *born April 9, 1943, in Sedan, Chautauqua County, Iowa. Became active in Agency as of*

2 Inactive agents.

24

September 4, 1969, with A-13 rating in F.I.[3]. Moved to CI[4] May 6, 1974. Became staff member of C.A. with A-2 rating in November, 1974. Served as case officer in U.S. Embassy, Kadura, Nigeria, Africa, until June 7, 1976. Transferred to U.S. Embassy, Damascus, Syria, as C.A. observer for T.S.D.[5] Resigned December 6, 1977, to reorganize security department of American Metals, Inc., Newark, New Jersey. Married, three children, lives with wife and youngest boy in Marrison, New Jersey.

The Death Merchant's thoughts skidded to a stop and a tiny bell of warning rang in his mind. American Metals, Inc.! Where had he seen that name within the last few hours; in what case history? Methodically, he began going through the sheets he had already scanned. Finally he found the case history he wanted:

MEUNIER, GERALD BUSHROD: Born November 19, 1929, Elkville, Perry County, Illinois. Became active in Agency as of October 3, 1964, with A-9 rating for clearing in CHAOS[6]. Transferred to CIFAR[7] in January, 1967. Joined C.A. staff in 1970, as 4th assistant to COPS/DDP[8]. Worked in that capacity until January 6, 1974; transferred to File Section in Operations of C.A. Resigned August 10, 1978 to become Director of Security for American Metals, Inc., Newark, New Jersey. Married, two children, lives in Marrison, New Jersey.

Wheels of concentration spun in Camellion's mind. Okay, maybe it was only coincidence. But wasn't it odd that both Boden and Meunier worked for American Metals, Inc.? First Boden leaves the Agency to reorganize the security department of American Metals, then, eight months later, Meunier quits to become the Director of Security at

3 Foreign Intelligence, engaged in the clandestine collection of intelligence.
4 Counterintelligence: active operations aimed at penetrating foreign secret intelligence agencies or operations.
5 Technical Science Department.
6 Domestic Security Files and operations.
7 Central Institute of Foreign Affairs Research.
8 Chief of Operations in the DDP, i.e. in the Directorate of Plans: the clandestine services side of the CIA, of which the Covert Action Department is a branch. The Q-Section is a branch of C.A. Q-Agents are the elite of the CIA.

American Metals. Could the two men have been friends? If so, it would be natural for Boden to help Meunier to obtain a plush job. There was also the fact that Meunier had worked in the File Section of C.A. Operations for almost five years.

No way! It's all too much of a coincidence! Camellion picked up the two sheets and turned to Grojean, Wyland, and Tuskin, all three of whom were watching him with keen interest.

"You've found something?" inquired Grojean. He and the two other men looked expectantly at Camellion.

"I'm not sure," declared Camellion, who then went on to explain the similarity between the two case histories. He finished with, "I want to see the dossiers on Boden and Meunier. And bring me anything you might have on American Metals in Newark, New Jersey. I've a feeling that we're going to find that outfit is somehow mixed up in this."

Grojean exhibited no surprise; not a muscle in his face moved.

Tuskin said, "It will take me about fifteen minutes." He put his glass on the corner of Grojean's desk and left the office.

Clark Wyland looked at Camellion incredulously, a look of cool appraisal coming into his eyes. "Without checking their dossiers, I'm not familiar with the two, but I can't believe that either of them would leak information. We consider such an act more than an offense to be punished by a term in the pen, even a long term."

Camellion, sitting next to the table, reached out and picked up the half-empty glass of apple juice. "I know," he replied. "Motor-mouths receive total neutralization—and rightly so. You needn't worry. If Boden and Meunier are guilty, I'll do the job for you."

"Just so the Agency is not involved," Wyland said tersely. He sat down in an armchair and glanced from the Death Merchant to Grojean, who had walked around his desk and was dropping into his swivel chair.

Wyland turned again to Camellion. "We don't blame you for wanting to avenge the murder of Sontoya and—"

"His knockoff plus other annoyances," Camellion cut in. "A neighbor had to take the time and trouble to move my stock, including my two pet pigs. I've had Damon and

Pythias since they were piglets, and they're not used to being away from home."

Grojean scrutinized Camellion and smiled but did not comment.

In contrast, Wyland did his best to radiate magnanimity. "Well, pigs for pets. Aren't they rather big to have trotting around the house?"

"They're not all that big," Camellion explained. "Damon and Pythias are S-1 miniature pigs—one of several strains of scaled-down swine specially developed for lab-research purposes."

"But aren't they dirty to have around?" said Wyland, somewhat dumbfounded.

"Hogwash! Pigs in general are among the cleanest of God's creatures," Camellion said with a laugh. "Damon and Pythias prefer a swimming pool to a patch of mud. They have a very clean wallow in Little Cuba. They're as clean as we are."

"Little Cuba?" echoed Wyland, frowning.

"Their wading pool," Camellion explained. "The pool itself is the Bay of Pigs."

"Camellion, you're something else!" chortled Grojean, finding it difficult to maintain his composure in the face of Camellion's sincerity. "Of all the people I know, you're the least likely candidate to have pigs—shall I say, in the parlor?"

"That's because you don't know me," an amused Camellion said, "and you don't understand pigs. Consider other animals. Horses, cattle, sheep are either suspicious or shrinkingly submissive. A goat's damned impudent and often cantankerous. Geese are usually hostile; cats always condescending, while dogs are flattering parasites. A pig is totally different. He regards us as brothers, as fellow-citizens, and takes it for granted—or grunted—that we understand his language."

There was nothing in the dossiers of Hugh Boden and Gerald Meunier to arouse the slightest suspicion. In an attempt to learn more of the two ex-CIA agents, the Death Merchant studied their psychological profiles.

Damn it! I'm getting nowhere at a slow pace! Both men had scored high on the Strong Campbell Interest Inventory Profile (SCI), their score indicating that they were interested primarily in "realistic activities: technical and out-door activities;" plus a pattern of related interests in scientific and social-service activities.

Conclusion of SCI profile: Boden and Meunier were serious and sober-minded, relaxed and composed.

The Sixteen Personality Factors Test (16PF Test) Profile further strengthened the findings of the SCI.

There were other tests which Camellion perused. Gerald Meunier's ACL profile (Adjective Check List) showed that he scored high on the total number of adjectives checked. Therefore, he could be described as being adventurous, conservative, enthusiastic and frank, but with a tendency to make blunders.

Huge Boden had scored low on the ACL Profile, this indicating he tended to be quiet and reserved, more tentative and cautious in his approach to problems and, at times, unduly taciturn and aloof. Boden was more prone to think originally and inventively; yet he was less effective than Meunier in getting things done.

Both men scored "Average Range" on the Minnesota Multiphasic Personality Inventory (MMPI), this meaning there was no indication of deception or of neurotic reactions. Furthermore, both men had T-Score = 37 on Scale 7—a clear indication toward a behavior pattern of displaying little worry or anxiety. Much to Camellion's chagrin, he saw that both scored high on Scale ES: Boden T-Score = 65; Meunier T-Score = 71, these scores giving evidence that both men had a tendency toward unusual ego-strength and/or the inner resources needed by an individual in order to deal effectively with distressing experience. Such individuals would make very dangerous enemies.

The Death Merchant came to the last test, the HRP, the Human Reliability Program. Conclusion of the six psychiatrists who had given the test: Hugh Bernell Boden and Gerald Bushrod Meunier did not suffer from any emotional disorders. They were "trustworthy" and "dependable" and in any emergency could be counted on to do their share.

Camellion threw down the folder in disgust and made a grim face. Boden and Meunier were so damned "pure" that any American company would be only to happy to hire them. Yes, sir! Those two would be a valuable asset to any corporation. They had been checked, double checked

28

and triple checked by the CIA and had been proved as clean as newly fallen snow.

The Death Merchant made up his mind: The tests had to be wrong. The tests had not spotted a hidden evil streak in Boden and Meunier—*or can it be that I'm wrong?*

Simon Tuskin, who couldn't conceive of two Q-Agents turning traitor, shifted around in his chair. He couldn't resist saying, "It's like I told you, Camellion. All our IAAs are honest and moral."

"Are you boasting or apologizing?" responded Camellion, reaching for a slim blue folder marked American Metals, Incorporated.

AMI was owned by Stemplin Steel Corporation of Pittsburgh, Pennsylvania. The report further stated that Stemplin was a branch of Global Construction, which controlled 82 percent of the preferred stock.

A little earlier, he had wondered why the CIA had compiled a report on AMI, which was not one of the giants in the aluminum industry and why Tuskin had brought two folders, the thin blue one and a thick green one. Now, as he read on, he found part of the answer: Global Construction was involved in a lot of building work for ARAMCO, the Arabian American Oil Company, in Saudi Arabia. AMI furnished Global all the aluminum used by the world-wide construction company.

Camellion stared in surprise as he read the next two sentences in the Domestic File report:

> Global Construction, Ltd. is a subsidiary of Silvestter International which is controlled by the Silvestter Foundation. In turn the Silvestter Foundation is directed by the Cleveland Winston Silvestter Estate.

Bells rang in the Death Merchant's head. Suddenly it was Christmas and his birthday, all rolled into one. Conscious that his heart was beating faster with the feeling of victory, he closed the blue folder and smiled faintly at the other three men, who stared back in puzzlement.

"I've found the connection," Camellion announced in satisfaction. "I'm almost certain that it was Boden and Meunier who fingered me. I'm convinced that it was Meunier who put it together while he worked in the File Section of Operations."

"I can't believe that!" Tuskin said pompously with an air of natural superiority. Then, realizing that he had spoken too quickly, without thinking, he hurriedly left a way out for himself. "I suppose anything is possible. But for two of our agents to be involved—impossible. Where's your proof? Give us some evidence!"

"Camellion, you're forgetting our internal checks," Clark Wyland declared fiercely. "Your own personal file and the files of your exploits are coded by heterogeneous impulses on an Aktiebolaget Cryptograph. The completed reports are then double-scrambled on Enmat[9] before being impulsed onto tape. Neither Boden or Meunier were master cryptanalysts."

"Meunier did have access to the tapes, did he not?" pursued Camellion.

Tuskin glanced uncomfortably at Grojean who ignored him, whose face was without emotion.

"Well, yes. Meunier could have gotten to the tapes," admitted Wyland, hedging. "Yet it's all an assumption on your part. With the tight security we have in Files, it would be impossible for any agent to decipher H.I.A. reports, even a master cryptologist."

The Death Merchant was blunt. "Bunk! Your security isn't all that good. At times, it plain stinks. If it didn't, a watch-officer wouldn't have had access to a file cabinet and have been able to steal a top-secret manual for one of our spy satellites[10]. And that's what happened during the early part of last year—unless all the news magazines lied."

Angry looks flashed across the faces of Wyland and Tuskin.

"What that man did was one of those rare flukes," Wyland said coldly, thrusting out his jaw. "Such a theft could never happen again. It doesn't concern you and we can't discuss it."

"I don't give a damn if he kidnapped the Deputy Director," Camellion said jovially. "But keeping my file a secret is a different field to plow. You people haven't done the job."

9 An acronym for a monoalphabetic cipher machine that's tied in to a computer.
10 A low-level watch-officer who was only a lower-rung GS-7 employee allegedly stole an 85-page technical manual for the Keyhole-11 satellite and sold it, for $3,000, to a KGB officer stationed at the Russian embassy in Washington, D.C.

All this time, Courtland Grojean had been studying the Death Merchant with minute care, preoccupied with juggling facts against possibilities. In the intelligence game, things were never what they seemed to be and, in the past, Richard Camellion had always been right. Grojean couldn't comprehend the strange intuition the man of death apparently used. He didn't. He didn't care. It was a matter of priorities. The Death Merchant was one of the most valuable agents in the employ of the CIA. Camellion insisted on doing things his own way; he ignored all authority, had no respect for people in high places, and made more tax-free money from just one mission than Grojean made in a year. In spite of his unorthodox methods, he always got the job done. That's what counted; that's what made the difference. And that is why Courtland Grojean was careful of what he said to Richard Camellion and how he said it.

Now, not giving Wyland or Tuskin a chance to answer Camellion's charge of negligence, Grojean said to the Death Merchant, "Simon asked for proof. I'll merely ask for evidence. If you think you've found something to implicate Boden and Meunier, tell us what it is and we'll begin from there."

Nodding, Richard picked up the bulging green folder and looked at the silver printing on the polythene cover: *Silvestter Family, History of:*

"Tell me, Tuskin. Why did you bring the history of the Silvestter family?" Camellion asked in a soft voice.

Surprised, Tuskin pulled back in surprise, both he and Wyland failing to notice Grojean's renewed interest at hearing the mention of the Silvestter family.

"After you cut through all the holding companies, it comes out that the Silvestter family owns American Metals," Tuskin replied hesitantly. "On that basis, I thought you might also want to see the Silvestter file."

"The name means nothing to you?" Camellion mused. He turned from Tuskin to Wyland. "Or you?"

Wyland frowned and shook his large head. He knew there was a wind, but which way was it blowing? He played it cautious. "Should it?"

"The Silvestter family is one of the richest in the country," Tuskin said slowly, his voice full of hidden question marks. "They receive little publicity, although I understand they could buy the Rockefellers several times over and still have more than enough for a rainy day—in fact a cloud-burst."

Grojean motioned with a hand toward Tuskin and Wyland and fixed his keen eyes on Camellion. "They weren't in Covert Action when you worked on Plan Poaka. Now tell us what you have."

The Death Merchant told all three of them, beginning with Cleveland Winston Silvestter—for the edification of Tuskin and Wyland.

"He inherited two hundred million bucks from his father and proceeded to build one of the largest fortunes in America. Silvestter was a business genius; yet he had two of the worst flaws possible: he worshipped Satan, and he wanted to rule the world."

Speaking in crisp tones, Camellion explained to Boden and Meunier how Silvestter's own personal brand of insanity had led the billionaire to believe that he, as the "Chosen of Satan," would destroy world civilization[11]. Toward this hellish end, Silvestter, and Jerry Joseph Steel, had organized *New Dawn,* a worldwide secret society supposedly dedicated to world peace. However, the real purpose of the society was not "peace" nor "brotherhood among all men," but violence and death, and, ultimately, the annihilation of the entire human race, this destruction coming about when the world was plunged into a full-scale nuclear conflict. The *Gotterdammerung* of world civilization—World War III!

Wyland suddenly sat up straight in the chair, an excited look on his face. "Wait a minute! It seems I remember talking to another 'Q' who worked on that project. Wasn't it Silvestter who had a few world leaders assassinated back in 1973?"

"And in 1974," Camellion added. "Silvestter was diabolically clever, and he had the millions to make his concepts reality. He even managed to make the Saudis think it was the KGB that tried to kill the Arabian king by blowing him to smithereens with a rocket; and he succeeded in another plot, in that the Red Chinese became convinced that the Soviets had tried to poison Chou En-lai. Silvestter had also marked the U.S. President and the Russian Premier for death."

[11] See Death Merchant #8, *"Billionaire Mission."*

"But how did he intend to start World War III?" asked Tuskin.

"The old trick of setting nation against nation, in this case the Russians and the Chinese. His plan was to get the Soviet Union to employ a preemptive nuclear strike against the Red Chinese. The Soviets almost did. To trigger the Soviet attack, Silvestter intended to launch a rocket with a hydrogen warhead against Moscow. His plan was to do this from his secret base in Australia."

"Australia!" Wyland exclaimed.

"From 'New Eden,' on his sheep ranch in Queensland. His plan failed. Obviously, or none of us would be here. There wouldn't be a civilization, as bad as it is."

Tuskin and Wyland stared frozen-faced at the Death Merchant. Grojean's studious eyes remained fixed on Camellion.

"The last I saw of Silvestter was in his 'Hall of Conjuration,'" Camellion said. "I had him cornered and he was screaming for Old Nick to pop up and help him. The devil didn't. I broke Silvestter's back on an altar and that was the end of the nut." Camellion sighed and picked up the thick green folder. "Unfortunately, his damned ghost has come back to haunt me. . . ."

Wyland and Tuskin, instantly deducing the Death Merchant's chain of reasoning, became solemn and reflective.

"It's too fantastic," Wyland said meekly. "Two ex-Q men—trusted agents with good reputations—betraying you to someone in the Silvestter family who wants revenge."

"It's possible!" Courtland Grojean said in a tone all too familiar to Tuskin and Wyland, one that indicated he was in complete agreement with Camellion, who had opened the Silvestter family file. "Jerry Joseph Steel, Silvestter's right hand man, was an ex-company man. To our eternal credit, he wasn't in C.A."

Camellion noted that Silvestter's wife had committed suicide three months after her husband's demise in Australia. The couple had had only one son, Cleveland Winston Silvestter II. Born August 5, 1955.

The Death Merchant pursed his lips. *So! Silvestter No. 2 was 19 years old when his crackpot daddy went to his own private infinity. Now he's just turned 25. He was in college when I sent his old man to sit on Satan's lap. How about that?*

The file gave the names of aunts and uncles and various cousins, all highly respectable people. Cyrus Louis Silvestter, Cleveland's brother, was Chairman of the Board of the Silvestter Foundation.

No. He's not the brains behind the plot.

The Death Merchant quickly scanned the three page history of Cyrus Louis Silvestter. The man lived simply with his family (one son was a doctor; another was pursuing graduate studies at MIT), was religious (had been all his life) and was noted for his programs involving the poor.

Reading the history, Camellion found himself admiring Cyrus Silvestter. Once in Martha's Vineyard, Massachusetts, he had gone to the aid of a black attorney whose car had been hit by another vehicle containing three young drunks. The three men, who assumed that their families' wealth placed them ten steps above the common man and twenty steps above a black, had turned on Cyrus Silvestter and had given him a severe beating, to the extent that he had required hospitalization.

Camellion turned the pages, thinking that Cyrus' moral character was the exact opposite of his brother's. A man like Cyrus Silvestter would not seek revenge. He'd do a lot of praying for his brother's soul and that would be the end of it.

While Camellion studied the file, Grojean gave Wyland and Tuskin the details of *Plan Poaka,* the operation by which the Death Merchant had smashed Cleveland Winston Silvestter's mad scheme to make the horror of WW III a reality.

The final section of the file contained photographs of most of the family. Going on a hunch, Camellion thumbed through the pile and soon found the black and white 5" X 7" photograph of Cleveland Winston Silvestter II, noting that the photograph was a reprint, made from the original that had been taken on June 4, 1970, when Silvestter II had been 21 years old. There he stood, grinning, dressed in white tennis shorts, a racket in his hand.

For a long time Camellion stared at the photograph of the husky, good looking young man with rather long hair. Although the young man did not have a shaggy mustache, the Death Merchant was confident that he had not made a mistake.

The man in the photograph and the man he had seen

in Mexico—*the dude who escaped in the chopper!*—were one and the same! *I settled with your father, Junior! Now I'll settle with you!*

"Camellion, what's your next move?" he heard Grojean ask.

Chapter Four

Expectation is one of the cures for boredom. However, Richard Camellion's anticipation of an ambush on the highway did not free him from the kind of tension necessary to keeping alert, which is in turn necessary for survival. The catch is learning to control the strain and to not let it color one's thinking and/or interfere with one's health. Psychological and physiological changes involve the two basic defense emergency systems used by humans and animals to defend themselves against danger. The *flight-fight mechanism* mobilizes the body's resources for massive and quick motor activity. Acting as a counter-balance, the *conservation-withdrawal mechanism* prepares the combatant for disengagement and inactivity when the danger becomes too great and is impossible to overcome. The give and take between the two systems—usually finely balanced —sometimes causes them to break down, particularly when psychological uncertainty exists. Rapid shifts from one response to the other can seriously affect heart functions and circulation, with death resulting from a derangement of the cardiac rhythm.

Fortunately for Camellion, his cold blooded realism acted as a preventative against the dangers of stress—or he would have had a coronary on the long drive from the "Center" to Richmond. He had expected some kind of bushwhack; yet the drive had been as peaceful as the inside of a cathedral. If anything, it was the lack of danger that irked Camellion, the absence of the tug of war between Life and Death that bored him to the brink of melancholy.

He turned the Chevette onto Route 64, confident that while he had been in Grojean's office, the DD/O's agents had installed a hidden transmitter in the car and that they were now tailing him. Camellion didn't mind. He hadn't expected Grojean to sit by and ignore the situation. Camellion had a lot of secrets buried in his head. When he was threatened, the Agency was threatened.

Never one to underestimate any enemy, Camellion had taken into consideration another strategy that Silvestter II might employ. Since the ambush in Mexico had failed, Silvestter and his people might assume he would be expecting a similar attempt, in which case Silvestter might strike from another direction. *When he thinks I will least expect it!*

Accordingly, Richard had taken the proper precautionary measures, using equipment taken from his lab at *Memento Mori.* He had attached an ordinary FM bug to the back of the couch in the sitting room of his hotel suite. The bug broadcast on a remote part of the frequency spectrum, in the 70 to 90 megahertz band, far from the commercial FM broadcast band of 88 through 108 megahertz. The special receiver, needed to listen in on the transmitter, was in the front seat of the Chevette. By like token, the same kind of receiver could find the bug, provided that Silvestter and Co. suspected he had hidden one and had brought a receiver with them—*if they're waiting for me at the Lyndon Johnson.*

All they would have to do is dial the receiver. When they dialed past the frequency the bug was using, they would encounter the "quiet spot" amid the background hiss. This "sing-around" would indicate the presence of a bug. Or they could have brought a spectrum analyzer or a spectrum monitor with them, devices that check a broad range of radio frequencies simultaneously for the telltale presence of a microtransmitter. Such detectors would also find the second bug Camellion had planted in his two rooms at the Lyndon Johnson Hotel, a subcarrier transmitter that employed the same principle FM stations use to broadcast special background music services or other special programs. The stations send out their regular programming on their FCC-assigned frequency and simultaneously transmit their special programs on virtually the same frequency, using what is known as a "subcarrier" or "sideband." The special programs are not heard on conventional FM radios and must be separated from the main signal by a special receiver.

Slowing down, then coming to a stop for a red light, Camellion speculated on the course of action the opposing side might take, provided they had gotten into his rooms and had discovered the hidden transmitters. They could leave; he didn't feel that they would. He didn't think either that they would destroy the bugs. To do so would be foolish. Dead transmitters would mean a dead receiver and indicate discovery. Men with nerve, men with determination, would wait in silence, careful not to speak, even in whispers.

The light turned green, and Camellion put the Chevette in motion. Traffic was thick, but he was only six blocks from the Lyndon Johnson. He reached down and flipped the ON switch of the special FM radio next to him on the front seat. He then reached over and pressed the ACTIVATE button of a much smaller receiver. This was the receiving station of the third bug Camellion had planted, a Sender only twice the size of the head of a pin. He had carefully pushed it underneath one section of the molding in the doorway between the living room and the bedroom. And it couldn't be detected by even the most sophisticated bug-snooping devices. It couldn't because it didn't broadcast. It wasn't a transmitter, at least not one of the conventional types. Extremely sensitive, the Microwave Short Warning gadget—Camellion's own invention—could be activated only by heat from the human body. One person would be insufficient. In order to be triggered, the MSW required body heat from at least two persons (three if the inside temperature was below 55 degrees). Should two persons get within eight feet of the MSW station, a microwave oscillator would then send out a single wave front which would spark the tiny alarm on the MSW's receiver.

The FM receiver was silent, except for the throw-back noise of the open channel. The MSW receiver was also silent. Camellion had expected it to be. The range of the station was 1,750 feet and the Lyndon Johnson was still five and a half blocks away.

Camellion reasoned that Silvestter, Jr. & Friends didn't have to be waiting for him. On the other hand, he had to act on the assumption that they would be. In death-hunts, the target could only remain alive by paying meticulous attention to all factors and all possibilities. Only perfection in performance was acceptable and the target had to work on the law that if things can go wrong, they will. In such situations, the man who stays well and healthy assumes the worst and acts accordingly.

A block and a half from the Lyndon Johnson, the MSW's receiver began to beep, much to the Death Merchant's satisfaction. He had been right. Cleveland Winston Silvestter II had prepared a trap. Frustration, joined by speculation, also began to trot around in Camellion's mind. This second ambush meant that—*they managed to trace me. But how did they do it? Coming from Texas to Virginia, I was so cautious that God would have had to work extra to keep track of me.*

Was it possible that Silvestter company scientists had developed some secret method by which a person could be traced at a distance? Sure it was. But damned improbable. Then again, so was the atomic bomb. Until it was invented and exploded.

Drawing closer to the hotel, Camellion backtracked his thinking processes to what he had read about Silvestter II in the Agency's files. Several months after his father's death in Australia, Silvestter II had quit Harvard, where he was majoring in business administration, and switched to the Massachusetts Institute of Technology, taking courses toward a degree in electronic engineering. He quit MIT after a year and a half. That was the end of his college career. Nor was he interested in his father's various business enterprises. He didn't have to be. Silvestter, Sr. had left him two hundred and twenty-six million dollars.

The latest CIA report, put together in 1977, revealed that the young man did have a strange circle of friends, that is for the son of a billionaire. There was Nario Hokakawa, a 40-year-old Japanese, who was a martial arts expert; he was Silvestter's chauffeur; and Laban Denbro, the boss of National Investigations, a detective agency with a reputation as odious as its founder. Silvestter had four bodyguards, all four supplied by Denbro, all four ex-convicts who had been convicted of crimes of violence—one for attempted murder, two for assault with a deadly weapon, the fourth for assault to commit homicide.

Camellion turned the car onto Blossom Avenue and headed for the Lyndon Johnson's parking lot. He concluded that if it wasn't Silvestter and his crowd who were trying to kill him, they were certainly wasting a lot of know-how and talent. He also congratulated himself for having had the foresight to stash spare Auto Mags, his makeup kit, and other necessary equipment at a motel in Dumbarton, a tiny town north of Richmond. A brand new Omni/Horizon, for which he had paid cash, was also at the Admiral Oasis Motel.

He pulled into the parking lot, slowed at the entrance to let the attendant see the hotel sticker on the windshield, then drove to the center of the lot, found an empty slot and pulled in. In one respect, he was lucky. While his suite on the third floor faced Monument Avenue, he would be able to enter from the side the parking lot was on, from the rear entrance on Blossom Avenue. Not that it really mattered. Silvestter would have a man posted at each entrance. Cause for another question mark in Camellion's mind. How could they spot him? Even if they knew what he really looked like—*I doubt if they do!*—he was in disguise.

He looked around, from left to right; he turned and looked out the rear window. No one was in sight. He reached for a small bag under the front seat and a horrible thought crossed his mind: could it be that he was marked in some strange way, so that no matter what disguise he used, he would still stand out like fresh blood on a snow-white sheet? He was pretty certain that he would not be in any danger in the lobby. Silvestter would want to make sure he had him. The Death Merchant's suite was the logical place for that kind of certainty.

Richard opened the bag and took out a .25 Budischowsky TP-70 auto pistol and a very thin Citofine face mask. He dropped the B-TP-70 into his left side coat pocket and added another 15 years to his appearance by expertly slipping the mask over his head. He turned around, leaned across the top of the seat, reached down and picked up a cocoa brown vinyl shoulder tote that was on the floor in front of the rear seat. He got out of the car, looked around again, then reached under the front seat and pulled out a plain hickory cane with a curved handle. After slinging the tote back over his left shoulder, he started walking from the parking lot. To the casual passer-by, he was just another old man . . . one with a limp, one who had to walk with the aid of a cane. Only the average elderly person does not walk around with two .44 magnum Auto Mag "Backpackers," each with a Jurras-designed noise suppressor (or "silencer") on its four-and-a-half-inch barrel. Nor does the average old man shuffle around with tear gas canisters and tiny detonation buttons in shoulder totes.

Camellion, who had registered at the Lyndon Johnson

as Clifford W. Bottsford, of Tampa, Florida (and had all sorts of forged ID to prove it), limped to the corner of Cherry and Blossom, crossed the street and walked to the door of the hotel. Soon he was in the lobby, peering furtively at his surroundings. All seemed normal. Several women and a man, engaged in conversation, were standing near the small gift booth in the center of the lobby. Other men and women, singly and in pairs, sat on couches or in deep leather chairs. No one was at the desk; only one clerk was in sight. A beat cop was kidding the young woman at the tobacco shop counter. The only thing unusual about the lobby—at least to Camellion—was the sign, on an easel-type stand, next to the potted Walking fern: *DRINK BILLY'S BEER.*

At the moment, Camellion had the feeling that if he bought a praying mantis it would turn out to be an atheist, just like the long walk to the elevators, halfway across the lobby, could turn out to be the last seventy feet he would walk on this earth. However, there was no other way. The bank of self-service elevators were placed an equal distance from either entrance of the hotel, to the north center-side of the lobby.

But the odds are with me. They'll wait until I'm inside the suite. Or they wouldn't have gone upstairs in the first place.

He ambled across the lobby, the metal tip of his cane tap-tapping against the imitation marble floor. He turned at the gift booth and walked to one of the elevators that was opening, wondering if the men in his rooms had discovered the FM bug or the subcarrier transmitter. Suppose they had? They still would not know if he or the CIA had planted them. It was a foregone conclusion that Hugh Boden and Gerald Meunier, having discovered that he was the Death Merchant, knew of his involvement with the Central Intelligence Agency. Surely they and Silvestter realized that the Agency would swing into high gear to save him, to save one of their most valuable agents. Why then had they fingered him? There was only one frame of logic which could supply the answer.

They hope to kill me before I or the Agency can figure out who the enemy is! Boden and Meunier wouldn't be involved if they thought there was any chance of their being suspected; they wouldn't dare risk execution by Q-Section neutralizers.

41

Camellion punched the No. 2 button. The doors closed. The elevator lifted and came to a smooth stop at the second floor. The doors opened. Camellion stepped out and looked up and down the carpeted hallway. Only a man and a woman, and they were walking away from him. Richard turned to the right and limped to the stairs, taking out the explosive button on the way.

The button was not a button. It was a round metal disk the size of a silver dollar, a magnetized compartment filled with a tiny pinch of ammonium sulfide mixed with powdered acacia. The disk also contained a bubble chamber, which could be broken by pulling the length of six inch wire protruding from one edge of the button. Half a minute after the air reached the two chemicals, they would explode with the force of a medium-sized firecracker.

Toward the top of the stairs, seeing that no one was ahead or behind him, Camellion reached into the shoulder tote, pulled out a Backpacker Auto Mag and jammed it and its six-inch-long silencer into his belt on the left hand side.

He came to the third floor, his feet silent on the thick brown carpet. The day before, right after he had checked into the hotel, he had reconnoitered the area, so that now he didn't have to stop and speculate. Due to the hot weather, the hotel's central air conditioning was going full blast, and the two bedroom windows in his two-room suite were sealed. The bellhop had told him that in case of fire, he could smash the glass with a chair and reach safety on the ground by means of the fire escape outside his bedroom window.

Camellion hurried down the passage which was actually shaped like a T, with his rooms being toward the center of the right side of the T. This top section of the T moved in a north-south direction. The short hall to the right was not quite thirty feet long, its end opening into another hall that stretched east and west. For the moment, the Death Merchant was not concerned with the longer hall. He turned right and hurried down the short hall, his only concern the fire alarm close to the end of the hall. There was a bit of a problem: to get to the alarm, he had to walk past his own door, Number 317. He calculated that he would be in no danger. Whoever was inside waiting was expecting him to unlock his door and walk in. That's when they'd blow him away.

Camellion hurried forward, moved past his door, and

closed in on the fire alarm on the left side wall. The alarm was a small glass box, with slots in the wall side, the alarm working on the vacuum principle. Should air get past the glass and reach the sensitive exclusion membrane behind the slots in the wall, alarms would ring on every floor of the hotel, as well as in the lobby and the other sections of the ground floor.

Richard slapped the button on one corner of the alarm box, in such a manner that the magnetized side of the disk grabbed the steel frame of the box. He put down his cane and prepared to pull the wire. He was about to put a thumb on the button, to hold it in place while he pulled the wire, when Fate spit in his face. A man and a woman, coming from the east/west half, turned the corner on the left side. At the same time, a bellhop came around the right corner and saw Camellion reaching for the disk on the alarm.

"Hey you! Get away from there!" the bellhop said angrily and hurried toward what he presumed to be an old man. The man and the woman, a young couple in their twenties, pulled up short in surprise.

The bellhop, reaching Camellion, attempted to grab his wrist. Richard could sense that the man, thinking that he was dealing with an old geezer who was perhaps senile, did not intend to hurt him; yet the Death Merchant couldn't afford to waste a single second. His left hand moved so fast that it was only a blur of motion to the bellhop; he had even less time to feel the pain from the expertly delivered sword hand strike against the center of his chin. His eyes spun in their sockets, his legs turned to jelly and he went down. Camellion, not wanting to hurt the bellboy who was only doing his job, had only given him a "love-tap." The young man would be out cold for half an hour and have a helluva sore jaw; otherwise, he wasn't harmed.

"Oh my God!" gasped the woman, putting her hands to her mouth.

If she screams, she'll wake the dead! Camellion thought in disgust. *Oh boy! Here comes the all-American hero!*

The man, blond, broad, and built like a Notre Dame halfback, glared at Camellion and started what was intended to be a right uppercut to Camellion's jaw. The blow didn't even get off to a good start. Camellion slammed him in the solar plexus with a right Seiken forefist, then clipped him with a left hook to the jaw. Blondie folded, fell flat, as still as if frozen.

"Sister, you scream and I'll kill you!" Camellion snarled at the terrified woman. He hated to frighten her, but he didn't have much of a choice. His words did have the desired effect: the woman slumped down in a faint. In her yellow dress, she didn't exactly resemble the Yellow Rose of Texas.

Camellion reached up, jerked the wire on the disk, then turned and ran in the opposite direction, pulling the Auto Mag from his belt and thumbing off the safety catch. His goal was the door to his own suite. He was almost there when the ammonium sulfide and the powdered acacia exploded with a loud bang and broke the glass in the box. Next, the fire alarm went off. Simultaneously, the door across from Camellion's suite opened and two men stepped out.

I'll be damned! This hall is getting to be more crowded than the Gaza Strip!

The men jerked around in the direction of the loud ringing which was coming from a round bell over the broken box. That's when they saw the Death Merchant, holding the Auto Mag, and almost knocked each other over in their attempts to get back inside the room.

In spite of the interruptions, Camellion's plan matured. The heavyset man with the long sideburns was turning the knob as the door to Camellion's suite opened and a man stepped out into the hall—a stocky yoyo with a round, red face and long, sun-bleached hair. He wore a blue and white seersucker suit.

For a fraction of a second the man stared at the two men hurrying through the doorway across from him. Another moment and he swung around toward Camellion, who was only eight feet away. It was then that he knew, knew that all of it had been a clever trick to get him—to get anyone inside Camellion's suite—to think there was a fire and to open the door and investigate.

Richard could see the surprise and shock stamped on the man's face, and the fear and the hair-trigger realization that he was staring straight into the portals of hell!

The man's mouth opened almost as wide as his eyes and his right hand made a dive for the revolver in his shoulder holster. But all the man was doing was performing an exercise in futility. The noise suppressor on Camellion's Auto Mag went BBZZITTTTTTTT. There was a thudding sound, and suddenly the gunman did not have a face. The big .44 medium point bullet had dissolved it in a bloody shower of flesh and bone, along with his head, skin, bone, brain and blood splattering against the door and wall and over the nitwit's seersucker suit.

The decapitated corpse—part of its chin hanging on a bloody strip of skin and tendon—rocked back and forth, then sagged against the door. The Death Merchant charged forward, fired twice more, and pulled the second Auto Mag from his shoulder tote, as happy as a first-time father, when he saw the two slugs chop through the door and heard a low, agonized cry.

It was now or never at all. An AMP in each hand, Camellion jumped over the corpse of the first man he had smoked and kicked the door wide open. Wishing he were somewhere else, he stormed into the room, hunched so low that he was almost in a duck-walk position.

In a fire-fight, you don't take time to think, to figure out moves. It's not like chess. You can only react, past experience and technique impelling each action. With the Death Merchant, it was like women cooking—he didn't use rules. He just *knew.*

It all happened within a blink of an eye. Amazed, fearful faces flashed in front of Camellion. One man to the left. Another to the right. Both raising automatics. A face on each side of the doorway between the bedroom and the sitting room. One was Oriental! The other—*It's Cleveland Winston Silvestter Two!*

Camellion, almost stumbling over a dead man on the floor, the gunsel he had iced through the door, jumped to the end of the couch and fired at the two men who were closest to him. He would have preferred to take care of Silvestter and Nario Hokakawa first. However, the other two jokers, being closer, were the more dangerous.

The man to Camellion's left was slightly faster than Silvestter, Hokakawa, and the other man. He pulled the trigger of his Smith & Wesson automatic at the same time that the Death Merchant sent .44 slugs at him and at the man to Camellion's right. The S&W roared, the 9mm slug missing Camellion by at least three feet. The man to the right wasn't any more successful. His .45 projectile, fired from a Llama IXA auto pistol, buried itself in the edge of the door.

There were two BZIITTTTTSSSSSS from across the room, from the silencers attached to Silvestter's Walther P-38 and Hokakawa's Heckler und Koch autoloader. Both slugs, while coming close to the Death Merchant, might as well have been aimed at the ceiling, for all the good they did. They buried themselves in the couch's cushy arm, their trajectory halted by the thick polyurethane foam.

Camellion hadn't missed. The man to the left dropped his S&W and fell sideways, his eyes closed, his mouth open, his tie newly decorated with a hole almost an inch in diameter. The man to the right took a slug in the stomach that doubled him over and kicked him back to the wall.

For the moment, the Death Merchant was safe, protected by the big couch and its thick, tufted cushions. He didn't dare rear up to fire from behind the arm; instead, he crawled on the pile rug to the rear of the couch, hearing five more BZITTTSSS in quick succession and the thud of slugs striking the thick arm. Determined to kill Silvestter and the Japanese he was sure was Nario Hokakawa, the Death Merchant placed the muzzles of his silenced Auto Mags sideways against the back of the couch and pulled the wide, grooved triggers twice more. The powerful .44 projectiles would lose some of their power in cutting through the thick material, but they'd still have more than enough force to blow away anyone they might hit.

There weren't any cries of pain or the thud of bodies hitting the floor. Either the men had gone or he had missed.

Damn! To prevent Silvestter and Hokakawa from gauging his position, Camellion moved away from the bullet holes he had put in the pin-whale corduroy upholstery. He crawled to the end of the couch closest to the doorway and listened, the roar of the enemies' .38 and .45 still ringing in his ears.

He couldn't look underneath the couch because its bottom was flush against the rug, nor did he dare rear up and look over the top edge of the back. Yet time was running out, the grains of sand falling rapidly in the hourglass of survival.

The sound of glass breaking in the bedroom might have made a man of less experience jump up and charge into the bedroom. But not Camellion! Since two men were in

46

the bedroom, the breaking glass could be a trap—one breaking the glass while the other waited at the door, his pistol trained on the couch.

Not willing to take the chance, Camellion pictured the location of the door and again jammed the muzzles of the AMPs against the couch, this time against one corner, and fired twice. His reward was not a scream of pain but a loud metallic ring, as if one of his slugs had struck a stainless steel gong! What mattered was that there wasn't any return fire, no soft hissing sounds from noise suppressors.

Now he had to take the risk. He looked around the corner of the couch. The doorway was empty. The breaking of window glass hadn't been a trap.

Camellion leaped to his feet, raced to the doorway and, just to be on the safe side, fired twice more, toward each side of the opening—well aware that he was balanced evenly on the scales of life and death.

Seconds later, he was in the bedroom, ducking toward the right, his eyes scanning the room. The room was empty—and so was the bottom windowframe to his left, except for large slivers of glass ringing the inside of the aluminum. Silvestter and Hokakawa had broken the glass and had escaped by way of the fire escape.

The rear of Camellion's bedroom overlooked an enormous courtyard, and it was a moot question whether Silvestter and Hokakawa were climbing to the roof or retreating to ground level. Camellion assumed they would seek the route of least resistance, which would be the ground level, only two stories down. The roof was another five stories up. And once they reached the roof, where could they go?

Camellion gritted his teeth in frustration. He couldn't follow. He couldn't risk a shootout in public—certainly not on a fire escape where there wasn't any cover and where their chances of killing him were equal to his of killing them. Worse, to go after them now would only interfere with his own chances of escaping. By now, the police had to be on their way to the Lyndon Johnson.

The Death Merchant's face twisted with cold fury. That which is, is! Silvestter and his men had tried to kill him and had failed. He had hoped to kill them in his rooms, but he too had blundered. Winston Silvestter II had escaped. Now, that's all Camellion could do—escape!

He was about to leave the room when he saw the case on the floor, a gray metal case that resembled an attaché case, only it was larger. There was a bullet hole toward one corner. *So that's what my .44 hit!*

Richard got down on one knee, laid one of the Auto Mags on the rug and opened the top section of the case. Curiously then he stared at the panel over the top of the bottom half of the case. There was an assortment of dials and meters and several rows of colored push-buttons. On one side of the panel, up toward one corner, was a 4-inch square opening, thick slivers of glass protruding from the metal sides. Camellion could see that his bullet had broken the glass on its passage through the case. There was another jagged bullet hole in the cover.

Camellion stared at the shattered screen. A small TV set? The glass shards did have an aquadag coating like a cathode-ray tube.

It's a cathode-ray tube (abbreviated crt) that produces a television picture. A crt is a tube in which an electron beam can be focused to a small cross section on a luminescent screen, a beam that can be varied in position and intensity to produce a visible pattern.

But this isn't a crt! Camellion muttered. Below the opening there wasn't any bullet-banged wreckage of vertical and horizontal deflection plates, no first and second focus anodes; there wasn't a control grid or a cathode heater enclosed in a grid cylinder. Beyond the opening, there was only a tangled mass of wires. Some of the top ends of the wires were attached to tiny stylus arms; other tops to what seemed to be tetrodes[1]. But it was the labels over five of the dials that interested—and worried— Camellion. All the lettering was in red. One was marked HYPOTHALAMIC READ-IN. Another, LIMBIC ADJUSTMENT. Above a third dial was PONS INSET. A fourth dial was marked THALAMIC COORDINATOR. The final dial was designated AURA PATTERN & ADJUST.

The Death Merchant felt icicles stab up and down his spine.

By God! All parts of the human brain! But not 'AURA!'
Was it possible? Could this machine be the answer as

---

[1] A four-electrode vacuum tube containing two electrodes in addition to the cathode and anode.

to how Silvestter had been able to keep track of him, as to why Silvestter had always been a dozen steps ahead of him? To think of it was mind-boggling—as if being able to see one's own soul in all its spiritual nakedness. Think of it! A machine that could focus in on an individual who might be a hundred miles away and pinpoint his location! Or a thousand miles away! Anyplace on Earth! Incredible!

Uh huh. . . . And the H.M.S. Titanic had watertight compartments!

Camellion would have liked to take the contraption with him. He knew that he couldn't. He'd even have to dump his shoulder bag. *The Richmond Police will never be able to figure out what the device is—if it is what I think it is! I'll make sure of that.*

He pulled the labels from the panel, then stood up and calmly put six .44 AMP slugs into the device, turning the contraption into useless junk. He sure had news for Courtland Grojean. With such a machine in existence, the CIA would have to possess it!

After reloading the Auto Mags, Camellion hurried to the sitting room. The *au-wuga, au-wuga, au-wuga* of the fire alarms had stopped, but he could hear voices out in the corridor, not far from the door. Damn it. All he needed now was to run into fools with more nerve than sense, or worse, the police.

An Auto Mag in each hand, Camellion stepped out into the hall. He had expected a welcoming committee and he got it. Not only were people peering out of doorways up and down the length of the hall, there were knots of them, rubbernecking in all directions, where the end of the short hall opened into the much longer east/west passage.

A woman, standing in front of an open door, was the first to spot Camellion. In her mid-30s, she wore thick mascara, heavy make-up, rings, bracelets and a low-cut dress.

There must be a convention of Gypsies in this dump! mused Camellion. *I wonder if she wants to tell my fortune?*

He decided she didn't when she jumped back and screamed, "Look out! He's Going To Kill Us All!"

Heads jerked toward Camellion. The woman fell into her room and slammed the door, starting the domino effect. Doors closed, faces disappeared. The people at the end of the hall scattered faster than quail flushed by a pack of over-anxious hounds.

Camellion tore down the hall, his feet pounding on the thick carpet. He reached the long hall and once more his appearance set off shouts and screams and a mass exodus from the corridor.

Camellion, considering the length of the hall, surmised that some curious soul might see him use the stairs, unless he made sure the hall was empty and all doors closed. He stopped a dozen feet from the four elevators, shoved the Auto Mags in his belt, took a couple of CN canisters from his shoulder bag and pulled the rings. He turned and tossed the canisters down the hall. He started toward the elevators, and by the time he reached them, he could hear the tear gas hissing from the canisters behind him. No, not very long. He estimated he had several minutes before the eye-stinging, lung-choking gas reached him.

He darted past the elevators, stopping in front of the last one, and pulled another CN grenade from his tote. Carefully measuring the distance, he tossed this canister almost to the end of the hall. He pulled an Auto Mag, turned and looked behind him. The gas, filling the hall, was drifting lazily toward him. Turning, he looked at the last canister he had thrown. It had just begun to spew out its green-white gas.

With the sweet confusion of the universe coursing through his veins, Camellion took the last canister from his tote bag, pulled the pin and tossed the grenade to the floor of the elevator. Next, he reached inside the elevator and pressed the number 5 button, after which he quickly pulled back to avoid the CN gas, which began to hiss from the slots while he was racing to the door marked *Service Stairs*, six feet past the last elevator.

He opened the door, moved into the stairwell, closed the door and glanced around, first at the top flight of steel steps, then at the flight leading to the second floor. He could hear sirens from outside the hotel, not too far in the distance. The police were only blocks away.

This was the risky part of his escape plan, the odds 50/50 because he could neither influence nor control Fate. The great danger was that someone would come along within the next few minutes . . . hotel employees or the boys-in-blue. Camellion sighed. He would just have to take care of them. . . .

Conscious of the tension mounting in him, he removed

the Citofine mask, ripped it apart with quick motions and tossed the shreds to the concrete floor. The shoulder bag, now empty, followed, but not before Camellion had removed from it a dark brown Ferrari cap and put it on his head. Next came the coat; however, Camellion did not toss it to the floor. He turned it inside out. There wasn't any lining on the inside that was now the outside. There was only another "coat," a dark brown coat that, with handkerchief and side pockets, matched his tan trousers.

He was almost finished, but not quite. He bent over, pulled up his left pants leg and, using the narrow straps already on his ankle and calf, strapped on one of the Auto Mags. He strapped the other Auto Mag to his right leg. Again he thought of the strange machine that Silvestter and Hokakawa had left behind. *Aura? That's something right out of occultism. The aura is a luminous appearance seen surrounding the human body. I'm convinced it exists and that it's made up of numerous elements of the human forcefield, including perhaps heat radiation, electromagnetic fields, and many other things unknown to modern science. But did 'Aura' on the label mean the kind of 'Aura' I'm thinking of? What other kind of aura is there? Plus parts of the human brain! What does it all mean?*

The Death Merchant stood up, transferred the Budischowsky .25 automatic from the left inside pocket of his coat to the right outside pocket and made sure the safety catch was on. Finally he took a pair of amber-lensed sunglasses from his shirt pocket and put them on. At last he was ready.

He hurried down the stairs, taking care that his feet did not make a noise on the bare, knobbed steel. Very quickly he came to the level that opened to the service stair door on the second floor. He didn't even bother to glance through the small wire-reinforced window in the center of the metal door. He kept right on going until he was at the door of the service stairs on the ground floor. The door was in the lobby, right around the corner from the registration desk. With only a few sprinklings of luck, he could slip out unnoticed, provided a crowd had gathered. He had assumed that touching off the fire alarms would draw a crowd of confused, frightened people. He looked out the window and saw that he had been right. People were milling about aimlessly, glancing fearfully at each other. Those who had just come into the hotel were afraid to go to their rooms, while those who had come downstairs were afraid to return.

The Death Merchant could see only a small portion of the lobby; nonetheless, he could hear the loud, nervous voice coming from about the center:

"There isn't any danger. There isn't a fire. It was a false alarm. There has been some shooting on the third floor, but the danger is passed. But please do not go upstairs to the third or the fifth floor until the tear gas has cleared. I repeat: there is no danger. There is no fire. The police are on the way, and I assure you—"

Now! Camellion adjusted his sun glasses, opened the door and stepped into the lobby. He had no way of knowing if anyone saw him. If anyone had, he or she had not been suspicious. No one shouted a warning. No one yelled "There he is!" or "That's one of them."

Camellion went through the motions of milling around with the other people, letting an expression of confusion creep over his face. All the time he kept edging toward the main entrance on busy Monument Avenue. Soon he was close to the double doors and walking behind a young woman hurrying from the hotel with her little boy in tow. He followed them through the doors and walked out onto the hot sidewalk, his eyes scanning the immediate area. All was normal enough. He paused for a moment under the canopy, gave the doorman a brief glance, turned to the left and started toward the Two Doves, a restaurant which was halfway down the block. He was almost to the restaurant when three police cars, sirens dying down, pulled up in front of the hotel.

For several minutes, he gaped and gawked with other pedestrians, who had turned to watch the fuzz charge into the Lyndon Johnson, remarking that "No one is safe these days" to a woman standing next to him. Satisfied that he was in the clear, he continued on to the Two Doves, thoughts dancing in his mind. Call Grojean through the C.A. section's toy-store-front in Richmond? Why bother? He'd relay his conclusion about the device to the contact who brought him the license plates.

The later the better. I don't want those C.A. dummies getting in my way in Massachusetts.

Walking into the restaurant, he made up his mind about

the strange device, convinced that his theory was correct. Somehow, Silvestter was using the human aura to keep track of him—*My aura!*

He wondered if the Two Doves served vichyssoise. . . .

Chapter Five

The Death Merchant did not like surprises, especially when they came from people on his side. The schedule had called for the C.A. section contact to meet him at St. John's Church, where Patrick Henry made his famous "liberty or death" speech.

"Contact will be made at 15.00 hours," Grojean had said. "All you do is go into the church and pretend to be one of the tourists. Our man will know you from the photograph taken automatically at the gate. He'll have the Virginia license plates for your new car."

Contact had not been made at two o'clock in the afternoon. Indeed not! At 6:00 A.M. the C.A. agent had knocked on Camellion's door at the Admiral Oasis Motel. The second part of the surprise was that the agent was not a he. It was a she—an attractive woman of about thirty, with well-rounded curves in just the right places of her off-white pants suit. An oval face. Dark hair clustered in tight curls at the top and close to the sides. Very little lipstick. She was the type one expects to meet in a business office, or in an elegant cocktail lounge. She hadn't seemed surprised that, after she had given him the proper code-pass-cipher through the closed door, he had opened the door holding an Auto Mag in his hand. She had sat on the bed smoking a cigarette, her back turned, while he dressed.

Surprise Number 2! Sandra had not come alone. She had brought some highly polished brass with her. Courtland Grojean, and an agent Grojean had introduced as "Howard," had been in a delivery van whose sides bore the lettering *ACE DELIVERY COMPANY. We Deliver Anything But Bad News.*

"Why the change?" Camellion asked, after he had gotten into the van and moved past the blank-faced driver

54

into the rear section, where Grojean and another man were sitting on metal chairs bolted to the floor. Both were drinking coffee from paper cups.

As usual, Grojean was impeccably dressed, this morning in a dark blazer and gray slacks. His silver-gray hair was neatly combed, but his eyes were slightly bloodshot from the late night before. As usual, he was playing the role of friend and protector of Mother, America, and Apple Pie.

"The gadget the police found in your rooms at the hotel," he said, waving Camellion to a chair. "You must have seen it?"

"Your tattletales in the Richmond P.D. are on their toes," Camellion answered. He sat down and crossed his legs. Behind him, the driver closed the sliding door between the two compartments. "What do the police think the device is?"

"They're so dumb they think Sherlock Holmes is a housing development," Grojean said, his sharp eyes on Camellion. "I'm asking you. Or didn't you have time to inspect it?"

"The way the bullet holes were spaced, we are of the opinion that you deliberately destroyed the machine," intoned the other man, who was pudgily built, wore shell-rimmed glasses and whose large beard looked like crushed brown wire. He reached out to the edge of the folding shelf-table to steady himself as the van got under way.

"Cream and sugar?" Sandra asked Camellion in a matter of fact voice. She had moved to one side of the van and had poured coffee for herself and Camellion from an automatic coffee machine fastened to a wide metal shelf.

"Black," Camellion said. Not the least bit concerned about Grojean's growing impatience, he accepted the steaming cup from Sandra and murmured his thanks. Only then did he give his attention to Grojean.

"All right, Camellion," Grojean said grimly. "Tell us what you know. Tell us what happened at the Lyndon Johnson."

Camellion turned his head slightly and stared at the man with the beard.

"Oh, him!" muttered Grojean. "He's Jeffrey Howard. He's with the Office of Science & Technology. Miss Kaaston is an attorney with the Domestic Affairs Section. Get on with it."

55

The Death Merchant got on with it, beginning with his parking in the hotel's parking lot and finishing with how he managed to leave the hotel and elude the police.

"Four hours later, I drove here, to the motel. It's a risk. It's only a matter of time before some wise and observant person connects me with the description of 'Clifford Bottsford.' The police artist didn't draw a very good likeness, but it's too close for comfort."

"The gismo in the attache case," insisted Grojean, putting down his paper cup.

Camellion explained in detail what he had seen on the panel, explaining why the broken glass had not been a part of a television set. He completed the report by stating his theory that he believed that Silvestter research scientists had developed a method by which an individual could be tracked by locking on to his electromagnetic aura.

Grojean looked gravely at the Death Merchant. "At all costs, we must obtain the secret of the device. If you're correct and the Silvestter people have discovered such a fantastic method, I wouldn't put it past that young monster Silvestter to sell it to a foreign power. He hates the U.S. Government as much as he hates you. He blames us and you for the death of his father."

"We can't arrest him," Sandra said pointedly. "We don't have the legal grounds. However, I do think we have enough to obtain a court order for electronic surveillance." She blinked at the Death Merchant. "You are sure that it was young Silvestter you saw?"

"I'm positive. I recognized him and Nario Hokakawa from photographs in O-files."

"I say, you only got a glance," poked in Howard. "You said that yourself. How can you be so adamant in your assertion?"

Camellion glanced annoyingly at Howard. "If I had the least doubt, I wouldn't be positive. So let's not waste time jawboning whether or not Junior is our target, my target. He is. And I'm going to put a slug in the bullseye of that target."

Howard scrutinized Camellion, as if trying to make up his mind, but he didn't comment.

"I detect a mean streak in you, Mr. Camellion." Sandra had a half-smile on her mouth.

"And it sure comes in handy at times," admitted the Death Merchant. "If it didn't, I might hesitate, and—"

56

"And 'He who hesitates is lost.' Isn't that what you were going to say?"

"Not lost!" Camellion corrected. "Dead! We only pass through this life once, and I intend to 'pass through' as long as possible." He tilted the cup to his mouth, watching her over the rim, wondering how she would look wearing nothing but a wristwatch and a smile. She was crisp, cool, and all business. He had met dozens like her, and everyone of them had been fire and ice in bed—at least those he had bedded down for the night. Or the weekend. Or, occasionally, for the entire week.

Grojean spoke with equal briskness, "I'm not waiting for any damned court order. I'm going to have side-feeders[1] put on the lines of Silvestter Foundation executives and on Winston Silvestter Junior's own phone at his Cape Cod mansion. The time involved will be enormous—a month or more at minimum."

"We could cut the time factor by tapping only the phones of the research labs," offered Howard, rubbing the tip of his nose with a thumb. "But which lab? Silvestter has steel mills, manufacturing plants and—his companies are into a little of everything. The Silvestter interests even have a small plant in Mesa, Arizona, that only makes doorknobs. Imagine that! Doorknobs!"

For the moment, no one said anything. The driver was swinging the van around a corner, and Camellion and the others were forced to brace themselves by holding onto chairs and the edge of the shelf-table and letting their bodies lean with the momentum. The Death Merchant looked at the six green telephones and the special FM radio transceiver on an opposite shelf and surmised that they were firmly fastened. They were, none of them moving half an inch as the driver completed the turn and headed the vehicle in a straight course.

"I wouldn't even bother," Camellion said to Grojean. "The time involved is not worth the effort. Silvestter isn't going to reveal anything worthwhile over any telephone. Furthermore, since the fracas at the hotel yesterday afternoon, Silvestter knows I'm onto him. He realizes we can't touch him legally, but he knows we'll be out to bury him. He'll be ten times more cautious and figure that he's now number one on my hit parade. He will also have to assume

[1] Slang for tapping a phone line.

57

that the Agency will want to get its hands on another one of those devices. Neutralizing him will not be easy."

Sandra tapped ash from her cigarette. "Your shooting the device from his hand was a lucky break for us, and a bad streak of luck for him."

"Don't underestimate Silvestster," Camellion warned. "He and Nario Hokakawa went out the window and either up or down the fire escape. Yet they escaped the police. Silvestster's only twenty-five years old, but he's every bit as clever as his old man was. He might be even more diabolical."

Deep in calculative thought, Courtland Grojean pulled a cigar from his navy blue blazer and bit off the end. Howard leaned forward as though he had not been hearing well but was determined to catch every subsequent word. He looked at Camellion, then craned his head toward Grojean. "I'm of the opinion that if we could somehow get harmonica bugs[2] and hookswitch bypasses[3] in the main offices of the Silvestster Building in New York City, we might learn something worthwhile. We might be able to develop leads that would let us move against them legally."

2 Also known as the infinity transmitter, or the "listen back." It's an eavesdropping device that must be wired into the telephone. To trigger it, the eavesdropper calls the target phone from another phone. Just before the phone begins to ring, the eavesdropper blows into a harmonica, this action sending a tone over the line to activate the bug. The bug turns itself on and prevents the telephone from ringing; but now the activated bug will pick up conversations within the room and transmit them over the line to the person who is listening. When he's heard enough, another tone of the harmonica turns the bug off and breaks the connection. Now the phone will react normally in a countermeasures check, this making it impossible for the bug to be detected, unless one takes the phone apart.
3 When a telephone is hung up, the weight of the handset pushes down two plastic pegs known as "plungers." These plungers open a switch called a hookswitch. This hookswitch disconnects the microphone in the mouthpiece from the line that links the phone with the local exchange. However, a very simple change in the wiring will shortcut the hookswitch and turn the phone into an open microphone even after it's been hung up. This trick is known in the trade as a "hookswitch bypass."

"Damn it, it's the time factor," Grojean said sternly. "Plus the fact that their own security setup is good! It should be! A man we trained reorganized Silvestters' protection system—Hugh Boden. Use your head. Boden probably has a weekly check for bugs."

Camellion stretched out his legs and watched Sandra crush out her cigarette against the upper inside of an empty coffee can. *Yeah, all fire and ice. . . .*

"Did you bring the license plates and the driver's license? I can't take the Horizon out of Virginia with only a temporary permit. The State Police would stop me."

Sandra shook her head. "No. We didn't bring them."

The Death Merchant turned and gave Grojean a stare that was twice as savage as his low voice. "That tears the rag off the bush! You know I can't linger around here. Or maybe you expect me to go north on a Greyhound! Or maybe use a pogo stick!"

"Why not use a plane?" Grojean said with a touch of schoolmasterly geniality. "We're going to fly you out of Virginia. A plane will save time and you'll be in less danger."

"I think we have some talking to do!" Camellion displayed no emotion, favorable or otherwise. What he thought was a different matter. *The gadget in the attache made you change your mind, didn't it. Now you're anxious to protect me. Now you want me to clean up the dirty laundry. . . .*

"Not about money we don't!" Grojean came right to the point and revealed that his own intuition was working in high gear. "The Agency is not going to pay you a hundred grand to save your own life. I know what you're thinking! You're right. We do want that device in the worst way, and we'll give you the usual help—unofficially of course. You might say the device—if you learn its secret—is a by-product, a 'gift' from you to us."

Grojean, his little speech finished, thrust out his jaw defensively. He didn't get the argument he expected. He drew back slightly in surprise when Camellion smiled, got up, and went over to the coffee machine.

Camellion pulled a paper cup from the holder. "At least you don't believe in adding cargo to a leaky boat." He pushed the button and watched the narrow column of coffee flow into the cup.

"I was referring to coordinating our activities. I don't

want to be bumping into any of your people in Cape Cod! Or any place else."

"It's a crazy scheme, Camellion." Grojean shifted the unlit cigar to the other side of his mouth. "Other than young Silvestter, any number of people in high places have their homes around Hyannis Port. Silvestter's mansion must be a fortress. Attacking it doesn't make sense."

"To polish a diamond one must have another diamond," Camellion said, steadying himself as he returned to his chair.

Jeffrey Howard shook his head. "Any shoot-out in Hyannis will create headlines all over the country, but"—he sighed—"as long as the Agency is not involved. . . ."

"We must begin somewhere," Grojean said, a note of finality in his voice. "*You* must begin somewhere, Camellion."

"How can you be sure that Silvestter will go to Hyannis from Virginia?" Sandra's voice was curious. "Aren't you only guessing?"

"Not in the sense that you probably mean," Camellion said. "Silvestter is aware that we're on to his scheme. He knows that we know about his gadget, whatever it is. The intelligent thing for him to do now is to retreat and plan his next move. He's no doubt in Hyannis right now."

"He might see it differently," Sandra said.

"If I were he, I'd retreat. I'm confident Silvestter's sense of survival is as sharp as mine." Camellion leaned back and eyed Grojean inquiringly. "I'll need special equipment and the help of several of your boys."

"Not to attack Silvestter's mansion you don't!" Grojean snapped.

"Quit trying to second-guess me," Camellion lashed back. "I need them to pilot a boat. They won't be anywhere near Silvestter's palatial dump."

"I suppose that's reasonable," Grojean growled, somewhat pacified. "I guess you'll want a wet-suit and other diving equipment."

"Be sure the suit has a closed circuit breathing system. That's a must."

"Mr. Camellion, if Silvestter is as clever as you think he is," asked Sandra, "how can you be sure he isn't expecting you?"

Camellion shrugged. "I can't be. At this point, I can't be sure of anything. . . ."

Chapter Six

There are times when a meat ax can get the job done better than a scalpel, those situations which require not so much patience and clever finesse but speed and a bulldozer. For that reason, the Death Merchant was taking the fight to Cleveland Winston Silvestter II, to his mansion several miles west of Hyannis, a resort community on the south central coast of Cape Cod. Cape Cod is a crooked arm peninsula that juts out from southeast Massachusetts into the Atlantic Ocean, a huge sandpit of low, rolling hills covered with scrub pine.

South of Cape Cod, in Nantucket Sound, are the two celebrated islands of Martha's Vineyard and Nantucket, separated from each other by Muskeget Channel. Important resort areas, both are triangular in shape and similar in character. Some people include a third island, Chappaquiddick, although Chappaquiddick is considered a part of Martha's Vineyard. At its closest point, it lies less than a mile east of the much larger island.

02.00 hours: Lamar "Dusty" Miller eased the cabin cruiser to a full stop, hurried down from the flybridge, went to the stern and tossed the sea-anchor into the dark water. With quick movements, he turned and hurried across the deck of the small, bobbing boat and went to the salon below the bridge.

Miller didn't know the name of the unsmiling passenger whom he and Lynn had picked up earlier that night off Popponesset Beach. He knew only that the lean, taciturn man had an important job to do—and that he had the most unusual blue eyes Miller had ever seen. They were almost a cobalt blue, eyes that not only looked right through you, but made you feel vaguely uncomfortable.

Miller saw that their passenger was already suited up and fastening the straps of the air tanks on his back, while

Lynn, wearing only a bikini, sat on a bunk, swinging her long legs and smoking a Tiparillo.

Camellion, as snug in the black wet suit as a large bull in a small bomb shelter, finished buckling the strap around his waist and looked toward Miller. "You're sure of the distance?"

"Yes sir. We're just inside Hyannis Port, 3.2 nautical miles southwest of Hyannis.

"Don't call me 'sir.' Do you have the rest of your orders straight?"

Lynn Mitchum brushed blond hair from her forehead, a trace of a smile on her lips. "What should we call you?"

"Frank will do."

"OK, Frank," agreed Miller. "Lynn and I sit out here and wait for you. If you're not back on the boat by 07.00, we forget about you and blow. That's it. There isn't anything else for us to do."

Camellion finished checking the regulator of the Emerson closed circuit OBA[1]. It functioned perfectly.

"You two shouldn't be bothered by the Coast Guard," he commented, his eyes darting to the red heart tattooed several inches above Lynn's navel. "This time of night, you're harmless kooks."

Miller's screechy laugh rang throughout the tiny cabin. "Hell yes, they'll believe us. All they have to do is look at us."

For the first time since he had been on the boat, Richard grinned. Although he didn't say so, he couldn't have agreed more. Miller—*he can't be over twenty-five!*—had a full beard and hair down to his shoulders. Put him in Arab robes and he could pass for Jesus Christ! As it was, he was wearing a faded yellow shirt and old blue jeans cut off at the thighs. Around his neck was a large pink ankh.

Lynn, who looked a few years younger than Miller, looked as off-beat as her supposed husband. Practically naked in a bikini that could have gotten lost in a man's shirt pocket, her uncombed blond hair fell loosely from her head. A long, four-strand necklace of wooden beads hung from her long neck, and she jangled when she walked, the clang-clang, tinkle-tinkle generated by the

[1] Oxygen Breathing Apparatus.

numerous metal bracelets on her arms, almost up to her elbows.

"Let's get up on deck," Camillion said and picked up a pair of swim fins. "Time is precious."

"Yes, even if it isn't money." Lynn laughed and swung her lithe body from the bunk.

Once on deck, Camellion inspected the four and a half foot long by 18 inch in diameter aluminum cylinder lashed to the deck, making sure the Demis clamps were closed all the way.

"I checked it earlier," Miller whispered, knowing that voices carry over the water on a still night. "It's watertight and the pump's working."

The Death Merchant, stooping over and putting on the swim fins, nodded. He stood up, and glanced at the ink-black sky slashed with the Milky Way.

"Let's get the carrier into the water," Camellion said to Miller. "I'll give the line a tug. Listen for my signal from shore. I'll transmit as soon as I'm ready to move inland."

They picked up the underwater carrier by its side handles and shoved it over the top of the railing. It dropped into the water with a loud splash.

"Good luck." Miller watched Camellion pull down the face mask and put the OBA mouthpiece into his mouth.

"Watch out for the tigers," Lynn said. With Miller, she watched Camellion climb up on the railing. He didn't use the standard procedure of falling backward. Instead, he carefully lowered himself over the railing and slid feet first into the water. Moments later, Miller felt a heavy tug on the nylon line. Staring down at the water, he could barely distinguish the bobbing black cylinder. But the line was free and he hauled it in.

"I'll go downstairs and send the arrival signal to the pickup in Boston," Lynn said. "You're finished up here, aren't you?"

"I will be, as soon as I lock the wheel. Go ahead. I'll be down in five minutes."

The Death Merchant swam toward the shore at a depth of 25 feet. The closed circuit SCUBA system worked perfectly. The primary advantages of closed circuit equipment are that it is quiet, can be utilized effectively on long swims, is hard to detect, is economical of gas, and is comfortable to wear. A further advantage is that 100 percent of the gas media can be utilized and the gas consumption is dependent only on the work rate, not on depth. Disadvantages include depth limitations—oxygen becomes extremely toxic at two atmospheres—and the delicacy of the equipment. Nonetheless, the closed circuit OBA lends itself well to SDV (Swimmer Delivery Vehicle) and/or sneak attack operations.

With a mix of $60/40_2O_2N$ in his tanks, Camellion could have gone to a depth of 6 fathoms (6 fathoms equals 78 feet), or slightly beyond, to 80 feet. He hadn't because he didn't need to; 25 feet was more than adequate and, at the same time, necessary. Sound can carry a long distance over the water, especially in quiet night air. The Death Merchant, having no way of knowing who might be parked in a boat ahead, didn't want anyone hearing him splashing in the water. As long as he kept at the 25 foot depth, no one could.

Even though he was an expert swimmer and in excellent physical condition, he still didn't force himself, preferring to pace himself and to conserve energy, mainly because of the carrier cylinder he had to pull. Twenty feet behind him, the metal tube was not simply a hollow cylinder. The space within the carrier was actually a cylinder within a cylinder, a 6-inch space between the two walls. This space was the water ballast tank. In the rear of the cylinder was a small but powerful Kimberly pump and two air pumps, by means of which water could either be pumped in or out of the space. The more water that was pumped in, the heavier the tank and the faster it would sink. When the water was pumped out and the ballast space filled with air, the cylinder would rise and float on the surface—the entire process similar to the "Dive!" and "Blow Tanks" system of a submarine.

Camellion frequently consulted his luminous Mod O wrist compass and the MK 1 depth gauge, as well as the SEALERS' watch. He had carefully plotted his landing point by using charts from the Defense Mapping Agency's Hydrographic Center and wasn't about to go ashore haphazardly. Ahead were long stretches of open beach, ideal for swimmers, sun bathers, and people who might want to spend the night under the stars, people who might run straight to the police, should they happen to see him emerge from the water and wade through the surf, pulling a long black cylinder.

However, there were those sections of shore that were broken up, sections that were nothing but foamy surf breaking over water-sculptured rocks. Camellion had chosen one of these lonely places, one that was 1.7 miles from the eastern edge of Cleveland Silvestter's property line.

02.46 hours. Camellion swam to the surface, pulled an underwater Starlight Viewer from his wet suit's equipment belt and snapped it on. With the waves washing around his neck and face, he looked through the eyepiece, shaking the infrared instrument to free the outer surface of the lens from water. Right on course! Fifty to sixty yards to his left were the two large rocks, poking upward like two dark swollen fingers. He had to kick repeatedly to keep afloat and to pull at the line looped over his shoulder, or the equipment carrier would have pulled him down. He had pumped a bit too much water into the ballast tank of the cylinder and it wanted to sink to a depth deeper than 25 feet. Carefully, Camellion studied the landing area and the beach to either side of it. Only rocks and empty beach, only water, sand and darkness.

He rehooked the infrared viewer on his belt and began to swim, staying on the surface, taking long, powerful strokes. Very soon he was being very cautious and fighting the surf, the sound of the foam breaking on the rocks, loud in his ears. In places, the dissolving billows pounded and roared, and Camellion had to fight the water crashing against him in his battle to get to higher ground. He finally won, the final victory coming when, standing on firm ground, he succeeded in pulling the cylinder to the side of a large protective boulder.

It took him ten minutes to open the end of the cylinder and remove the various items. Another fifteen minutes to dress in a flat black jump suit and arm himself. Plus ten more minutes to dig a grave in the sand, roll in the cylinder, and cover it. Lastly, he shoved the folding shovel in a group of rocks.

He started inland, wrapped in darkness. His eyes had become conditioned to the darkness; yet vision was limited. Always there were those overtones of shadows and indistinguishable objects looming on his route, invoking fleeting impressions and wavering illusions. In reality, the slabs of shadows and blackness were rolling hills and trees.

His booted feet crunching in dew-moist sand, Camellion paused now and then to check his wristwatch and wrist compass and to peer through the Starlight Viewer. No matter what he might do or the precautions he might take, he was in great danger from Silvestter's security system. The main house and other buildings were in the center of a one mile square section of land, every inch behind a 15-foot high chain-link fence topped with four strands of barbed wire. A few years earlier, Silvestter had attempted to electrify the fence, but local authorities had stopped him.

The top strand of barbed wire was tied in with a central alarm system at the main house. To have made the entire fence intruder-sensitive would have been useless. The property and the armed guards patrolling the fence were always objects of curiosity, people often wandering up to the fence and staring in. Many of these tourists, either accidentally or intentionally, often touched the fence. On this basis, the guards would have had nervous breakdowns investigating, each time the alarm went off. It was different with the sensitized top strand of barbed wire. Someone would actually have to be trying to crawl over the fence in order to set off the alarm.

There had been very serious legal difficulties over the guards, many of whom carried automatic rifles and submachine guns. In 1977, eager beavers of the BATF[2] had raided the compound, on the assumption that the weapons were illegal in the first place and being carried by ex-cons in the second place[3].

The BATF ended up with egg in its face. The automatic weapons were legal. Laban Denbro, the head of National Investigations, Inc., had purchased the weapons and had paid Uncle Sam the necessary "possession" tax. Another blow for the U.S. Treasury Department was that none of the weapons were being carried by any of the ex-convicts who worked for Silvestter.

---

2 The Bureau of Alcohol, Tobacco & Firearms, a branch of the United States Treasury Department.
3 In accordance with the 1968 Street Crime Bill, any person convicted of a felony, whether in state or federal court, is not allowed to own/possess a firearm.

The Feds were another worry for Camellion. All he needed was to bump into some BATF, perched in some tree and watching the area through a night viewer. If that happened, the guy would have to go. . . .

Camellion took each step with extreme caution. It was bad enough that the guards were heavily armed. Worse that they carried walkie talkies and night vision scopes. First, he had to get through the fence. The distance from the fence to the mansion was half a mile, but if he was spotted at the fence, he'd have to retreat and return to the boat. Once inside, the danger would increase proportionately. His best weapon was stealth and in remaining "invisible."

Once more he looked through the Starlight Viewer and this time saw that he was only thirty or so yards from the fence. Time now to use his smarts. He crept to the top of a long rise, got down between two masses of gulfweed and, using the S-L viewer, stared down at the fence. The east section of the fence was not a straight mile-long line of steel; neither were the other three sections. To avoid trees on each side of the fence, and to make sure that the steel chain-link barrier was in the open, the fence zigzagged, first one way and then another, reminding Camellion of the fences separating East Berlin from West Berlin. The important thing about the fence was that guards patrolled the inside perimeter, day and night, every hour on the hour.

From his position on top of the rise, Camellion could see several hundred feet to the east, and an equal distance to the left and the right. Through the viewer, the infrared infusion made the landscape appear to be bathed in twilight, each rock, each tree, each bush standing out in an eerie clarity; and so he was sure that his eyes were not playing tricks on him.

There wasn't anything to do now but wait. He pulled the M11 submachine gun from its hip pouch, thrust in the special 70-round magazine and pulled out to full length the metal telescoping stock, privately chuckling as he thought of what Grojean expected him to do. *He's expecting the impossible, and he knows it.* Obtain the secret of the Aura-tracing device? *Impossible! I'll be lucky just to get in and out. I'll be two times two lucky if I don't get killed!*

Camellion had only one goal: to find Cleveland W.

Silvestter II and kill him—*and anyone else who gets in my way*. The Death Merchant had already pronounced sentence on any person in the compound. That sentence was death.

Camellion pulled a noise suppressor from the M11 pouch and screwed it to the stubby barrel of the Ingram machine gun, which could be fired as an automatic carbine, or could be carried as a pistol with the stock removed and a shortened 16-round magazine. Sure that the silencer was properly attached, he next attached the Starlight Viewer to the special mount on top of the M11 and set the firing selector to 4-round bursts. He then began scanning the area by the fence.

Presently, he saw them, to his right—two men abreast, walking at a steady pace behind the fence. Camellion aimed in at the two security dummies, lining up the man who was closest to the inside of the fence, in the wedge sight. He didn't feel the least twang of conscience over neutralizing the two men. Had he been their target, they would have blown him away without a second thought.

The Death Merchant gently squeezed the trigger. A short and soft *bzzzittttt* issued from the noise suppressor and the weapon jumped slightly. The guard jumped a lot, as if hit by a cannon ball, the left side of his face and skull exploded by the brutal knock-out power of the .380 slugs.

The second guard died at the height of his astonishment. Turning in amazement toward his instant-dead buddy, he caught the next four .380s squarely in the chest and was dead within the blink of an eye.

Camellion removed the night vision device from the machine gun, rehooked it to the wide belt supporting the holstered Auto Mags, got to his feet, ran down the rise to the fence and went to work. What bothered him was that he had no way of knowing how soon the two dead guards might be missed. Were they on a schedule to report into a central station? Every fifteen minutes? Every thirty minutes?

He took capsules from one of the large pockets of his "Furnace Creek" fishing vest, removed the strip of tape from the side of each capsule, and, one by one, stuck them to the steel strands of the fence, all the while thinking that he was taking an enormous chance. Out in the open, he had no protection against other guards spotting him through a night sight device.

After he had placed the last capsule, he took a needle from his vest and quickly punched a hole in the end of each capsule. Within seconds, after a hole was punched, each capsule was smoking and hissing like a snake as the air activated the three chemicals, which then combined to form H6m-G1, an extremely powerful corrosive, with an active life of 5.3 seconds. But long enough for the acid to cut through the steel strands.

Camellion put his fingers through the wire, tugged, and a section of the fence came loose, leaving a five-by-three-feet opening. He moved around the two dead men and, at a fast pace, headed west, doing his best to keep as close as possible to the numerous rises or to clumps of scrub pine, although now other trees were becoming more numerous. Again, there were those times when he had to slow down and creep around fallen branches or practically tip-toe through patches of leaves, afraid that he might step on a dead branch and that the cracking sound might telegraph his presence to any guards who might be in front of him. Other times he stopped and checked out the area through the night sight scope, making a complete circle-sweep.

He spotted the two guards on his third sweep. A hundred feet in front of him. Both men leaning against a beech tree. A turkey shoot! Camellion's elation dropped to zero when one of the men picked up his automatic rifle, moved to the other side of the beech and sat down. All Camellion could see was his foot and left ankle.

Damn! Damn! Damn! The Death Merchant's knowledge of firearms was comparable to Einstein's knowledge of astrophysics. There wasn't any problem about blowing off the man's foot and ankle with a burst of machine gun fire. Nine times out of ten, the man would pass out within 60 seconds after being shot. But it was that minute that bothered Camellion. During that span of time, the man could trigger off a burst of warning shots.

Camellion was too much of a realist to waste time on useless regrets. He removed the two carry-all bags and placed them and the submachine gun on the grass. He settled down on one knee, opened one of the compartments of a bag and removed a CIA "Assassination Special," a .22 Magnum High Standard HD autoloader. The entire weapon was midnight black, the silencer being an integral part of the weapon, since it was built around the barrel.

HD in hand, Richard started to creep forward, a step at a time, gingerly testing the ground before he let his weight settle on either foot. As silent as a shadow, he crept closer and closer to the two guards, pausing now and then to reevaluate his position. In due time, he was close enough to catch snatches of the men's conversation.

". . . . cool night. . . ."

". . . . I heard on the weather radio we're supposed to get a storm before morning. I hope so. This heat—"

Richard released the cover of a narrow holster on his belt and, with his left hand, pulled out the Iron Butterfly, an unusual knife that had a very heavy 44OC stainless steel blade and a curved, well-shaped handle. Holding the knife by its handle, in his left hand, and the High Standard HD in his right, Camellion took several steps, then stopped and peered through the tall bushes between him and the two targets. He couldn't use the night scope and shoot at the same time. He could have mounted it to the sub-gun, but at close range, he preferred an ordinary autoloader. There was also a slim chance that he might be able to capture one of the men and force him to reveal the general security setup.

He could barely see the man leaning against the tree, the target who was facing him. Yes, about thirty feet. He put his foot down lightly and tested the ground. Only leaves. No twigs. No noise. He took another step, then another. He paused, stared through the blackness, listened.

"Say Chip. You notice how nervous they seem to be, up at the house?" he heard the man standing up say.

"Sure. You can bet something's in the wind," answered the man on the other side of the tree. "That's for sure. That's why we're doing extra duty. But hell, Harley! Where else can we make eighty bucks a day for just walking around?"

The muscles of Camellion's jaws knotted. Extra duty could mean more guards. *Damn it! I've got to take one half-alive and find out what's going on!*

Several more minutes, five more steps and eleven more feet passed. He would have liked to get closer, but didn't want to press his luck.

He waited until Harley had finished asking Chip if he

was still thinking of buying a new car, then raised the High Standard HD.

"I dunno," Chip said. "I was thinking that—"

The Death Merchant pulled the trigger twice, the two .22 Magnum slugs striking Harley in the center of the chest, the first stabbing projectile causing him to utter a loud but short *"UHhhhhh. . . ."*

Chip, hearing Harley's cry, didn't immediately connect it with danger, or he wouldn't have called out, "Hey, was that you? What's wrong?"

He picked up the Armalite M16 rifle and was turning around when Harley's corpse toppled sideways to the grass. It was then that Chip heard Camellion crashing through the brush toward the tree.

A veteran of Vietnam, Chip was at home with violent death, and he was very fast. He brought up the M16 and spun around from behind the tree—to the left of the Death Merchant, who was now only eight feet away. Harley was stone dead, but Chip was very much alive. Yet the fingers of his left hand never reached the safety lever of the M16. His right shoulder exploded with burning pain, the savage agony draining him of strength and shattering his will power. By the time that he put it together he'd been stabbed by a thrown knife, the attacker was all over him. Chip's finger, pulled by reflex, squeezed the trigger, but the safety was on and the M16 would not fire. The next thing he knew, the rifle had been jerked from his hand and the attacker was shoving the muzzle of a strange looking weapon in his face. He thought of pushing the ON button of the walkie talkie on his belt. A moment later, his attacker had jerked the set from his belt and was whispering, "Yell or try to sound a warning and I'll blow both your eyes out."

Chip sagged against the tree, blood pouring from his shoulder. He stared at the hard-faced man and had to make an extra effort to keep from vomiting.

The Death Merchant put a hand on Chip's left shoulder, shoved him to the base of the tree, got down in front of him and shoved the muzzle of the HD under his chin.

"How many of you are guarding this estate?" Camellion demanded. "Don't stall or I'll blow you in ten different directions."

Chip's mouth was very dry, his tongue a monstrously parched worm. Trembling from pain and fear, he looked at his right shoulder and saw the handle of the Iron Butterfly sticking out like a large black splinter. He heard himself saying in a strange voice, "I'm not sure off-hand. There's maybe fifty or sixty of us."

"Don't tell me that many of your crumbs are protecting the fence!" snarled Camellion.

"No, no! I don't mean that," croaked Chip. "Some of the guards are at the main house. Half of the force is sleeping. They're the day shift. They'll take over at seven in the morning."

"Is Silvestter at the main house?"

"I think so. At least I saw him about eight last night with Mr. Meunier. They were in back of the house seeing the others off."

"What others—and how did they leave?"

The others turned out to be Hugh Boden and Nario Hokakawa. The two men had left by helicopter. But Chip didn't know their destination.

"Honest, I don't know," he said, groaning with pain. "Look, I'm just a guard. I don't know anything about Mr. Silvestter and his associates. I don't know anything."

"I don't suppose you know anything about a gadget that tracks by locking in on the human aura?"

In spite of his pain, Chip stared incredulously at the Death Merchant. "I don't know what you're talking about. I never heard of it." He groaned again. "Listen, I don't want to die. I—"

"Then you shouldn't be working for Silvestter!" Camellion pulled the trigger of the silenced High Standard, the slight sound from the noise suppressor a whispering elegy for Chip whose eyes rolled back and whose mouth filled with blood. The bullet had torn through his lower jaw, his tongue, the roof of his mouth and, passing through the Sphenoid sinus cavity, had lodged in his brain.

The corpse fell forward, the bloody head coming to rest between the knees. Camellion pulled the Iron Butterfly from the shoulder of the corpse and carefully, almost tenderly, wiped the bloody two and a half inch blade on the dead man's back.

"Fifty or sixty of us." That's just great. But Silvestter's there. For now, he is all that matters.

Camellion hurried back to where he had left the shoulder bags and the Ingram M11 submachine gun. He slung the bags over his shoulders, picked up the deadly little chatter box and once more headed west through the darkness. He thought he heard a rumble in the west. Thunder? He couldn't be sure. But he hoped it was. A storm would create confusion and cover his retreat.

His progress was fast, yet limited, his speed determined by the amount of leaves and branches in his path. Once he heard faint voices. Two men, far to his right, maybe thirty yards away. Ready with the M11, he waited until the voices faded in the darkness; then he moved ahead, picking his way around clumps of thick knotweed or bitterdock.

The house suddenly confronted him. There it was, in a wide wall of unbroken blackness—Wind Whirl, the Silvestter mansion, a magnificent structure that rose boldly and beautifully. Regardless of its imposing immensity, Wind Whirl stood out like some monstrous monument misplaced in time and locale.

Built by Cleveland Winston Silvestter II's grandfather, the Victorian house was enormous, and it was proud . . . an arrogant house that seemed to be personified with the fierceness and determination of all three Silvestters— grandfather, son, and grandson. The turreted gables, rounded dormers and other Victorian features suggested past glory and musty secrets, while the long, straight lines of feudal greatness and strength gave the impression of embrasures and battlements, there to defend and destroy all Silvestter enemies.

The Death Merchant stared at Wind Whirl, noticing that a dozen windows shone with yellow light. *Yes sir. It's something right out of a Hitchcock movie. I'll bet Dracula is the butler and Frankenstein is the gardener!* He had the feeling that the house was alive, poised and waiting, as if taunting him, daring him to as much as touch one of its massive gray stones.

It was the fence and the modern addition to the house that added to the grotesqueness of the place, as if youth and age were sharing an unstable marriage.

A chain-link fence, 12-feet high and set several hundred feet away from the house, formed a square around Wind Whirl. The fence was not supposed to be there. But there it was. The CIA had goofed. Camellion wasn't unduly surprised, only frustrated.

The Death Merchant looked around him. "Burning" his way past the fence would be a risk that only a madman would take. There were small lights at each corner and in the center of the fence.

Camellion thought of turning back, of scratching the kill-probe. Certainly, to continue was to increase his chances of getting his head blown off. But he couldn't keep running and dodging the forces of Silvestter II for the remainder of his life. To do so would be to negate the very purpose for his existence. *I'm damned if I do and I'm damned if I don't. I might as well go ahead and take my chances right now. I can expect no less, living among these savage and primitive human beings!*

He moved from tree to tree. He would stop, wait, look around, then move again. Much closer now, Wind Whirl became more three dimensional, taking on a fierce reality. The lighted windows widened, the house became more massive, more virulent, more deadly. Alive! A cold-blooded enemy waiting to devour him!

Only a hundred feet from the eastern section of the fence, Camellion could see the other buildings within the confines of the chain-link barrier—a long garage that could hold a dozen cars; a Victorian carriage house, looking completely out of place, like a Boy Scout at a convention of the Mafia! There was an L-shaped building made of brick, and Camellion assumed it was the barrack where the guards made their quarters. A few smaller buildings.

He unhooked the night sight scope and listened for voices. Crickets. That was all. Watching for guards, he crept to his right, toward the north, until he could see the entire new section, a two story brick rectangle with a top sun deck stretching the length of the roof. Steps leading from the sun deck to the concrete patio. A round swimming pool north of the patio. Deck chairs and other furniture around the pool.

It looked very peaceful. He couldn't see any guards. But there had to be security men inside the house. And Silvestter was there, unless the guard had not told the truth.

Camellion studied the fence. The section directly in front of him—due east—would do. Beyond the fence, the east side of the house was dark. In the center of the east side, a solarium jutted out like a huge boil, its base flat on the ground.

A deep rumble to the west. This time Camellion was positive. Thunder. A storm was brewing in the kettle of black sky. He looked to the left, to the right, and behind him. He set his jaw; his eyes glittered strangely. They might get him, but they would sure know he had been there.

Come, Brother Death . . . let's go to work. . . .

The thicket ended seventy to eighty feet in front of the east fence, although there were tall, massive oaks and carefully trimmed shrubbery around the mansion itself, on the inside of the fence. It was the wide open space in front of the east side fence that annoyed the Death Merchant. He became downright troubled when, only thirty feet from the fence, he saw two sets of headlights moving along the fence on the north side, and, to his left, four guards moving out of the bush. There had to be a reason for such activity. There was.

They've either found the guy in the woods or the two jokers I terminated by the fence. Maybe all three!

The four guards spotted Camellion at the same time he sighted them. They did have a disadvantage. They were grouped together and wasted precious seconds in an effort to spread out. By then it was too late.

The Death Merchant, dodging and weaving from side to side, triggered the M11, the compact submachine gun shuddering in his hands. He hoped to cut down the four guards before they could fire a warning shot. If he could, he might then be able to smear the jokers in the jeeps before they could swing into action and throw lead in his direction. No such luck. His streams of .380 hollow cavity projectiles chopped into the four men, almost at the same time that one of the guards got off a short burst from his automatic rifle, the rapid reports ringing out across the countryside.

A swarm of AR18 slugs buzzed to the left of Camellion, only inches from his body, one boat-tailed bullet coming so close to his head it almost kissed him. His own slugs hadn't missed. Two of the guards went down with bullets in their chests and stomachs. The third man was about to fire a burst at the Death Merchant when a .380 projectile struck him in the manubrium, the bone above the sternum, and zipped through the lower part of his trachea. He was almost dead when two more slugs punctured his

75

lungs and made an exit from his back. The last man, who had gotten off a burst at Camellion, caught two slugs in the stomach, yelled, stumbled, and fell.

The quick-thinking Camellion ran for his life. He sprinted to the dead men on the ground, flopped down among them, and aimed toward the north, his body close to Valmet M-71S semi-automatic rifle. He realized that, unless he was wrong, the guards in the two jeeps wouldn't fire until they were sure that they weren't trying to kill any of their own kind. Camellion was right. The guards in the jeeps didn't fire. Side by side, the jeeps proceeded toward Camellion and the four corpses on the ground, increasing speed slightly when the drivers spotted the bodies on the ground.

A man in the left jeep stood up for a better look, as did several guards in the right vehicle. Not willing to wait any longer, the Death Merchant cut loose with a long, sweeping left to right burst, his first targets the drivers. Still firing, he also jumped to his feet. To remain a stationary target would increase his chances of dying by half.

The noise suppressor on the M11 buzzed. Windshield glass shattered. Guards yelled in pain and confusion, but not for long. The drivers were terminated instantly, as well as the two men standing in the jeeps. The drivers dead, the jeeps swerved and began an erratic course. The one to the left headed toward the trees and brush. Because the man next to the driver was also a brand new corpse, one of the guards in the rear seat leaned over and tried to grab the wheel and, at the same time, pull the driver to one side, since the driver's foot was wedged against the gas pedal and held there by the weight of the corpse's body. He stopped after a .380 slug hit him in the forehead, the impact knocking him back against the last man alive in the jeep. This man, who was trying to keep his balance and simultaneously get off shots at the zig-zagging figure ahead, quit living moments later, taking slugs in his left arm and chest. He fell out of the careening jeep, hit the ground and lay still.

The other driverless jeep swerved toward the chain-link fence, its only live occupants the two men in the rear, one of whom was doing his best to shove aside the dead driver while his companion succeeded in getting off a chain of

AR-10 slugs at Camellion, who was racing toward the jeep.

Camellion's deviating course, one that made him more difficult to hit than a terrified roadrunner, saved his life in more ways than one. Six slugs zinged by harmlessly. The seventh came so close that it ripped off the bottom end of a belt loop and grazed the belt of his pants on the left side. The seventh struck the round, metal body of the Starlight viewer. There was a loud WHANG. The full metal jacketed slug stabbed through the outside casing, then struck the inside casing on the opposite side and ricocheted inside the metal tube. For a moment the Death Merchant thought he had been hit, the King Kong impact smashing him backward with such force that he almost lost his balance. As it turned out, the bullet's striking the Starlight viewer saved his life.

A Thompson submachine gun roared from an open window on the second floor of Wind Whirl, while Camellion was righting himself, a chain of .45 projectiles thudding into the ground where the Death Merchant had been only moments before.

The gunner didn't have time to correct his aim. Camellion spun with incredible speed, jumped to the right, threw up the Ingram and snap-fired, basing his aim on sheer sound. The guard, five holes in his chest, died faster than a maple losing its leaves in a November gale. He dropped the submachine gun, fell out of the window and crashed through the glass roof of the solarium below.

The last two men in the jeep were next in line to find out that one can't build a cannon barrel around an empty hole. Camellion had lost neither his speed nor his sting. He swung toward the north, caught a flash of the jeep and the men and fired a short burst—short because the firing pin clicked on an empty chamber. He did, however, have the brief satisfaction of hearing one man scream and seeing both men go down.

Not about to slow down, Camellion pulled an Auto Mag from a holster, slung the sling strap of the Ingram over one shoulder, and raced toward the jeep. A few seconds later the jeep slammed into the fence with a terrific noise. At 30 MPH, the vehicle didn't tear through the fence; all the bumper did was put a long dent in the chain-links, making them bulge inward, and snapping a few of the steel strands. The jeep came to a full stop. The crash had jarred the dead driver's foot from the gas pedal.

Camellion was a scant six feet from the jeep when one of the men in back reared up with the unexpectedness of a hidden snake in the act of striking, his hands full of a Ruger Mini-14, an automatic rifle chambered for the .223 cartridge. The weapon roared, the muzzle winking flashes of flame. But the Death Merchant had jumped from the path of the trajectory a split second earlier, during that fraction of lag time, just before the man pulled the trigger, when the man had to adjust his line of sight.

The stream of .223 death breezed by Camellion, who fired twice while still in furious motion, the big 200/International AMP roaring with a deep BERRROOOMMMMMM. A .41 AMP cartridge is one of the most powerful on earth, 170 grains pushing along the projectile at 1900 f.p.s. What it did to the guard was ample evidence of its power. The first bullet tore a hole in his chest the size of an apple, the tremendous smash scattering tiny bits of shirt-cloth, flesh, bone and blood over the floor and the rear seat. The second projectile tore through the flap-door of the jeep, stabbed a hole through the dead man's stomach and came to rest against his backbone. The damn fool might as well have sat on a hand grenade.

The Death Merchant glanced at the corpse lying in a pool of its own blood and smiled. The man had only pretended to be neutralized, his life spared for a few minutes by the M11's running out of ammo.

Camellion went to work, sweat running in rivers down his chest and back. He pulled the dead driver from behind the steering wheel and dumped him on the ground, then got into the driver's seat, shoved out the other corpse in the front seat, started the engine and put the jeep in reverse, spinning the front wheels in his rush. He heard shouts from the north side of the huge house and spotted three sets of headlights to the south, the vehicles moving on the outside of the fence. Back toward the woods, he heard more voices as he slammed on the brakes and skidded the jeep to a stop, thirty feet to the east of the chain-link fence. He took a demolition grenade from one of his shoulder bags, pulled the ring, flipped it toward the fence and hunched down as low as possible.

He was reaching down and picking up a World War II Browning Automatic Rifle, dropped by the guard who had been sitting by the driver, when the grenade exploded with a roar that made the ground tremble. He swung around to the east and raked the wood with the BAR and watched the .30-06 slugs pepper the leaves, salt the trees, and chop off small branches—several cries of pain his reward. At least, he thought grimly, it would take a few minutes for the guards to reorganize. By then, he'd be inside the fence.

He threw down the BAR, shifted gears and jammed his foot down on the gas. The jeep shot forward like some wild animal bent on revenge. At better than 40 m.p.h., the vehicle shot through the jagged hole in the fence, accompanied by slugs that not only thudded into the vehicle but cut the air close to Camellion. Men in the approaching jeeps were firing, but the half a minute head start had made the difference.

The Death Merchant didn't put on the brakes. On the contrary, he put on more speed and deliberately aimed the jeep at the east side of the solarium.

"Mighty is the arm of the Lord!" he muttered with a low laugh.

Now he was practically on top of the solarium. He got down in the seat and covered his head with his arms.

The jeep slammed into the glass wall, the sound of the crash bursting out over the countryside!

The Death Merchant was in Wind Whirl. . . .

Chapter Seven

Courtland Grojean and Lybrand Hayes drove through the Dolly Madison entrance, one of the three gates at Langley, parked, and hurried into Administration.

"It's good to be back, damned good," Hayes said.

Grojean didn't reply. He knew the feeling, having experienced it years before when, after a tour of duty overseas, he had returned to CIA headquarters. It was more than a feeling of pride, a feeling of personal achievement. The white marble walls and huge columns of the immense foyer were the beginning of security, reminding Grojean and Hayes that they were employees of the world's second largest intelligence agency[1]; moreover that they were more than members of the clandestine service[2]; but that they were the elite of the very exclusive Q-Department, so ultra-secret that, theoretically, it didn't exist.

Once the guards had checked their print-and-punch IDs, Grojean and Hayes turned left to the "red" elevators and rode up to the fourth floor where they turned right and hurried down the length of "B" corridor, then left into "C" corridor. The bare walls were off-white, the floors covered with gray-green vinyl tile. Only the doors added

---

[1] The Soviet KGB is the largest. But the best is probably the Israeli intelligence service; the Iranian and the South Korean the deadliest.

[2] There are 4,500 employees in the CIA's clandestine services. They share the building with 10,000 overt employees. About a third of the employees of the clandestine services are also overt CIA, coming and going with the sensitive undercover officers. The Q-Department has less than 500 members; these men and women are overt and covert. Some of the best, like Camellion, are neither, officially. Officially they don't even exist.

life and color. They were painted red, green, blue, or orange.

The two men hurried to an unmarked green door, opened it and walked into a small room containing only a plain wooden desk and a wooden straightback chair. They went across the room to a blue door and Grojean pressed the buttons of the combination lock, setting them into the proper sequence. The door swung open. Grojean and Hayes stepped inside. The door swung shut, automatically locking itself and turning on the light, which was a single bulb in the center of the ceiling. To make sure the door was locked and the "white-sound" generators operating, Grojean glanced at the small bulb above the door. It was glowing pink.

"It must be important, Court," Hayes said, "or you wouldn't have brought me to a 'talk-in'[3]. I assume we are in a 'talk-in?' "

Grojean nodded at his old friend and indicated that he should sit down in one of the chairs in front of the desk. The room was an eight-by-ten-foot cubicle, with a steel desk, credenza, rug, and two stuffed leather chairs.

Grojean sat down across from Hayes, who was slender, of medium height, with gray hair and eyes, and who had just arrived from London, England, where he had been attached to the CIA station. In rank he was a GS 14 field case officer, working both overt and covert; but first, last and always he was a "Q-man."

"Ly, I think we have a leak," Grojean said thoughtfully, tension and worry reflected in the lines and shadows of his face. Grojean talked for ten minutes and when he had finished, Hayes' expression was as apprehensive as his own.

"This disconnect man of yours," began Hayes, tamping his pipe, "the one Silvestter is trying to kill. I suppose his true identity doesn't make any difference?"

"You wouldn't know him," Grojean said and settled back in the chair. "What matters is the leak. I know that Boden and Meunier had a hand in it. They're not important. We can terminate them any time. But I'm almost positive that those two had help from someone high up, someone well placed . . . maybe in Q itself."

[3] An Agency acronym for a room in which "white sound" generators cancel out any "bugs" or hidden transmitters.

"My God, Court! If you're right, if Q's been penetrated!" Hayes' eyes focused directly on his boss. "But as you yourself said, you don't have anything *tangible* to connect Boden and Meunier. You know they made the leak about your man. OK. They might be operating independently of an agent-in-place. They might not even know of his existence, if he does exist. We could be dealing with two entirely different matters."

"I've thought of that," admitted Grojean, watching Hayes light his pipe. "Right now, I'm up against a stone wall. If I attempt any kind of probe, I'll tip off the creep 'in-place.' We have got to do it another way."

Hayes took the pipe from his mouth. "Which is why you brought me back from London."

Grojean looked mildly at Hayes, whom he had known for sixteen years and trusted implicitly. He was pure CIA. His career had cost him his wife, and his children, grown and married, no longer spoke to him. Now, his only home, his only refuge, was the Agency.

"As far as the London station is concerned, you're on indefinite leave and getting a suntan in Florida," Grojean said. "You'll have more than enough time and cover to head the network I'm forming. You'll meet the others tomorrow morning—seven men I've hand-picked, old Q hands like yourself. Three are especially valuable. Technically, they're CI-covert."

"Any designation?"

"SBY[4]. By the way"—Grojean tried to sound casual, "how many years till your pension? I know that you're close to fifty."

"Two more years. I'm forty-seven," Hayes said.

Grojean regarded Hayes with patient eyes. "Of course, you realize that what I am proposing is strictly illegal. If we're found out, the DDCI[5] will have to cashier all of us. Think about it, Ly. You could be throwing away twenty thousand dollars a year for life."

4 All CIA agents and operations are identified by special cryptonyms. Usually these cryptonyms begin with two letter digraphs. The letters are pronounced individually. "SBY" would be "S," "B," "Y." Now and then the desk people at the Agency will blend the digraph into a pronounceable word, for example PIC-NIC, or a phrase, HI-BOTTOMS-WEST.

5 Deputy Director of Central Intelligence.

"Wrong," Hayes said primly. "My Grade GS 15 came in just before I left London. My pension will be $21,500 a year—provided I'll be able to collect it."

Grojean wasn't amused by what he considered to be irrelevant.

"I want you to know what you're getting into and what it could cost you."

Hayes smiled tolerantly and blew a cloud of smoke into the air. Expensively dressed in an Italian suit, he looked like something right out of Esquire.

"As I see it, there won't be much of an Agency if we've been penetrated and we don't find the mole. Personally, I'm somewhat curious about this disconnect[6] of yours. As I recall, it was the Death Merchant who settled Silvestter senior's hash—in Australia, wasn't it? Your disconnect has to be the Death Merchant, not that I give a damn."

Grojean swallowed Hayes' imputation without batting an eye or feeling angered. The man wasn't waltzing him around. He had arrived at a logical conclusion and had stated the results of his analysis. After all, Hayes was too much of a pro to be clouded for very long.

"It's the Merchant," admitted Grojean. He looked at his wristwatch—2:34 A.M. "And right now, he should be doing something about Silvestter Junior."

Hayes smiled knowingly. "Uh huh. Night work." He carefully adjusted his eyeglasses and put down his pipe. "Let's get back to SBY. How do we begin the actual operation?"

Grojean thought for a moment. Again he looked at his wristwatch. His eyes then moved to Hayes. "We're going to tap three phones for a start—Clark Wyland's, Simon Tuskin's, and the DDCI's!"

Hayes started to cough, choking on the smoke he had inhaled.

---

[6] Any individual who works for the Central Intelligence Agency on a covert basis but is not a member of the Agency. However, such "civilian" disconnects are extremely rare in Q.

Chapter Eight

Cleveland Winston Silvestter II was an unhappy man, so miserable that if his frustration could have been measured in degrees of heat, the mercury in a thermometer would have burst through the top of the tube. The ambush in Mexico had been more than simple failure. With the exception of Silvestter and the pilot of the helicopter, the Death Merchant had annihilated the entire force. The trap at the Lyndon Johnson Hotel had been a catastrophe. Richard Camellion had done far more than kill everyone but Silvestter and Nario Hokakawa: he had shot the Auraic Transfinder from Nario's hand. Now he had a lead as to how he was being tracked. It followed that the Central Intelligence Agency had to be involved and perhaps the Federal Bureau of Investigation. To make matters worse, the Death Merchant could not be found, not until a bigger and much better Auraic Transfinder was put into operation.

"Mr. Silvestter, I can assure you that the Federal authorities can't move against us," Gerald Meunier said. "They haven't the evidence. Naturally, the Agency will work very covertly to find out the nature of the Auraic Transfinder . . . what it does, who made it, etc."

Silvestter, who was pacing up and down on the carpet, turned and regarded Meunier with cold, cruel eyes. "I'm not paying you a hundred thousand dollars a year to tell me what I already know," he snapped. "I'm not concerned what the Government can do legally. It's what that damned Camellion will do *illegally* that bothers me."

Meunier was neither impressed by money, power, or people in high places, nor was he the kind of man not to defend himself, either verbally or physically.

"You pay me a hundred grand a year to have the best industrial security system in the country," he said. He leaned back in his chair, crossed his legs and folded his arms over his chest. "In the first year at American Metals, I saved the company over $180,000. The same system is in use in all your factories. Last year alone, it was estimated that the overall theft factor was reduced 96.4 percent. That means millions of dollars in tools and other items that weren't stolen from your factories. I'm worth a hundred grand a year and you know it!"

One of the bodyguards, playing poker at a table with three other guards, glanced over at Meunier, surprise on his face, but he didn't say anything. Finally he turned away from Meunier's unflinching eyes.

Silvestter acted as if he hadn't heard Meunier. He strode over to a swivel recliner and stretched out; he placed his hands in back of his head and looked up at a Calder mobile hanging from the ceiling.

"Gerald, you're still convinced that Camellion won't try to come here?" he said at length.

"Richard Camellion is extremely intelligent," Meunier replied confidently, "and he has more nerve than twenty angry Turks. But he's not a fool. It's too bad he isn't, or he'd maybe take the risk. If he came here, we could kill him."

Silvestter made a disdainful noise. "The gospel according to 'Saint Meunier!'" He sat up on the recliner and looked sternly at Meunier, who stood six feet three inches tall, had wind-blown dark-blond hair and the physique of a powerfully built athlete. "It was your idea and Boden's to try to assassinate him at the Lyndon Johnson. A little more and Nario and I would have been trapped by the police."

"Hugh and I warned you not to go to Mexico," Meunier said calmly, getting up from the chair. "We pointed out that with Camellion's unique talents, you'd be taking a risk. But you insisted on being there. We told you not to go to the hotel in Richmond. Hell no! You had to go!"

Without looking at Silvestter, he walked to the built-in bar in the wall, leaned over the top and opened a cooler.

Silvestter got to his feet, his face as dark as the sky before a storm, his brown eyes as cold as steel. He watched Meunier take out a bottle of root beer and open it. Meunier was a non-drinker, for which Silvestter admired him.

"You know why I insisted on being there," Silvestter said, his voice bitter. "Richard Camellion murdered my father. It's my bullet that's going to end his life. I don't care how many years you were in the CIA. Camellion will come here. When he does, if the guards outside don't kill him—I will!"

Once more Silvestter began to pace, to walk back and forth like some sort of caged animal, a terrible look on his face.

Meunier left the bar, went back to his chair and sat down, an enigmatic smile fixed on his face. During the course of his career with the Agency, he had met all kinds of people: the ruthless and the stupid, the brutal and the dumb. Young Silvestter was something else. If anything, he was sinister, almost diabolical in his hatred for Richard Camellion, a hatred that lived and breathed and burned continuously within him. In spite of his youth, he wasn't reckless, never making a move that wasn't well planned, down to the last detail.

Meunier took a long swallow of root beer, then placed the bottle on a carved stand next to the chair. *Half-genius, half-clown, and all psychopath*—that was Hugh's assessment of Silvestter. Meunier recalled that Silvestter hadn't flinched a bit at paying him and Boden $200,000 each to finger Richard Camellion.

They were taking an enormous risk, Boden had pointed out to Silvestter. Suppose something went wrong? Suppose the CIA somehow learned that they had revealed secrets from Q-files? The CIA had its own way of dealing with traitors within its own ranks. The sentence was always the same—termination. Silvestter had not put up any kind of argument, and the $400,000 had been deposited to Swiss bank accounts.

Many months later everything had fallen apart. The Death Merchant had eluded both carefully planned ambushes. One of the Auraic Transfinders had fallen into Camellion's hands. Or had it? Had he gotten the device out of the hotel? For that matter, had he even found it? Probably so. But he couldn't have had time to examine it very carefully. So what? None of this pointed an accusing finger at Boden and Meunier—not legally. Little nagging darts of fear and doubt jabbed at Meunier. It wasn't the legal angle that counted. It was Richard Camellion and Courtland Grojean who presented the real danger. Grojean thought like a mobster and lived like a con man, the vicious wheels of his mind always turning. The Death

Merchant was even worse. From what Meunier had read in Q-files, there was a quality of deadliness about Camellion that defied all rational analysis. Another nagging thought. Had they gotten themselves into something too big? Well and good to say that it was Silvestter who was after Camellion! More likely than not, Camellion and Grojean might put two and two together and come up with Boden and Meunier. Maybe so. Yet it was too late. You can't jump out of a window on the tenth floor and change your mind halfway down. Meunier knew that he and Boden were up to their necks in the plot; all they could do now was see it through. Even so, Meunier was convinced that the Death Merchant wouldn't dare come to Wind Whirl.

Or would he?

And Silvestter? Meunier felt like laughing. When Silvestter was wearing a business suit, he looked like a successful young lawyer. Right now, he looked like a damn fool, dressed as he was in a blue and white-striped kaftan that reminded Meunier of a long nightgown. He certainly had a gift for rationalizing, for making his own kind of "truth." Camellion "murdering" his father! What nonsense. Meunier had read the report, immaculately typed and in the crispest form of Washington's bureaucratic English. Silvestter senior, nut that he was, had attempted to promote World War III, and the Death Merchant had killed him for it. Murder? It was a justifiable execution.

Another thing about Silvestter Jr. was that the millions, left to him by his nutty father, hadn't gone to his head. He wasn't queer, but neither was he interested in girls. He didn't drink; he didn't smoke. But he didn't try to "reform" those who did. There wasn't anything ostentatious about his life-style either. And Wind Whirl! My God, the foyer was larger than the living room of most American homes. Beyond the foyer was a huge space with four clusters of antique furniture, something like a hotel lobby. That was the living room. There were two dining rooms. A wall of french windows opened onto the swimming pool that contained no water. The right wing of the house contained nine bedrooms, each with its own bath. None of them in use. The left wing contained servants' quarters; yet there were no servants. Silvestter cooked his own food and slept in a small room in the new addition he had had built. The main part of the house went uncleaned. Dust piled on dust, except when one of the guards, in one of the unused rooms, got tired of looking at the mess and brushed off this or that piece of furniture.

Silvestter's constant pacing began to annoy Meunier. Why bother to say anything. No point in arguing with the psychopath. He glanced disdainfully at the four guards playing poker. Stupid types, without breeding or any intellectual curiosity, men who saw the world in shades of black or white, for whom everything could be reduced to a simple answer; the kind of men who fought wars and shouted patriotic slogans! Trash, too dumb to know their real worth . . . who would risk their lives for a pittance.

Damn Silvestter and his pacing! "There's another element that increases our safety factor," began Meunier. "Should Camellion suspect what the device is, he has no way of knowing its range, which is to say he doesn't know how effective it is." He went on as Silvestter walked over to a chair, gathered up the silk kaftan to his knees, and sat down. "Since he was ambushed in Mexico, only hours after arriving from the Far East, he might even believe that our little gadget has a world-wide range."

"The larger model that Boden is bringing from New York will have a three thousand mile range," Silvestter said triumphantly. He jabbed in the air with a finger that was abnormally long and thin. In fact, all of his fingers seemed to be articulated with knots rather than joints. "And if Camellion is the superman you and Boden think he is, he could deduce the truth about Mexico and suspect how we knew he would be in Valle Hermoso." He gave the guards a brief, suspicious glance, leaned closer to Meunier and lowered his voice to a whisper. "He might suspect that we had help from the CIA. Have you considered that, Meunier?"

Meunier had and said so. "There's a difference between what he knows and what he suspects. Wherever he is at this moment, he has to be wondering if we're locking in on him with the Auraic Transfinder. There's no way he can know its range is only seventeen hundred miles and that it consists of two components." He chuckled. "Two or twenty sections. It couldn't make him any difference."

"I wish we had stayed in Richmond," Silvestter said bitterly. "We might have been able to track him with the L-Model. I doubt if he left the Richmond area immediately."

"He hid out in an emergency station," Meunier said. "Some out-of-the-way motel, or maybe even an Agency 'house.' He wouldn't have stayed there long enough for us to probe his E.L.M. field. That's a day and a half job." He thought for a moment, then added brusquely, "From Richmond, I think he went to New York. He did have a secret base there. He mentioned it once in one of his reports."

Silvestter's eyes became shrewd. "None of his other personal stations were mentioned? If I were he, I'd hole up on familiar home ground. I'd go back to the Big Thicket."

"Keep thinking like that and we'll lose him," warned Meunier. "Don't try to plot Camellion's course on the basis of your own strategy. He's far too clever to be tracked or tricked by any kind of logical deduction." His eyes lidded thoughtfully and he finished with a triumphant flourish. "I say this, and you will do well to remember it: it would be suicide to go after Camellion in the Big Thicket. He'd terminate all of us before we even got off to a good start."

"I was under the impression that he had a string of bases across the country." Silvestter's tone was impatient.

Meunier's face crinkled. "Not a 'string.' Maybe three or four, from what I've been able to learn. You keep forgetting that Camellion is the best disconnect agent the CIA has. Very, very little about his personal life was in the Q files. Only *he* knows where the bases are. I know about the one in New York City because he mentioned it once in a report. It was attacked. I doubt if it's there any more."

"We'll soon know if you're right," Silvestter said stubbornly. "If Camellion is in New York, Boden and Nario will pinpoint his base with the larger unit." He waved a hand impatiently. "Yes, yes. . . . His old station might be closed and he might be at a new base. Finding him is all that matters." Carried away by his own rhetoric, Silvestter shook a finger at Meunier. "But you're wrong. You'll find out that Camellion isn't the type to hide out and wait for us to come to him. You'll see. . . ."

Meunier sneered with his eyes. "He's not a crash-in hotdog either." He picked up the empty pop bottle, went to the bar and put the bottle in a wooden case, glancing at the four bodyguards as he straightened up. Tired of playing cards, the guards had pushed back their chairs and were getting up from the table. Displeasure flashed in Meunier's eyes. Mawbecker and Wainwring had been twenty-year-men in the U.S. Army, both retiring at about the same time. They were clods but socially palatable to Meunier. They knew their place and recognized their betters.

Leonard Banta and Jasper Mines were cut from a different bolt of cloth—pure gunnysack. A 320-pound slob, Banta was built like a balloon, had a face like a muddy road map that had been stepped on, and a mind that would have frightened a cobra. Somewhere along the dirty route of his thirty-four years, he had picked up the moniker of "Little Beans."

Half the weight and size of Little Beans, Mines was a weasel of a guy, with a gray face that looked like he had been born with a veil over it. He had made his face more repulsive by sporting a mustache that grew downward to link with a short, fuzzy beard. Everytime he opened his mouth, he reminded Meunier of a whiskered fish.

The four guards went to the bar. Meunier walked to his chair and sat down, feeling satisfied and superior. All four guards always addressed him as Mr. Meunier, including Little Beans, who fancied himself an expert in karate. A great teaser because he was a sadist, Little Beans had once grabbed Meunier in a rear underarm body hold—that is, he tried to. Meunier, who held belts in several schools of karate, had dislocated Little Beans' left shoulder and had barely missed shattering his right kneecap. Little Beans had limped for more than a month.

"Watch your drinking!" Silvestter called out to the guards. "No hard liquor."

"We're only drinking three-two beer, sir," Bernie Wainwring said.

"No more than a couple of cans each!" Silvestter said sharply, as befitted one whose belief was being questioned. "Alcohol slows the reflexes and makes mush of the brain."

Meunier yawned. He didn't bother to put his hand over his mouth. His years with the CIA had conditioned him to function at all hours, day or night, and with a minimum of sleep, but there wasn't any sense in staying awake when he didn't have to. Silvestter could sit there in his silly looking kaftan. He was a "night person," who functioned best after the sun had gone down. The later it got, the more "awake" he became.

"I'm going to bed," Meunier said. "I—"

The distant reports of an automatic weapon being fired cut off his words in mid-sentence.

The guards froze, hands around cold aluminum cans.

Cleveland Winston Silvestter II jumped to his feet, the look on his face so ferocious and demonic that, for a moment, Meunier could not believe what he was seeing.

"New York, you said!" Silvestter hissed. "You idiot! He's here! He's right outside!"

Chapter Nine

This is definitely not one of history's immortal moments!
The loud crash of the jeep, smashing through the glass
wall of the Solarium, knocked the ridiculous thought from
the Death Merchant's mind and slammed him back against
the seat. His arms over his head, his face buried against
the back of the rear seat, he felt a terrific jolt and heard
glass falling all around him. The jeep half-spun around,
then jerked to a stop, the momentum throwing him to
the floor of the vehicle. Several more large pieces of glass
fell and broke. A wooden frame, half in, half out, groaned.
Then a chilling silence.

His breath rolling back in his throat, Camellion crawled
out of the jeep, shook slivers of glass from his clothes
and looked around in the gloom. The entire east side of
the octagon-shaped solarium was gone and many panes
on the north and south sides were broken. Others were
cracked.

The doorway on the west side of the solarium was
framed in mellow light coming from the second room
beyond. Avoiding the wide slanting shaft of light, Camellion, his feet slipping and sliding on wet soil, went to one
rear side of the jeep. The jeep's spin-around had been
caused when the front end had smashed a wooden planter
whose flowers had recently been watered, and the front
tires had slid in the wet dirt.

Camellion looked outside through the debris littered
opening where the glass wall had been. The two jeeps full
of guards screeched to a halt outside the blasted fence
and men were now racing through the hole in the wire.
A few of them were already close to the house. Camellion
raised the Ingram and hosed the attackers with a sweeping
fire. Two men went down, slugs having ripped across
their midsections. A third guard almost succeeded in
avoiding the rain of lead death pouring from the snarling

little Ingram M11—almost, but not quite. He threw himself to the ground. He wasn't fast enough. Two bullets stabbed into his left foot, one into his right calf. He screamed horribly while parts of his foot, flesh, bone, leather, went flying. So did he—to the ground, unconscious and bleeding to death.

I can't remain here, and I can't have them dogging my tail.

Camellion tugged a grenade from one of his shoulder bags, pulled the pin and tossed the grenade through the opening. The explosion, the deafening concussion, produced a twinkling of orange flame and shrapnel that pinged against the fence, the two jeeps and several other guards. Both guards yelled, one getting the steel in the face and neck, the other getting peppered in the chest.

Convinced that the rest of the guards would not follow him, at least until they got up their nerve, Camellion jumped up from the jeep and darted to the doorway of the half-dark room west of the wrecked solarium. He sized up the room, his eyes raking the couches and chairs draped with white dust covers. *Maybe a sitting room!* He crept across the room, ready to spray .380 slugs at any head that might pop up from behind a piece of furniture. He saw that the door to his left was open to a hall. The door to the next room was also wide open. His feet making no sounds on the thick carpet, he darted into the room which was lighted by a crystal chandelier hanging from the middle of the ceiling. More furniture that stood like white-sheeted ghosts, and a small marble fireplace, the ashes gray and cold. Three more doors. One to the west and one to the north, both closed. The door to the south was wide open. And there he was, out in the hall—a man in a bright red jumpsuit was levelling down with a Gwinn Bushmaster machine pistol. Hunched down, Camellion was just beginning to duck to the right and to bring up the Ingram M11 when the Bushmaster exploded with a deafening roar and the muzzle of the 10-inch barrel erupted into blinding muzzle flashes. The stream of .223 projectiles streamed past Camellion, zipped through a covered Queen Anne sofa and struck the white marble of the fireplace, some burying themselves behind the marble, others, having lost their power, zinging off.

"Red Jumpsuit," seeing Camellion swing around the M11, tried to jump to the left, to the side of the doorway, and put the wall between himself and the Death Merchant. His reflexes were too slow. Camellion's .380s stitched him up the right front of his body. His thigh, stomach, chest, and shoulder punctured, the gunman breathed a short UHHH, dropped the Bushmaster and fell unconscious against the wall. He was a bloody mess, wine-colored blood flowing on Chinese red poplin.

"This way, you guys! Over here!"

The Death Merchant, moving closer to the west door of the adjoining room, estimated that the voice had come from the center of the downstairs. He hesitated, the wheels of his mind spinning with extra speed. He had never seen a floor plan of Wind Whirl. Even so, this was not the first time he had been in such a mini-palace. The largest rooms were usually up front and toward the center, as well as the stairway to the upper floors; bedrooms and servant quarters upstairs. Camellion had no intention of retreating. He suspected, too, that Silvestter would be in the new section. With all the numerous other rooms in Wind Whirl, why would Silvestter have built the addition if he hadn't intended to use it? To get to the new addition, there was only one direction to take—through the door to the west. The stretch of hallway was too open, thus that route was far too dangerous.

Camellion shoved a new magazine into the Ingram and in five quick steps reached the closed door. He gingerly pushed it open, waited a moment, then stepped inside, looked around and saw that the guards had been using the room as a lounge. No dust covers draped the expensive antique furniture. Empty beer cans and beer bottles were scattered on the floor. Three coffee cups and part of a sandwich were on a walnut oysterwood center table. An overflowing ashtray was on a cushion at one end of an enormous floral cut velvet medallion sofa. A hundred thousand dollars worth of furniture being treated as if it had been bought from a discount store.

Camellion didn't get the opportunity to move across the room to either the hall door or the door to the next room west. A head poked around one side of the doorway in front of him, then was gone before he could fire. Pulling up short, he spotted another face at the casement of the doorway in the hall.

Damn! They're all around me! A less experienced fighter would have raked both doorways. The Death Merchant

94

knew better. He wasn't about to waste precious lag time by firing at empty space, and then he caught, seconds later, with his armored pants down.

The heart learns by trying. The mind learns by doing. Men of death stay alive by doing some things better than others. With blinding speed, Camellion threw himself to the right and jumped on the thickly padded sea of a Louis XVI gilded Fauteuil, a type of armchair. He made another leap, this time headed for the security of the medallion sofa. His body sailed over the sofa. His feet struck the floor. Just in time, too! He was ducking down behind the sofa the instant three automatic weapons opened fire and dozens of solid based projectiles tore into the general area where he had been standing. The roar was terrific. Slugs chopped into the oysterwood center table and sent splinters flying. A small cloud of dust and ground-up weave rose from the bullet-riddled rug while echoes bounced back and forth from the walls and ceiling.

Four men stormed through the west side door behind a barrage of slugs sprayed by Vito Campalli, who was joyfully firing a 9mm German Erma submachine gun. He waited until Carns and Roscow had crawled behind a massive eighteenth-century walnut cabinet and McGraph was protected by a late seventeenth-century cupboard before he too got down and crawled behind the oak-and-pine cupboard.

On the other side of the room, Bernie Hinnland and Clyde "Moses" Yearian stopped firing and tore through the hallway door. To their dismay, the two gunsels saw that the only possible cover on their side was a tall walnut and burlwood secretary and that it rested solidly against the wall and on the rug, on very short thick legs that ended in carved claws holding a round ball of dark glass.

"Move it! Move it over!" Yearian yelled in panic at Hinnland, who looked as if he were about to dive behind a Louis XVI gilded canape. On its high legs and with its thin back, the canape would not have offered any protection. . . .

Fear giving them extra strength, Hinnland and Yearian dropped down at either end of the secretary, their subguns beside them. They put their hands under the slight space at the ends and tugged and pulled with all their might, until the veins in their arms and neck stood out. Empty, the secretary was not too heavy. The ball ends slid easily over the slick rug. Soon the two men had moved the fine piece of furniture three feet from the wall and were behind it. Since they had entered the room, only 43 seconds had passed.

With the medallion sofa in front of him, the Death Merchant didn't bother to curse his bad luck; he was too busy planning to get out of the trap. At the moment, he wasn't at all sure how to do it. There were three or four men at least. It was difficult to tell. It was even more difficult to move. Bottled up as he was in the northeast corner of the room, he wasn't exactly in a position geared to increase his longevity. He was almost ready to rear up and spray the room with a sweep of slugs, but the voice ahead stopped him.

"Bernie! Moses! He's Holed Up Behind The Couch!"
Well now! Two more than I thought! The idiot should have kept his mouth shut.

A reply, to the south. "Okay. We'll Get The Sonuvabitch In a Crossfire."

Worried now, Camellion made like a postage stamp on the carpet, as helpless as a legless spider, as submachine guns chattered and spit out projectiles. Lying there, he could hear the thud of slugs tearing into the sofa, and ping as they struck springs in the thick padding. There were more smacks from slugs that bored all the way through the back of the sofa and hit the wall.

He was halfway safe behind the heavy sofa. Although projectiles could zip through the back, they couldn't penetrate the thick cushions and the bottom section of the sofa, which was almost a yard wide. There was a two or three inch space between the bottom of the sofa and the rug, not enough space for his enemies to try to fire at him by placing their weapons on the floor. Nor could he fire at them.

He had to take the chance, or they might get up enough nerve to charge him. Between enemy bursts, Camellion reared up and swept the south side and the west end with a long burst of .380 projectiles. During those six seconds, as bullets bored into old wood, he deduced that the men were hiding behind the secretary and the cabinet, and maybe a man or two behind the large cupboard.

Camellion dropped back to the rug and once more Silvestter's security men cut loose with raking bursts of fire, the chains of high velocity bullets ripping into the sofa, cutting away more cloth and padding. The guards began to fire wildly—to each side of the sofa and above it, hoping that one of the ricochets might sting him out of hiding and force him to run for it.

The four men behind the walnut cabinet had no intention of charging the sofa. Why should they? The lone enemy wasn't going anywhere. No matter what door he might try to reach, he had to expose himself.

Martin Roscow motioned to Denny McGraph, who was behind the cupboard. "Denny," he whispered, "you get out the door and go around and join Bernie and Moses. There ain't no telling what that sonuvabitch might do." McGraph, a man with a nose like a small red apple, didn't appear to be too happy with the idea. "Go on," Roscow urged. "We'll cover you."

Roscow nudged Carns, and while Roscow leaned around the edge of the cabinet and triggered a burst, and Carns, standing up, fired above and around him, McGraph jumped from the cupboard, made the six foot dash to the west door and ran into the next room. He ran down the hall, stopped by the south-side door, and waited against the wall. When he heard all three machine guns roaring, he looked around the casement and saw that the sofa was being shredded by slugs, cotton padding and patches of cloth flying up and sideways. More than a little afraid, he threw himself through the doorway and jumped behind the secretary.

"We can use some help," Hinnland rasped, looking at McGraph. He grinned, showing his missing front teeth. "We got an idea, me and Moses. We're going to push this big desk close to the sofa and tip it over on him. We can do it easy, now that you're here."

"Hell, why don't we wait him out?" grumbled McGraph. "Why take the chance of him shooting the piss out of us? He's a damned good pro, or he wouldn't have gotten past the fence and the boys outside."

"We're not going to wait," growled Hinnland, putting his hands on the bottom rear edge of the secretary. "Get your ass in gear and give us a hand."

Together, the three began to push the secretary across the rug, shoving it inch by inch on the claw-held glass balls at the ends of the legs. In a short time, they managed

97

to shove the secretary almost half way across the room, to a position that partially obstructed the view of the three men behind the cabinet. Only Vito Campalli had an unobstructed view of the sofa, so that, while he leaned around the edge of the cabinet, Roscow had to fire over him. Alonzo Carns did his best to shove the barrel of his M3A1 submachine gun under the bottom of the cabinet, but there wasn't enough room. Cursing and muttering to himself, he quit trying.

Hinnland, Yearian, and McGraph continued to huff and puff and push. They listened to the periodic firing of Roscow, Carns, and Campalli and hoped that they would be able to push the secretary over on Camellion before he suspected what was happening and try to do something about it. Desperate, he might charge around the sofa as a last resort and blow away one of them by sheer accident.

They stopped pushing when they felt the right corner of the secretary nudge another object and act as if it might hang up.

"I know what it is," whispered Yearian. "It's that short couch. We hit the end of it. Push a little to the left and we'll be able to get around it." Being on the end, he got down on his knees and looked around the left-hand corner of the secretary. "We've only three or four more feet to go," he said gleefully. "We're about seven or eight feet from the couch."

"How are we going to do it?" McGraph asked in a low voice. "This desk bookcase thing ain't going to smash that big couch he's behind."

"I know that, stupid!" Yearian said angrily. "We all do! Tell him, Bernie."

"We tip it over," Hinnland said. "Whether it smashes the couch or not ain't important. One thing for sure, it'll scare him and rattle him. We'll be able to pump slugs into him before he figures out the score."

"Well, let's finish it," McGraph said.

Having pulled a grenade from one of his supply bags, the Death Merchant was about to pull the pin when he felt something push gently against the left front end of the sofa. Grenade in one hand, M11 in the other, he walked on his elbows to within a foot of the left rear end of the sofa, put the M11 on the rug and pulled one of his Auto

98

Mags—all to the racket of another blast of machine gun slugs from the trio behind the cabinet, the storm of projectiles stabbing away more cloth and padding from the sofa.

Ignoring the savage firing, Camellion looked around the left rear end of the sofa, surprised to find that the secretary was now very close—and moving!—at an angle so that its carved front was cattycornered to the front of the slug-slashed sofa.

Camellion saw at once what it was that had nudged the sofa. The secretary had pushed one end of a gilded canape against the end of the sofa. The secretary was also the reason why the jokers behind the cabinet had been concentrating on the right side of the sofa for the past three or four minutes. *It's blocking their line of fire. My, my. They no doubt intend to push it right up to me and then charge around it. Or maybe the damn fools think they can tip it over. Well, well. . . .*

He pulled back his head, laid down the AMP and, in his mind's eye, measured the distance to the cabinet at the west end of the room. He pulled the pin and threw the grenade with enough force to make sure it cleared the top of the secretary. It did. It sailed across the room and landed with a plop on the carpet, several inches from the right front leg of the cabinet. Inhaling the sweet aroma of Death, Camellion counted. *Three, four, five—*

Six! The grenade exploded, the thundering concussion as loud as a 1000 millimeter cannon shell going off.

As far as the hoods behind the cabinet were concerned, the grenade might as well have been an atomic bomb. The wood of the 250 year old cabinet was bone dry, and very brittle. The explosion reduced the cabinet to thousands of pieces of splinters of various sizes, splinters that travelled with the force of missiles.

Alonzo Carns died with a chunk of wood sticking out of his chest like a pump handle, but the only thing the handle was pumping was blood, gushes of red that flowed out all around the 'handle' and its six-inch tip protruding from his back.

Vito Campalli was not as lucky as Carns. Tiny splinters had poked out his eyes. Larger splinters had used the front of his body for a cushion. Somehow, the larger splinters had missed him, all save one which had stabbed him in the abdomen. Looking like some kind of monstrous porcupine, he sagged against the wall, moaning, his hands pressed tightly over his eyes. It would take him hours to die.

Martin Roscow was already dead. He lay flat on his back, a two-foot long sliver of walnut sticking out of his throat.

The explosion hadn't harmed the other three men, who had begun to tip over the secretary at the same time that Camellion had tossed the grenade. The secretary fell on the sofa just as the grenade exploded—and saved Camellion's life!

The secretary didn't crush the sofa; however, its momentum and weight did tilt the sofa backward, the sudden slant knocking Camellion off balance and throwing him to the floor on his left side. At the same time, the explosion shattered all the plans of Hinnland, Yearian, and McGraph, or the three gunmen would have reached Camellion before he had time to get up from the floor. As it was, the explosion stunned them. McGraph spun around and threw himself to the floor. Hinnland and Yearian jerked back in alarm, their faces petrified with shock. By the time the three realized that they weren't hurt, Camellion had jumped up from the floor and was racing around the left end of the sofa. He almost stumbled over McGraph, who surprised not only the Death Merchant but himself by doing the only thing he could do: he threw his arms around Camellion's lower legs and pulled with all his might, yelling, "I got him! I got him!"

McGraph pulled forward. Camellion fell backward, landing on his rear end before he could swing the AMP and part McGraph's thick hair with a bullet.

Bernie Hinnland and Clyde Yearian didn't take time out to pick up their weapons. For one thing, McGraph was in the way, his arms still locked around the Death Merchant's ankles. For another, Hinnland and Yearian were afraid that Camellion would blow up McGraph and then throw slugs at them. They were half right.

Muttering *"Hurensohn!"*[1], Camellion pushed himself up with his left hand, threw down the Auto Mag with his right and pulled the trigger. The big autoloader roared. The .41 bullet thudded into McGraph's forehead, and the man's

[1] German for "son-of-a-bitch."

cranium, dissolved into half a dozen bone fragments, went flying into space. So did the boob's brain.

Camellion attempted to fire again as he stumbled to his feet, but fear had put wings on Yearian and Hinnland's reflexes. With a choked cry, Yearian grabbed Camellion's right wrist with both hands, a fraction of a second before Richard's finger squeezed the trigger. Yearian pushed the Auto Mag up and over as the Auto Mag roared, the muzzle flashing flame. No hit. The .41 bullet missed Yearian and struck the ceiling. Yearian began twisting Camellion's wrist, in a double play with Hinnland, who jumped behind the Death Merchant and threw his arms around Camellion's chest in a rear underarm body hold. Actually it was only half an underarm body hold, since Hinnland also had Camellion's left arm pinned underneath his own left arm. And while he squeezed with all his might, he attempted to trip the Death Merchant by knocking his left foot out from underneath him. It had occurred to both men that, since they now had hold of Camellion, it would be more than a feather in their cap if they could take him alive—it would be an Indian headdress.

Hinnland failed. The Death Merchant jerked up his left foot and stomped with his heel on the toes of Hinnland's left foot. Hinnland howled in pain, but he didn't release his arms. He only squeezed harder, trying to get even.

Yearian, a large and powerful man, didn't have any difficulty in forcing Camellion to drop the Auto Mag. As the AMP fell to the rug, Yearian let go of Camellion's wrist with his left hand and tried to jab him in the face with a closed fist piledriver and knee him in the groin with his right knee.

Camellion, finding it increasingly difficult to breathe, pulled his head to one side and managed to push Hinnland backward four or five inches. Yearian's fist, instead of connecting with Camellion's chin, skimmed by his left cheek. Yearian also scored zero with the knee lift, his knee finding only empty space.

Not about to give Yearian time to formulate a new attack, the Death Merchant used the heel of his left foot to stomp down on the man's right instep. He knew that such a strike would automatically trigger the right reflexes and cause the upper part of Yearian's body to lean

101

forward. Yearian did. And when he did, Camellion slammed him with a very fast right-legged snap-kick. The tip of his foot connected solidly with Yearian's testicles, the force of the slam crushing the testes against the pubic bones. A cry of hideous pain leaped from Yearian's throat and his face turned the color of cigar ashes. Even so, to gain that extra margin of time and safety[2], Camellion followed with a devastating *Fumikomi*—a front stamp kick—to the lower abdomen, just below the navel into the bowl of the pelvis. The Death Merchant's foot did the rest. It crushed the bladder and the lower large intestine, as well as giving the femoral arteries and the profusion of spinal nerves an H-Bomb shock. Sliding into unconsciousness from the hideous pain, "Moses" Yearian crumpled like old chalk.

The Death Merchant, his right hand now free, proceeded to go after Hinnland, who, having seen the heavier Yearian go down, became terrior-stricken. Yet he didn't dare release his hold. He didn't dare let Camellion get his left arm free. Hinnland didn't know it, but he didn't have to.

Camellion bent over, as much as he could, and put his right hand between his legs, up at the crotch. He reached backward and grabbed a handful of Hinnland's sex machine, digging in his fingers and twisting. However, the short reach prevented him from getting a firm hold. It was the surprise of the sudden move that caused Hinnland to relax his hold for a moment and let Camellion jerk his left arm loose from the man's bearhug.

The Death Merchant didn't try to stand erect. He kept right on bending at the waist, and, as Hinnland tried to get his right arm around Camellion's neck and jerk him back, Richard grabbed the man's right ankle with both hands and pulled, this sudden move putting unexpected pressure on Hinnland's right knee. Hinnland now had a choice. He could either release his hold and fall on his back, or

---

2 There is a second delay between a testicle smash and the resulting agony; therefore, some combat karate systems train their students to make use of this second or so between injury and the collapse and to follow through with another strike. A full second to work with is more than enough time for an expert to land several potentially lethal blows.

retain his hold, in which case he would still fall, but with Camellion on top of him.

Making gasping noises, Hinnland pulled his arm from Camellion's neck, his plan now to give Camellion a rabbit punch to the neck and a left jab to the kidney. Camellion had other plans. Quicker than a released spring, he put his left leg behind Hinnland's right leg and moved his left hand under Hinnland's left knee and his right hand under his right knee; he then locked his arms and jerked, lifting Hinnland off the floor, so that the man's feet and legs were higher than Camellion's head. Hinnland squawked like a plucked chicken. His head struck the rug. He made an attempt to free himself by twisting his body. For a moment he thought he had succeeded when Camellion let go of his lower legs. He hadn't. The Death Merchant jumped up, then fell sideways on top of Hinnland, employing a double Empi strike. Camellion's right elbow smashed into Hinnland's stomach. A moment later, the point of his left elbow crashed into the agonized man's nasal bones. Pain flowed in waves through Hinnland's body. Through a fog of torment, he found himself staring into the big muzzle of an Auto Mag held by a man with strange blue eyes, eyes that—were they glowing? And he heard a soft but deadly voice—

"Where is Silvestter?"

It didn't occur to Hinnland to lie. "In back. He's in back, where he always is, in the Hall of Revenge."

"This 'Hall of Revenge!' How do I get to it from here?"

"There's a hall to the left of the double stairs," moaned Hinnland. "The big room up ahead." Red-hot nails were being hammered in his stomach and he could hardly talk. "That narrow hall leads to the Hall of Revenge."

"Tell me, do you believe in a hereafter?"

Tasting blood, his face and stomach on fire, Hinnland could only choke on his own spit and, through a red haze, stare in horror at the man peering down at him. The bomb in his head exploded too fast for him to feel pain. Total blackness dropped over him and he became nonexistent. Camellion had done what most men couldn't do and few boys at all. The only safe enemy is a dead enemy. Camellion had blown Hinnland's head off with a .41 slug.

Camellion moved to where the secretary had fallen on the sofa and took two demolition grenades and two ther-

103

mite grenades from his "bomb" bag. He first threw the thermite grenades, sending them, one after the other, through the east door. The two grenades didn't explode in an ordinary manner. There was only a loud whooshhhh as each thermite canister burst like a beautiful star-shell, into petals and streamers of intense blue-white fire. Within a twinkling of an eye, the entire room, from floor to ceiling, was burning. Nothing alive could live in such a roaring hell, for thermite, a mixture of powdered aluminum and powdered iron oxide, burns at a temperature of about 4,000 degrees. He wasn't at all concerned that the mansion would burn to the ground. Reducing Wind Whirl to a pile of hot ashes was only a partial payment of what he owed Silvestter.

He threw the first demolition grenade through the south doorway into the hall. The thunderous explosion was gratifying, as were the high pitched screams of two or three men. He had been right: other guards had been creeping in toward the room.

The second demolition grenade went into the next room to the west and tore into splinters and rags more antique furniture. Camellion didn't wait for the echoes of the explosion to die down. He tore across the room to the west doorway, glancing only briefly at the corpses of Carns and Campalli and Roscow. He sprayed a long burst of M11 Ingram slugs into the next room, then jerked back, pulled out the empty magazine, shoved in a fresh one and pulled back the cocking bolt. He moved around furniture that was half-demolished, stepped on splinters and other rubble and moved to the southside hallway door. He chuckled. He could hear the flames roaring in the room to the east and smell the results of the all-consuming fire—the mixed stink of burning wood and cloth, of metal, paper, leather, padding and paint and other materials; and drowning out the cackle of the fire were occasional peals of cannon-loud thunder. The storm was at its height, crooked streaks of lightning crossing and cutting the black sky . . . wind-driven rain slashing in through the tall windows which concussion from grenades had emptied of glass.

The Death Merchant tore around the side of the doorway into the hall. Thinking of how nice it would be to see Silvestter stretched out dead, he triggered the M11 in short bursts, moving the short muzzle from side to side, raking the walls and the mouth of the hall where it opened into the huge living room. Two men, at the end of the hall, cried out, died, and crashed into infinity, their bodies riddled. Another halfwit, who stuck his head out from the doorway of the room Camellion had hosed with slugs, had his face erased by slugs that scattered his brain and exploded his head into numerous skull fragments.

Halfway down the hall, to the Death Merchant's left, was a suit of 12th century armor. Camellion skidded to a stop and crouched down beside the suit of armor. He finished off the M11 clip by spraying the doorway to the north and the end of the hallway to the west. Not bothering to reload the Ingram. He slung the submachine gun over his shoulder, pulled out a TH3[3] canister, jerked off the double tab and pitched the fire-bomb through the doorway to the north—at a slant, in order to carry it well into the room. *Plop. Whooshhhhh!* And the burn-bomb began to do what it had been designed for—consuming everything it touched, including six guards who had been out in the hall, but had charged into the room after they had heard Camellion firing from the room next to it. They died in hideous agony, the molten thermate, as clinging as molasses, burned their clothes like tissue paper and, just as rapidly, melted the flesh from their bones.

The Death Merchant ignored the shrieks of the dying men—*I'll light a candle for them later, when icebergs float on the sands of the Sahara.*

The west end of the hall was thirty feet in front of him. Beyond was the living room, as large in area as the average sized house. Camellion pitched two demolition grenades into the room, thinking that his time was running out. The explosions had to have been heard in Hyannis, and by now the entire east side of the mansion was blazing, flames leaping up into the floors above. The police and fire departments of Hyannis, such as they were, would be coming out for a look-see.

The Auto Mags in his hands, the Death Merchant raced down the hall and stormed into the room.

Kill Cleveland Winston Silvestter II was his only thought.

---

3 Also known as THERMATE. It's a mixture of thermite, barium nitrate, and sulfur in an oil binder—not quite as hot as thermite but it burns longer.

Chapter Ten

We have him! Silvestter had screamed at Gerald Meunier and the four bodyguards. *We know he's after me. He'll head this way. We'll wait for him out front. And remember! He's mine. I want the pleasure of killing Richard Camellion!*

Silvestter had not even taken time to shed his kaftan and put on more suitable clothes. He had grabbed holsters filled with 9-millimeter Smith & Wesson autoloaders and had snatched up a COLT CAR-15 submachine gun.

At the time, the guards had believed Silvestter. Sure, they'd get Camellion, provided the other guards in the mansion didn't. Hell yes! Silvestter could kill him. They didn't mind.

The cynical Meunier was not so sure. His only thought was to save his own neck. Stay alive and, much later, make sure that the U.S. couldn't indict him on some Federal charge. It was Grojean who worried him. It was Grojean he had to convince. Or he would be dead. Q-men would find him, eventually, no matter where he hid.

Now, crouched down in the large living room, the guards were having second and third thoughts about what Silvestter had said. The other guards had not killed Richard Camellion. Hell no! It had been the other way around.

The guards had never been told the full story about Camellion; neither had Silvestter's personal bodyguards. All the regular security men knew was that they were supposed to keep everybody out of the compound and that there was one individual in particular that Silvestter both feared and hated. However, the bodyguards knew that Silvestter had twice tried to kill Richard Camellion and had failed.

Waiting in the living room, the guards asked themselves: how did Silvestter expect to kill him at this point? Whoever this Richard Camellion was, the four bodyguards had the distinct feeling that he must be very, very good, almost superhuman. He was using explosives and was burning Wind Whirl down around them. Smoke was already beginning to drift into the theater-sized living room. In spite of the downpour, the house was doomed, and every man knew it. And that young punk Silvestter was going to snuff such a man? Highly unlikely.

The six men waited. Nine, actually. Three guards were crouched by the second floor railing, their automatic weapons trained on both the hall opening and the door to the room east of the living room.

Silvestter and his group were well-positioned. Silvestter himself was not far from where the hall opened into the east arch of the room. Wisely, he had protected himself by having the bodyguards place an early eighteenth-century black and gold lacquer cabinet to within twenty-five feet of the arch. Behind the cabinet was an oak and pine press cupboard. And there he waited, behind the heavy cupboard, crouched by the right hand corner.

Eight feet to Silvestter's left, Anton Mawbecker was all set by the right hand corner of a mahogany breakfront (circa 1800). Jasper Mines was at the left hand corner. The two men had moved the breakfront so that it faced the east. They had then overturned a tall cherrywood corner cupboard and had lain it on one side in front of the breakfront.

Fifteen feet to Silvestter's right, Willard Wainwring was very worried, and he was also protected by a dower chest turned up on one end. On one side of the chest, he had placed an upholstered love seat. On the other side he had put a massive Wainscot armchair.

Lennie "Little Beans" Banta and Gerald Meunier were toward the northwest corner of the room, not too far distant from the narrow hallway that led to the Hall of Revenge. The two men had overturned a pedestal dining table which Meunier, who knew something of antiques, estimated to be worth $3,000, if not more. They had arranged the table in such a way that the top was toward them, the twelve legs of the three pedestal columns on the outside, facing away from them. They had then leaned the tops of a George II gilded and painted eagle console and a Georgian mahogany side table against the bottom ends of the pedestal legs.

Meunier had no intention of fighting it out with the

Death Merchant. Some men were lovers. Some were fighters. Meunier was neither. He was a survivor, and he intended to remain one. His intense eyes darted to the left. The end of the hall was only twenty feet away. The hall was seventeen feet long. Thirty-seven feet to the Hall of Revenge. A stupid name for anything, much less a room built of ordinary brick and plaster. From the loony brain of a psychopath, of a "half-genius, half-clown." Meunier was convinced that the thing to do now was save his own skin. Worry about the Feds and the neutralization boys from 'Q' later. He glanced slyly at fat-freak Banta. No problem there. The man was a sadist, but he had the mind and the reflexes of a snail. It would be a simple matter to swing the Beretta sub-gun around and fill his blubber-belly full of 9mm slugs, should Little Beans try to prevent him from leaving.

Meunier and the rest of them had expected the Death Merchant to use a grenade. The first explosion showered shrapnel over the furniture protecting Silvestter and the three bodyguards scattered out with him—and splinters from the shattered George III "Croft" and a rosewood teapoy.

The second grenade tore a hole in the floor, sent pieces of carpet, slivers of floor wood and a Regency reading stand flying.

Would the Death Merchant toss a third grenade? Even Silvestter wasn't willing to bet. He kept his head down with the other men, and by the time he felt it was safe to look around the right side of the cupboard, Camellion was streaking into the room and throwing slugs at the furniture facing the east. Unwilling to risk a stray slug, Silvestter jerked back around the cupboard.

Camellion had even caught the three men by the upstairs railing by surprise. One did manage to get off a wild burst with his U.S. M3 sub-gun, but the only thing he hit was a lot of carpet and an open-shelf console table against the east wall.

Camellion was headed for a huge late gothic oaken chest close to the south wall, but he knew he'd never reach it if he didn't do something about the machinegunner upstairs. He changed course, darted to the east, spun around, raised both Auto Mags and fired four times. The man who had been firing the M3 took a .41 magnum slug in the chin. His chin went bye bye and so did the rest of his lower jawbone and all of his throat. A hideous sight of blood and gore, he fell over the railing and crashed into a $5,000 eighteenth-century side table inlaid with ivory and gold. The second man had been preparing to fire; he caught a .41 bullet in the stomach. He doubled over and went backstepping all the way to the hall wall. The third gunman, getting ready to trigger an H&K MP, felt a terrible pain in his left hand, heard a loud *Wanggg* and saw and felt the submachine gun flying from his hands. Odd. His left hand felt numb and wet. He saw then that the bullet had done more than knock the machine gun from his hands. All he had at the end of his left wrist was nothing! And a lot of blood spurting from the ragged stump. Horrified at the loss of his hand, Frank Skepto screamed, staggered back and fainted.

Silvestter looked around the edge of the cabinet. At the same time, Anton Mawbecker leaned out from the right corner of the breakfront. Mines, at the other end of the breakfront, stayed down. But not Willard Wainwring, who looked up over the back of a Wainscot armchair.

Toward the northwest corner of the room, Little Beans carefully looked around the edge of a dining table. Watching Little Beans from the corner of his eyes, Meunier listened.

The Death Merchant, by the east wall, saw all four simultaneously, a fierce wave of elation stabbing through him when he recognized Silvestter. Again he had been right—*The crackpot has come out to meet me. Good!*

Camellion did have an edge of a few seconds, in that he had total freedom of movement, not only with his body but with his twin Auto Mags, whereas his enemies had to move themselves and their weapons around furniture. It required twice the time to put a rifle or a machine gun into position than it did an autoloader.

With incredible speed, Camellion jumped to the left and, his arms in a kind of V, fired both Auto Mags. Silvestter's stream of CAR-15 projectiles missed Camellion by five inches, although two .223 slugs did rip through his clothes, one tearing through the cloth along his back, the other leaving a short burn line on his hip. The cloud of .223 caliber slugs then chopped into rubble the bottom of a gilded wall sconce and buried themselves in the plaster.

Wainwring didn't have time to fire. The Death Merchant's bullet tore into his right shoulder, broke the scapula and rocketed out his back, the terrible impact knocking him around and leaving his arm hanging only by some skin and muscle fibers. Bathed in blood, Wainwring gurgled a cry, fell to his back, slid into unconsciousness and began to die. In five minutes, he'd be in oblivion.

The .41 bullet from Camellion's other Auto Mag narrowly missed hitting Silvestter in the chest. But Silvestter was very fast. He also surprised the Death Merchant by being very battle-wise. Most men would have merely ducked down behind the cabinet. Silvestter, however, knew the power of an Auto Mag pistol. He did more than duck: he threw himself to the floor on his back. Camellion's slug, travelling at an angle, went through the rear side edge of the cabinet and stabbed out the back, leaving a hole several inches from the top edge and four inches from the side edge.

Camellion dropped a microsecond ahead of Mawbecker's getting off a burst with a Walther MPL machine pistol. Spitzer-shaped projectiles cut over Camellion, who snapped off two shots as he was dropping to the carpet. One bullet missed. The second .41 more than made up for it. The second slug sliced off Mawbecker's left arm at the elbow. Muttering *"Oh, oh, oh, oh,"* he sat down flat on the floor, then toppled over, his blood spreading over the rug.

Camellion scooted to the left, half-rolled over, pushed himself up slightly and triggered off the remainder of the shells in his Auto Mags, scattering the rounds toward Silvestter and the northwest corner of the room.

Two .41 projectiles struck the tables Little Beans and Meunier had piled in front of them. One bullet bored all the way through the George II Console, cut through the top of the pedestal table and, missing Little Beans by a mere six inches, thudded into a gilded torchere, a tall ornamental stand against the wall. The second slug clipped the edge of the tables, sent splinters flying, and buried itself in the wall.

Little Beans, beads of sweat glistening on his fat pumpkin face, stared for a moment at the big bullet hole, then looked at a calm-mannered Gerald Meunier. He didn't notice that Meunier was holding the Beretta with the muzzle pointed toward him.

"I'm not getting paid to fight in this kind of a deal,"

Little Beans said nervously. "That creep's pure death. He's knocking off everyone in sight. I'm going to get the hell out of here. If you got any sense, you'll do the same."

Little Beans didn't wait for Meunier to reply. He looked fearfully toward the smoke pouring in from the east, then crawled past Meunier on his hands and knees. Meunier followed him. The thing to do now was contact Boden in New York City.

Three of the Death Merchant's slugs stabbed the cabinet in front of Silvestter, each thud a warning that his first mistake would be his last. The Death Merchant was every bit as good as Boden and Meunier had said he was. Silvestter didn't mind. For years he had trained for this moment. He was a crack shot and in prime physical condition. The best martial art experts in the world had taught him karate, and he was good, very good. And he was almost fifteen years Camellion's junior.

On both knees, Silvestter turned and looked at the breakfront. Through the layers of gray-white smoke, getting thicker by the moment, he could see the corpse of Mawbecker; and there was Mines, crawling around to the left side of the breakfront. No doubt, he was going to try to fire on Camellion from the front of the breakfront.

Silvestter did some hard thinking. The Death Merchant could not retreat through the east archway because of the smoke. The north? No, that would be the long way. Besides, he'd run into the slugs of Mines. He would have to go south. He would have to seek refuge by the gothic chest or try to move along the south wall. *No, he won't risk my coming up behind him,* Silvestter told himself. *He'll wait by the chest. He has no choice.*

Silvestter's face twisted with dark, vindictive emotions and the anticipation of victory. He looked at the dower chest to his right. It was only a very short distance away. On the far side of the chest was a huge Wainscot armchair. Behind it was the body of Wainwring. At the other end of the chest, the side toward Silvestter, was a love seat. Yes, the risk would be worth it. Fifteen feet wasn't that great a distance. The Colt CAR would be too bulky and too unmaneuverable at such close range. He placed the submachine gun on the rug and pulled the two S & W automatics from their shoulder holsters. Each autoloader contained thirteen cartridges in the clip and one in the firing

111

chamber. He switched off both safety levers and began a quick duck-walk to the love seat.

While Silvestter had been planning his method of attack, the Death Merchant had ducked behind the oaken chest and had reloaded the Auto Mags. His concern now was that Silvestter might slink out or that the fight would degenerate into a standoff until the house tumbled down in flames around them. Already the ceiling was obscured by smoke, the numerous lights of the Ormolu chandelier barely discernible.

Camellion couldn't afford to wait. An AMP in each hand, he wriggled to the left end of the gothic chest, looked around the edge and saw nothing but smoke. Taking a deep breath, he jumped at the same time that Jasper Mines moved around the corner of the cherrywood cupboard that was in front of the breakfront.

Mines saw Camellion. Camellion saw Mines. Both fired, but with some difference. Mines, not wanting to lose the barest fraction of a second, triggered his M68 carbine instantly—six rounds in two seconds. Camellion, however, fired the Auto Mags while throwing himself to the rug—one, two, three, four times.

All six of Mines' 9mm projectiles missed Camellion's body. Two did come very very close. One cut through the left holster on his hip. The other bullet, also on the left, tore through the canvas strap of one of his carry-all bags.

Two of his .41 slugs missed Mines. Two did not. With a bloody hole in his chest, another one in his stomach, and two exit holes in his back, Mines never felt the double impact which lifted him off his feet and smashed him to the rug. He had never even heard the big booms of the AMPs, since it was the first two slugs that had struck him.

Silvestter certainly had! He had covered half of the fifteen foot distance to the love seat, but couldn't see Camellion because the love seat and the dower chest were between him and the Death Merchant. The four loud shots had sounded much closer than if they had come from the oak chest on the south side of the room. A horrible question stabbed itself in Silvestter's mind: Could it be that Camellion was headed for the dower chest?

Crawling like a runaway centipede, Silvestter headed for the love seat.

Camellion was uncertain as to how many men might

be hidden in the vicinity of the cherrywood cupboard. He had to move fast. He got halfway to his feet and launched himself sideways and landed heavily on his back, next to the Wainscot armchair. Concurrently, Silvestter reached the love seat whose back was facing the end of the dower chest. He put one knee on the middle cushion of the love seat, raised his right autoloader, looked over the edge of the back and saw the Death Merchant.

On his back, Camellion was pushing himself up on his left elbow when he saw Silvestter's surprised face and the 9mm automatic in the man's right hand. At the moment, most of Camellion's weight rested on his left elbow. His forearm was slanted and the AMP in his left hand was pointed at a slant toward the ceiling. His right elbow was six inches off the rug and the Auto Mag in his hand pointed east. Camellion more than realized that because of his awkward position, he wouldn't have time to rear up and swing either weapon toward Silvestter.

With a tremendous effort, Camellion used his left elbow as a spring and pushed his body forward, swinging to the left so that his legs turned toward the front of the dower chest.

A highly excited Silvestter pulled the trigger of the S & W automatic. However, his surprise at seeing the Death Merchant so close had caused him to hesitate. It was that microsecond that permitted Camellion to get his body in motion.

Silvestter's 9-millimeter bullet clipped Camellion's short hair at the crown and then struck the floor. The slug had just struck the rug when Camellion fired the Auto Mag in his right hand. He had not tried to aim the AMP. He couldn't. The muzzle was slanted slightly to the left and pointed at the smoke flooded ceiling; but there was a chance that the shot would confuse Silvestter and give Camellion time to get in front of the dower chest.

The sudden shot did startle Silvestter. He jerked back on the love seat, and by the time he realized that the Death Merchant had not been levelling down on him, Camellion had jerked up, was snuggling up against the front of the dower chest and pushing the right Auto Mag over the edge of the top, in the hope that a wild shot would whack out Silvestter.

Silvestter half-fell, half-pushed himself backward from the love seat just as the Death Merchant fired, the crashing sound of the Auto Mag hammering at his eardrums.

As if the loud sound had been a master shutoff switch, the lights in the chandelier went out, as well as the decorative bulbs on the walls. The flames had reached the wiring in the ceiling. In the northeast corner of the room, red and orange flames burst through the junction of wall and ceiling. And there were crashing and ripping sounds as burning beams and timbers fell in the hall and in the rooms east of the dining room.

The Death Merchant's .41 bullet rocketed upward and passed in front of Silvestter as he was falling, missing his body by only a few inches. Arms and legs moving wildly, he landed on his back and instantly swung both autoloaders in the direction of the dower chest and fired twice. Camellion could be coming after him.

The Death Merchant wasn't. Too wise in the subtle ways of Death, Camellion didn't believe in luck, and it would have required a truck load of good fortune to blow away Silvestter in the dark. And keep alive while doing it, especially since Wind Whirl was burning down all around him. Now was the time to get out, out of the house, out of the compound. Then into the woods, into the oceans and onto the *Gentle Mary*.

Camellion heard Silvestter's two 9mm bullets strike the back of the dower chest. Reluctantly, he congratulated the young crackpot.

He has moxey and a lot of know-how. A bit more and he would have blown me away.

Camellion leaned out to his right and fired off two rounds from each Auto Mag, spreading out the slugs. He heard no screams nor cries of pain. He pulled back and listened. The smoke was beginning to burn his eyes and breathing was becoming more and more difficult. He couldn't see anything, except falling beams and roaring flames eating along the eastern edge of the ceiling. He looked around the left edge of the chest. By the flickering light, he could see only furniture half hidden by smoke on which numerous reflections of flame danced.

This was not the time for a marshmallow roast. Camellion reloaded the M11 Ingram and the Auto Mags. He wished that he had not used all of his thermite grenades. He did, however, have five demolition grenades left. He took out two grenades, pulled the pin on one and tossed the

114

grenade to the northwest, then pressed himself against the front end of the chest. The grenade exploded, showering him with bits and pieces of wrecked furniture.

He threw the second grenade straight west. Another big *BLAMMMM* and the clutter and clatter of more broken and blasted furniture hitting the floor.

Camellion moved to the left. He kept a very low profile and all the while watched the entire area in front and to the side of him, prepared to shoot any shadow that might turn into an enemy. None did.

He moved west, wondering if he had succeeded in killing Silvestter.

Or is he doing what I'm doing—getting out before he's barbecued?

By this time the upstairs hallway of the second floor was a mass of fire, sparks and falling timbers. The stink of burning furniture became heavier, more pungent. Without warning of any kind, an area toward the center of the living room ceiling exploded downward in a shower of plaster and burning joists and flooring. Above the hole was hell, one solid mass of roaring fire.

I'll never make it to the front door—never!

Camellion ran to the nearest window in the south side. There wasn't any glass, due to concussion. He smashed the thin pane frames with the barrels of the Auto Mags, then holstered the weapons and removed the Ingram submachine gun from his shoulder. He looked out the window, forced to duck his head several times to avoid sparks and burning rubble falling from the upper floors. He didn't see any guards, but knew that the trees could be between him and some of them, trees whose leaves moved back and forth from the pressure of the heat. And there was the chain-link fence, outlined weirdly in flickering hues of light.

With less patience than a stuck bull, he crawled through the window, hurried from the side of the house and sprinted for a tall oak. Thirty to forty feet to the east he saw a jeep parked close to the inside of the chain-link fence. At the southwest corner of the fence were four guards, one pointing at the revolving red lights a mile away. The police and the firemen from Hyannis were on the way.

Camellion crouched by the tree, water from the rain

dripping all over him. The storm had blown by and the rain had quit; yet there was still some thunder in the distance and an occasional flash of lightning to the east.

There were eight more guards toward the fence on the east side. He saw them several moments before they spotted him. He was faster. The eight men went down yelling and screaming from the sweeping blast of .380 projectiles, down like kicked dominos.

The four guards at the southwest corner were caught flatfooted. One fell flat on the grass and triggered off a wild burst of automatic rifle fire. Two tried to run to the west side of the house. The fourth man lost his head completely. He ran along the fence, clawing at the chainlinks, as if seeking an opening.

The guard's burst of bullets took off a lot of bark on one side of the tree while Camellion fired from the other side. The man on the grass died with his skull blown apart, his back stitched with projectiles. The man clawing at the fence was smashed against the wire, projectiles chopping him horizontally across the small of the back. The two men running for the west side of Wind Whirl were knocked to a stop by .380s that butchered them into bloody mincemeat. They fell like wet tissue paper, twisting and turning in all directions.

The Death Merchant didn't bother to reload the M11. He dashed for the jeep, reached it, crouched down on one side and took two grenades from his bomb-bag. He threw them both at the side of the fence, forty feet ahead of the jeep. Only seconds after the explosions tore a ragged hole in the fence, Camellion was in the jeep starting the engine. Half a minute later, he was roaring through the fence, jagged strands of wire raking the sides of the vehicle.

Behind him, there were loud crashes from inside the burning house, mountains of sparks carried skyward by the hot updraft, then captured by the wind and tossed even higher, to fade and burn out in the lofty blackness.

The Death Merchant raced the jeep to the edge of the brush and stopped on the narrow road that moved along the inside of the main fence. He turned around in the seat and looked at Wind Whirl. The entire structure was a gargantuan torch, tremendous tongues of flame twisting upward. Even as Camellion watched, a large section of the roof on the south side caved in, the several pinnaclelike chimneys dissolving in a shower of bricks.

The Death Merchant smiled. Was it not better to light one small candle than to forever curse the darkness? Of course it was. And that is what he had done.

I've lit up the whole countryside!

He shifted gears and shoved down on the gas. The jeep moved ahead on the road. He glanced at the sky. Light was cracking the east sky. Dawn was about to rise from the Atlantic.

In another hour I'll be on board the Gentle Mary . . . .

Chapter Eleven

Standing in the stern of the moving boat, Lynn Mitchum gripped the railing and stared across the choppy water of Nantucket Sound toward Hyannis, which was now ten miles to the northwest. Dawn had crept into a sky filled with more than blue-gray rain clouds. There was a lot of gray-black smoke. Toward the ground the smoke seemed to roll and tumble into itself, as if composed of many individual clouds determined to crash into each other. Higher, the smoke merged into one huge cloud that drifted purposely with the wind.

Lynn and Dusty knew that "Frank" had done a thorough job on shore. It was mind-boggling! One man attacking Winston Silvestter's estate! And getting out alive! Frank —whoever he might really be—had not told them what he had done, but Lynn and Dusty had monitored the police radio in Hyannis and had heard the central order to investigate the "gunfire and explosions" at the compound. Then again, it was possible that Frank had performed another mission. Lynn and Dusty Miller didn't believe that he had. They couldn't ask him. Their orders from Control were to follow *his* orders—period.

The man who called himself Frank had returned from the mainland and had come aboard with only a small watertight drum, explaining that he had left the larger cylinder carrier behind on the beach and that the drum contained "special weapons."

Dusty had helped Frank remove the air tanks from his back, and Frank had said, "Dusty, take us out of here. Slowly, not more than ten knots. We don't want to stir up anyone's suspicions."

Dusty had gone to the flybridge and had started the engine. Lynn had lingered in the cabin, until Frank had told her to go topside.

"Or do you want to stay and watch me get out of my wetsuit?"

"Not especially." She was surprised, somewhat insulted. Going up the short flight of steps, she had then left the cabin.

Lynn stared abstractedly at the water churning behind the screws of the *Gentle Mary*. This was the third morning in a row that she had felt slightly nauseated. She hoped she wasn't pregnant. Abortion was out of the question, and Dusty wasn't the marrying kind.

"Oh Lynn!" She heard Frank call out to her. "Come down here, please." Wondering what he wanted, she hurried across the short deck and went down into the cabin. She saw that he had washed his face and had changed into tan slacks, a white Serape pullover shirt and tan strap-buckle demi-boots. There was no sign of the Scuba suit, air tanks, and accesories; he had put them away in lockers.

He didn't look at her as he opened the waterproof container.

"Lynn, what harbor is Dusty going to use in the Boston area?" he asked. He took two Auto Mags from the container, then pulled out the Iron Butterfly, two silencers, and the .22 Magnum High Standard autoloader with noise suppressor.

"The harbor in Quincy Bay," Lynn replied, watching him place the weapons in special compartments in an attaché case. "Quincy is a south suburb of Boston. Will you be coming with us?"

"Are you two based in Boston?"

"Yes."

Camellion turned and smiled at the young woman. "Tell me, has your Control ready access to a plane? I need a plane and pilot to fly me across country." He closed the top of the attaché case and moved the wheels of the two combination locks.

Lynn sat down on a lower bunk and grinned. "Why not use the plane and pilot who brought you to Providence. He's at the Boston station. The Cessna's at a private field north of Newton, which is west of Boston." Her grin broadened as Camellion turned and looked down at her. "I'll bet you thought we didn't know about the plane and pilot?" she said.

119

The Death Merchant had assumed that pilot and plane had flown back to the Richmond, Virginia, area. He didn't pursue the matter with Lynn. He had more important matters rolling around in his mind. There was the matter of the tracing device which Grojean had dubbed "The Box." Once he was at the Boston station, he would have to report by short wave that he hadn't obtained the device. There was Silvestter himself. Camellion would know whether Silvestter was dead or alive before the Gentle Mary even dropped anchor—by listening to news broadcast on the vessel's radio. If Silvestter had perished in the fire, that left only the problem of The Box. The first step toward solving the problem would be to kidnap one of the Silvestter scientists in New York City—*or could the device have been perfected outside the U.S.?* If Silvestter were still alive—*then my strike last night was a waste of time.*

Camellion did not entertain any thoughts about going after Silvestter again. He would be too well guarded, too well protected, *with only God knows how many traps. I'll have to wait until he comes to me, if he comes. But how will I know if he changes his mind and decides he's had enough? I won't know. Yet he can't quit. I'm out to kill him and he knows it. He can't quit, unless he's dead.*

The Death Merchant found out about Silvestter ten minutes later, the newscaster stating that "Several dozen armed men" had "invaded the estate of Winston Silvestter II, in an apparent attempt to kidnap the prominent multimillionaire." Then the next bit of broad bull—"During the gun battle with the would-be kidnappers, numerous employees of Mr. Silvestter lost their lives in a gallant attempt to protect the heir to the Silvestter fortune." The announcer then said that "the hoodlums, frustrated in their attempt to kidnap Silvestter, set fire to the palatial mansion" and that the "Hyannis police, the Massachusetts Bureau of Criminal Investigation and agents of the FBI's Boston office are investigating the bizarre case."

The dreary part was that Cleveland Winston Silvestter was alive and healthy, except for "smoke inhalation. Mr. Silvestter, who refused to be taken to St. Elizabeth's Hospital in Hyannis, told police that he has no known enemies and believes the attempted kidnapping was the work of organized crime."

You have one enemy, you bastard! He switched off the radio.

Lynn, carefully gauging the angry expression on Camellion's face, thought that the teeth bared by a twisted smile was very masculine. She couldn't resist the temptation.

"I didn't know you had 'several dozen armed men' with you!" she said jocularly. Her voice became serious. "Were you actually trying to kidnap him?"

"Who said I was even there?" responded Camellion.

"I do. You didn't go ashore with all that fire-power to shoot birds."

Looking at Lynn, Camellion assembled the pieces of the new plan forming in his mind. Through Boston Control he could tell Grojean what had to be done. There wouldn't be any problems in that direction. The CIA had a large station in Santa Fe. It would be a simple matter for several Q agents to meet him in Santa Fe, furnish him with what he needed and drive him the short distance north to Chimayo. Nuts to that. They can have a four-wheel deal waiting and I'll drive myself. A warm feeling welled up within him. It would be nice seeing Norberto again.

"Well, I don't hear you denying it!" Lynn persisted.

"I was trying to kill Silvestter," Camellion said matter of factly. "The next time I won't fail."

Lynn registered surprise. "And you have to fly across the United States to do it?"

Camellion nodded. "All the way to New Mexico, honey. I only hope he'll be able to find me. . . ."

Chapter Twelve

"Es muy bonito—it is very beautiful!" That is what the Spanish say about the Sangre de Cristo and the area surrounding the mountains. A shroud of mystery does hang over this range of the Rockies in northern New Mexico, these cloud-bound and forbidding great peaks that are flanked on the west by the Rio Grande and on the east by the High Plains.

Overwhelmingly Spanish, with only small numbers of Indians and Anglos, the 70-by-100 mile region has less than 50,000 people, the majority of whom speak a Spanish dialect as it was spoken 350 years ago. The reason for this purity of language is not at all mysterious. Conquistadores brought Spain's culture to the region in the 16th century, New Mexico became United States territory in 1850, yet didn't become the 47th state until 1912. After that, the rest of the U.S. forgot about the remote region. It had never been very well known to begin with. The Sangre de Cristo did the rest, insulating villages from outside influence and freezing customs and language in a time frame long eclipsed in other parts of the southwest.

The area harbors other things beside a pure Spanish dialect. There are also wise village elders, religious apparitions, and a shrine that is almost totally unknown to the religious world. For the people of the Sangre de Cristo, however, the Shrine of Santuario, in the little town of Potrero, has no equal. During Holy Week thousands of pilgrims, many bearing crosses on their shoulders, come to worship at the chapel and take sacred earth from a hole in the room next to the altar.

This area is also the home of the Penitentes. Some say that the sect's practices of scourging and crucifixion have given the mountains their name—Blood of Christ. Others maintain that the name was inspired by the mountains' color at sunset.

No matter the origin of the mountains' name, other centuries do live on in this isolated region, live on in manners, arts, and customs. Life is pleasant and quiet. Scattered through valleys bounded by forests of pine, fir, and spruce are hundreds of tiny ranchos, the remnants of those great land grants in the days of Spanish and Mexican domination. People are friendly, although not enthusiastic about tourists. In the little villages one sees freshly whitewashed houses, tended gardens and well-kept churches and graveyards. There is very little industry . . . a small mine here, a lumber mill there, or home workshops where items are made for tourists, products that aren't necessarily sold in the region but are shipped all over the West and Southwest. Some craftsmen make silver and turquoise jewelry. Religious items are very common, wooden and clay-baked figures of the hierarchy of heaven, for many of the people have the talent of *santeros*, those carvers and painters of religious figures, of long ago.

Norberto Martinez made rugs and blankets in his little shop on a winding dirt road, which was the main street of Chimayo, a tiny hamlet west of the Blood of Christ.

Working under a portal, Norberto looked up curiously when he saw the blue Ford pickup stop in front of his house. He smiled and stood up at the sight of Richard Camellion, who got out and walked around the front of the truck. His arms outstretched, Norberto hurried out to meet him, calling, *"Mi campañero,* Camellion."

Grinning, the Death Merchant called back in Spanish, "It has been a long time, good friend Martinez."

The two men embraced with a heavy Spanish *abrazo*, and Norberto used the common greeting of old Castile, *"Como estamos, Ricardo?"*—"How are we, Richard?"—instead of the modern *"Como esta usted, Ricardo?"*—"How are you, Richard?"

"Healthwise I'm fine, *amigo.* How has God been treating you and all that you hold dear?" asked Camellion.

They walked underneath the portal, the overhanging roof, and the wiry Norberto motioned for Camellion to sit down. "We will have wine and a good talk, *mi amigo.*"

Camellion nodded, sat down at a small table and removed his silverbelly sagebrush hat. Norberto hurried into the house and returned with a bottle of red wine and two glasses. Slim, his skin burned dark brown from the sun, he had strong gaunt features, intelligent dark eyes, and a lot of white hair.

Norberto sat down, opened the wine bottle and sighed. "My business is good," he said, pouring wine into the glasses. "I have seven weavers working in two villages near here, and I am selling more rugs and blankets locally."

"That is good," Camellion said politely. "Work gives a man pride. No work plus poverty breeds anger and resentment."

"*Si.* We will never have a lot of tourists though. As you know, there are almost no cafes and no motels, which is why few Anglo tourists come to this area. Perhaps it is for the best. On the eastern side of the Sangre de Cristo, there is much poverty in the Mora Valley. The people there are not as fortunate as we, here on the west side. In the Mora Valley, there are long, burning memories of land grants lost after 1850, when Anglos began moving into the region. The outsider is not welcome, and Anglos are not always safe."

One who understands the customs of the region remains patient and never interrupts a village elder. Camellion let Norberto talk.

"Our life is slowly changing," Norberto said sadly. "The old people are ashamed that they cannot read *Ingles,* and they are terrified by government documents. Here in Chimayo, they come to me with envelopes hidden under coats and dresses. Usually the letters turn out to be Social Security statements advising them how much they have been paid in benefits. I tell them and then they are relieved, and they say, 'Thank God. I didn't sleep all night, thinking I *owed* all that money.' "

Norberto shook his head and fingered the stem of the tall wine glass. "Ah, the young men. . . . They leave to seek jobs and new opportunities. Outside the mountains, they cannot speak the *Ingles* so good. They blame the problem on their Hispanic background, and they say, 'I am not going to speak stupid Spanish again, eat that stupid food again, go back to that stupid town.' "

Norberto spread his hands in a gesture of helplessness. "How can we old ones teach them that their Spanish heritage is something to be proud of? We cannot, my friend." He suddenly brightened and smiled at Camellion. "Has God been smiling at you, *mi amigo?* You look well and at peace with yourself and your fellow man."

"Norberto, *viego amigo*. Powerful men are trying to kill me. I need your help." Camellion put down the glass and looked at Norberto, who sat back and regarded him with thoughtful eyes.

Norberto did not know what business Camellion was in or how he made his money. Once Camellion had said, "I have an income." He had not offered an explanation. However, Norberto had seen a lot in his 72 years, and he was a keen judge of men. There was not the slightest doubt in his mind that Richard Camellion was a good man, a sensitive man, a generous man. Every year, Norberto, as the *Alcalde*—the Mayor—of Chimayo, received a check from Camellion for the poor children of the village. Camellion helped in other ways. When the village church needed extensive repairs, it was Richard Camellion who had paid for them. The people of Chimayo were very proud of their church, which displayed a brilliantly hued 265-foot-long tapestry that told the story of the region from pre-Spanish days.

And when Carlos, Norberto's eldest son, fell from his horse and needed extensive surgery on his hip, it was Richardo who had had him flown to Denver and had paid all his medical bills.

Si, Ricardo was a good man. *A strange man in many ways, but still a man of compassion and honesty.*

Norberto spread his hands in a gesture of compliance and said in the Spanish of Cervantes, "My humble house is your house, *amigo*. My three sons and I will do all we can to help you."

"Not your house, my friend," Camellion said quickly. "I do not want to hide out in your home. I am going to drive into the high country east of here. I'll go on foot into the Pecos Wilderness and camp on the *Mano de Dios*. I want you, or one of your sons, to drive my truck back to Chimayo and keep it hidden here. Once a week I'll need food supplies. I need you to bring them to me."

"These evil men who will try to kill you? They will seek you out, amigo? They will know you are camped on the Hand of God?" Norberto's long, ascetic face reminded the Death Merchant of an El Greco portrait.

"Yes. They have a marvelous invention that will enable them to find me," Camellion explained. "For that reason I cannot stay in your home. I cannot endanger you and your family."

Camellion could smell the pungent lanolin scent of wool from inside the house, where nine generations of the Martinez family had made rugs and blankets. Norberto could trace his forebears in the New World back to Hernando Martinez, one of the early colonizers of the Chimayo region in the 1700s.

"These men, they will pass through our village?" Norberto poured more wine into the glasses.

"Possibly. I really don't know. I think they will fly from the Santa Fe area in helicopters. If strangers do come through here, do nothing to hinder them. The only way you can help is to do as I ask. I will leave a walkie-talkie with you and we'll stay in contact after I camp on the rock."

Norberto slowly nodded. "The men will come to you. Either you will kill them or they will kill you. That is what you are saying."

"It is the way things are, Norberto," Camellion said. "Evil exists. Evil must be dealt with. That is the business I am in, old friend. I fight evil. I destroy those who would destroy good men and the way good men live."

Norberto looked sad. "It is strange because it is the good minds, the good people, who allow evil to exist." He tilted the glass to his lips, then put it on the table and looked at the Death Merchant. "Carlos will be here within the hour. He will be happy to see you, Ricardo. Were it not for your goodness of heart, he would be a prisoner of a wheelchair. He will go with you to the High Country and drive the truck back. We will put it in a large shed in back of the house."

"*Gracias, amigo.*"

Sitting next to Camellion in the truck, Carlos Martinez pushed back his short-brimmed sheepman's stetson and leaned back in the seat. He was in his late thirties, had ink-black eyes and hair and a friendly smile that revealed perfect white teeth. He was also considered a fool by many of the young men in Chimayo. Carlos, who had been in the U.S. Marines and had seen action in Vietnam, had not only a high school education, but two years of college. He was further blessed with an ability to speak the language of the Anglos, and speak it well. Yet he preferred to live in Chimayo and raise sheep. *Si!* He had to be *mucho loco!*

Carlos had lapsed into silence. The Death Merchant, watching the road, concentrated on Silvestter, wishing he had the answers to the two questions that troubled him most:

Could the tracing device lock in on a target 2,300 miles away? If it could and Silvestter could pin-point his position—*will he come after me? Or will he sit back and play the waiting game . . . strike months from now. I don't think he will wait. He'll come after me like a husband on a honeymoon! His rage and hatred will force him to move as quickly as possible.*

Miles of twisting dirt road vanished underneath the wheels of the Ford pickup. Headed east, Camellion and Carlos passed through Cordova. The softly contoured adobe houses, each with its garden of corn and chilies and beans, shone brilliant in the hot sun. Later, as the Ford turned into the cutoff and headed toward the high country, they passed postage-stamp ranchos laid out in rectangles. Camellion knew why there was such uniformity of size. It was the old Spanish way, with grandparents and parents dividing their land equally among their children, so that they would always have a place to come back to one day.

Carlos turned to Richard. "This is a fine truck, Senor Camellion," he said admiringly.

"*Si.* Its 'Fat Herbie' wheels and heavy-duty shocks are just the thing for rough country. There's nothing like duel shocks to help prevent major damage to the suspension when off the road. By the way, how good a mechanic are you, amigo?"

Carlos glanced in surprise at the Death Merchant. "Average. Better than some, not as good as others. Why do you ask?"

"This truck is yours, my friend. A gift from me to you. You might have to make two or three trips to the Hand of God. I want you to know that you might be risking your life. You can change your mind if you want to." Knowing that Carlos would be hurt if he thought the truck was payment for his help, Camellion quickly added, "The truck is not any kind of payment for helping me. It's simply a gift."

Carlos was thunderstruck. A Ford pickup that was almost brand new! Such things did not happen, at least not to him.

"Senor Camellion, you need not give me this truck!"

he protested. "Because of you I am able to walk. I would help you anyhow."

"And I appreciate it. But I bought this truck for just this job. I won't need it when I come down from the mountains. I can't use it. You can. *Compreder, amigo?* You'll find the title in the glove compartment. It's already made out to you."

Carlos could only nod. *"Gracias.* Thank you."

The Death Merchant smiled, recalling his radio conversation with Grojean. The DD/O had not raged; that was not his style. In a quiet tone he had demanded to know why he should order the Chief of the Santa Fe station to hurry up, pull strings and have the title of a truck made out to one Carlos Rafael Martinez.

"Because my life might depend on it," Camellion had lied.

The "front cover" of the Agency station in Santa Fe was Simco Industries, an outfit that made tinker toys and model electric trains. The Station Chief had wanted to know about the transfer of the title—why? Camellion hadn't gone all around the barn with him. "It's none of your business," Camellion had said. "Grojean has given you the order; that's all you need to know."

Came the time when there was no more road. The truck bounced along over uneven ground that became more and more rocky and continued to slant upward. Finally the terrain became too rough for even the truck. They could proceed no farther without risking broken shocks or springs, or becoming stuck in a mini-crevice.

From this point, Camellion would have to proceed on foot.

Carlos watched him pull two canvas angler shoulder bags and a heavy Loadmaster back-pack-on-frame from the rear of the truck. He said, "Getting supplies to you will not be difficult."

"You'll lose a day doing it," Camellion said. His keen eyes scanned the countryside. It was beautiful but devoid of human life.

Carlos, standing to the right of Camellion by the tailgate, finished lighting a cigarette. "I can start early in the morning and be at this place in several hours. Another three or four hours of hiking and I can be at your camp on the *Mano de Dios*. Three hours back to the truck. I can be home by five in the afternoon, at the latest."

He glanced up at the afternoon sky. "You will have to hurry to reach the Mano de Dios before dusk."

The Death Merchant, strapping on the Loadmaster pack, did not appear worried. "I'll contact your father every two days. I'll want you to come every Saturday. Is that convenient with you?"

"*Si*. Any day, except Sunday. I do not want to miss mass. I have a question. Suppose we do not hear from you. What do we do, Senor Camellion?"

"In that case, wait four days before you come looking for me." Camellion turned and looked at a serious-faced Carlos. "If you find me dead, don't be surprised. No radio contact will mean that the men looking for me have won."

Camellion pulled a canvas gun bag from the bed of the truck. He unzipped the bag and took out a $2,000 Mann-licher semi-automatic rifle. The fine weapon was .308 caliber, had a flash hider, a sling strap, and a 20-round magazine. Camellion threw the rifle over his shoulder.

"The keys are in the ignition," he said, smiling at Carlos. "I'll call tomorrow morning and let you and your father know I've established camp. *Hasta luego, mi amigo. . . .*"

Carlos sensed there wasn't anything more to be said. He nodded.

"*Hasta la vista,* Senor Camellion. *Buena suerte. . . .*"

The Death Merchant moved upward into the high country. He'd unpack the Ingram submachine gun and the Auto Mags once he reached the Hand of God and set up his light camp. For the present, he would be safe enough with the stainless steel Vega .45 auto in a belt holster underneath his bush jacket.

He was not a stranger to this beautiful country. All around him were the green-hued foothills, studded with pinon and juniper trees and rent with crooked, zig-zagging arroyos. Far below, at the end of the five mile slope, he could see the tiny houses of Cordova, and could imagine the strings of red chilies hanging on the portals of adobe houses. And he could see the green and brown and yellow squares of the lands, of the fields.

He thought of his position. To the north was the Carson National Forest, in two vast sections. Between the sections lay the Pueblo Indian Reservation—all of it part of the Sangre de Cristo.

Camellion trudged upward. Would he have to wait a week? Two weeks? Longer? He was prepared to wait a month. The time spent alone would not be boring. He would have to be on guard every second. Silvestter and his killers were not novices. They would not come in beating drums, and they would expect him to be expecting them, and to be prepared.

It was going to be that kind of situation in which the *why* was meaningless and only the *when* was important.

Camellion frowned. He had not liked planting the bugs in the Ford. Carlos was not the enemy. But it couldn't be helped; he couldn't take the chance. There wasn't anything in Q files about his friendship with Norberto. But suppose Silvestter had learned about Norberto from another source? Improbable but not impossible.

Then Camellion chuckled. Alone? No, he knew he had company. He couldn't see him. He didn't have to. He could sense him.

The Cosmic Lord of Death was walking beside him . . . grinning . . . waiting for his victims.

He'll get them!

Chapter Thirteen

"Such an operation is akin to playing with matches around hi-test gasoline," Hugh Boden said. Leaning on the table on his elbows, he frowned at Silvestter, who was standing, like a Rock of Gibraltar, on the other side of the oval table, a wooden pointer in his hand. "Such an operation is too risky. We could put Camellion to sleep—maybe—but we couldn't complete the hit without detection."

"And you know that the FBI is watching every move we make," Gerald Meunier said in guarded tones. He sat next to Boden. "And we have no idea what the Agency might be up to. Our inside man can't find out a thing. He is convinced that Grojean suspects a leak in Operations."

"The contact was certain that Grojean suspects you and Hugh of complicity in revealing Camellion's identity as the Death Merchant?" probed Silvestter. He shifted the pointer in his hand, now holding it as one would grip the handle of a dagger.

It was the tall, lanky Boden who answered. " 'Complicity' is not the right word. Grojean and Camellion suspect that Gerald and I are directly responsible. Grojean is like a starving leech. He won't let go until he gets the truth. Neither will Camellion. Gerald and I are on his death list, the same as you. But going to New Mexico after him is not the answer."

Boden screwed up his eyes, which always looked as if they were too close together, and made a systematic search of the faces around the table. Silvestter stared down at him with all the tenacity of a bulldog. Nario Hokakawa, looked straight ahead. He had a shaved skull, the body of a tank and hands the size of mine detectors. He would have jumped off the Empire State Building and have tried to swim in air if Silvestter ordered him to.

Meunier's expression was one of extreme worry. Gerald

had a right to be. He knew the score. Q-neutralization boys were something to worry about. The Death Merchant was even worse.

Laban Denbow didn't look happy either. Boden didn't blame him. Earlier in the day, before they had come to the Silvestter Building in mid-town Manhattan, Denbow had confided that they were in over their heads with Silvestter. Denbow had whispered, "There's no reasoning with him. His hatred for Camellion has unhinged his mind, and he's going to drag us down with him. I tell you, we must do something."

Yes, do something. But what? How can you reason with a crackpot whose destructive impulses have run off the track? Silvestter was a basket case to begin with. This penthouse office was proof. A normal person would have found it difficult to imagine the sun shining outside. From the inside, it might as well have been midnight. Silvestter had had the windows removed and the spaces filled, so that when the work had been completed, no trace of the windows remained.

Amazing! Boden thought. How could a slob like Denbow have built National Investigations into a successful detective agency, one of the biggest in the country, after the Burns and the Pinkerton agencies.

Denbow was short, plump, and had a network of blood vessels on each cheek. When in the presence of Silvestter his manner was always obsequious and his smile ingratiating.

Denbow blinked at Boden, then turned and looked up at Silvestter.

"We could give the FBI the slip," he began slowly. "Taking the large helicopter across country will require a week. As I see it, the problem is twofold. Camellion and the mountainous area he's in. He's not sitting in those mountains without a lot of protection, traps we don't know about."

"I must admit, Camellion is far better in electronics than I," Boden said, looking down at the large map on the table.

"There's the ranger station at Carson National Forest," Denbow said. He paused, then added solemnly, "I must vote against the operation, Mr. Silvestter. It's entirely too dangerous."

"None of you is here to vote." Silvestter's voice dripped

with contempt. He looked from Denbow to Boden and stared long and hard at Meunier. "You're here to help me implement the plan." He leaned down across the table, with a slow smile that exposed his teeth. They glistened wetly. An abnormal amount of saliva had collected in his mouth and his palms were wet with sweat. "And don't try to tell me that Camellion is not in those mountains. The new L-Model works like a dream, and you both saw yesterday how I finally succeeded in locking in on his electromagnetic field. The cross-references are complete. Camellion is somewhere in the Sangre de Cristo Mountains of New Mexico. Once we're within a hundred miles of him, we'll be able to pinpoint his precise location.

"We're not denying that you haven't located him," Meunier said abrasively. "It's the idea of going into those mountains to whack him out that we're against. We're saying we should wait until things cool off."

"Cool off!" Silvestter's voice shook with rage. "The ashes of the house my grandfather built were cool days ago. The Death Merchant might be cold in his grave if you and that fat freak bodyguard had done your part and hadn't run off. All alone, I almost killed Camellion. I would have succeeded if the lights had not gone out. And you two constantly telling me how dangerous he was! Bunk!"

Humiliation stabbed through Silvestter, shame at how he had been forced to crawl by the light of the fire to the opening that led to the Hall of Revenge. Burning timbers had fallen all around him. Debris, generated by Camellion's grenades, had rained down, a stick of wood hitting him on the head and almost knocking him out. He had escaped only minutes before most of the living room ceiling had caved in.

Police and firemen had invaded the estate. To cover the truth, he had been forced to answer questions put to him, not only by the Hyannis police, but by State investigators and agents of the Federal Bureau of Investigation. Reporters had pestered him. Photographers had snapped his picture dozens of times. It had taken a week to sift through the ashes and to make arrangements to protect the wreckage of the house from sightseers. Newsreel helicopters had flown over the area almost constantly.

All the police had found, two days after the fire, was a metal cylinder on the beach. And Silvestter had looked like a fool. Why was it, the police asked, that "dozens" of invaders had required only one underwater carrier to transport their weapons. The FBI was more than insistent. The agents made it plain that they didn't believe Silvestter. His answer had been quick: How did the FBI know that the cylinder belonged to the gunmen who had invaded his estate?

And now, Boden and Meunier—those gutless wonders! —expected him to wait, to sit around and do nothing about the man responsible for all the humiliation he had suffered! Those two—and Denbow, too—were like torpid dairy cattle whose lot was to live in fear.

"You were already in Camellion's proximity!" Meunier protested, red-faced. "Little Beans and I were across the room. We couldn't have reached you without Camellion's putting a slug in us. I'm not committing suicide for you or anyone else."

"Denbow said it," interjected Boden. Turning sideways, he draped his right arm over the back of the chair. "It will take a week to cross the U.S. in the Sikorsky—with 'Stemplin Steel Corporation' painted all over it. We might as well call the newspapers and tell them where we're going and what we're going to do!"

"We're not going to take the Sikorsky," Silvestter said. He dropped the pointer on the table and sat down. "We'll fly to Los Angeles in one of Stemplin's company jets. The Silvestter interests have a shipping company on the West Coast. I'll buy a new helicopter through the shipping company. We'll plan the rest of our moves from L.A."

Denbow rubbed his knobby chin. "We shouldn't be seen around Santa Fe."

The look of apprehension on Boden's face changed to total skepticism. "Now just a minute," he stated, looking at Silvestter. "Do you realize how much racket a chopper makes? What do you think Richard Camellion will do when he hears a helicopter in the area? Damn it, man. He *expects* us to use a chopper!"

Silvestter's grin was like the smile of a death's head.

"Who said anything about landing in a chopper?"

Chapter Fourteen

This was the 18th day that Richard Camellion had been on the Hand of God, a grassy, rock-strewn plateau that was a quarter of a mile long and eight hundred across at its widest point. In no way was it shaped like a hand—a mitten, but not a hand. There weren't any fingers.

Camellion wasn't bored. He was disgusted. He was beginning to have doubts about Cleveland Winston Silvestter II. It was not impossible that Silvestter had given up, at least for the time being. He hadn't, however, let down his guard, not for a single second.

During his first night on the Hand, he had holed up in a small cave, discovering to his delight the next morning that the cave twisted upward to a line of rocks, a hodge-podge of boulders and an outcropping of metamorphic rock on a slope several hundred feet above the fairly flat surface of the Hand. Camellion had set up a permanent camp in the mouth of the cave.

The morning of the first day, Camellion made a study of his surroundings. To the west, the plateau was ringed by a ridge that was curved, so that several hundred feet of the north and south sides lay beneath it. The east wall below the plateau was a sheer drop of three hundred feet. The north wall, while steep, could be climbed without difficulty; so it was possible for an enemy to approach from the north. It was the same with the south approach to the Hand, the route Camellion had travelled. To the west was a 500-foot-long slope.

That first day, Camellion had gone to work. First he had ringed the west ridge and its north and south sides with Model-9 Silent Emergency Alarms. Each unit, the size of a thimble, was actually a miniature transmitter, an extremely sensitive bug that could pick up the slightest sound within a 74-foot radius and transmit it to a central receiving station, warning the operator by a flickering red light. The closer the "target" got to the bug, the faster the light would flicker.

The Death Merchant spaced out thirty-eight of the S.E.A. units. A foot from each unit, he buried an explosive charge called "Little John"—an aluminum pyramid filled with tiny steel BBs and ten ounces of tetrytol, a powerful explosive that was 70 percent tetrytol and 30 percent TNT. Each Little John contained a transdiode transducer attached to a relay-trigger-transmitter. When the transmitter picked up the signal from the central station, it detonated the tetrytol. Each Little John was numbered. Its corresponding number was on the panel of the central station. The operator could detonate each Little John individually or, by pressing the master button, explode them simultaneously.

He had planted five S.E.A. units on the south rim and four on the north edge. But only the five on the south side were accompanied by Little Johns. He had also planted one S.E.A. unit and one Little John a hundred feet up in the cave chimney that twisted up to the first ridge on the west slope.

Camellion was not satisfied. First of all, the plateau was ideal for a helicopter. Half a dozen large choppers could land on the *Mano de Dios*. Yet he had not had explosives to plant on the flat areas of the landing regions.

During his first few days, he did make a map of the Hand's surface area, drawing each contour and feature, each dip and rise and boulder, then committing the sheets of paper to memory.

Physical discomfort added to dissatisfaction. The Loadmaster back pack had been filled with explosive Little Johns, S.E.A. units and the two central stations; other items had included tins of food, canteens of water, a collapsible aluminum pot, a small Primus stove, a Primus infra-red heater, and a Primus lantern. The shoulder bags had contained demolition grenades, six thermite grenades, ammo clips, a night sight scope and two noise suppressors, one for the M11 Ingram and one for the Mannlicher F.A.L. .308. A walkie-talkie had also been in one of the shoulder bags, plus a knife and fork and a bottle of vitamin pills.

Contact with Norberto and Carlos Martinez went off as scheduled. Carlos came twice to the Hand, carrying food supplies and propane fuel packs. On his second visit, Ramon, one of his brothers, came with him. On this second trip, both men had carried lever action 30/30 rifles. Ramon had lugged a sleeping bag, extra canteens of water, fresh fruit and three bottles of Zibba, a sweet red wine native to the area. All these items were in the cave, over whose small entrance Camellion had placed a thin sheet of black plastic to block out light at night from the stove and the lantern.

At night, holed up in the cave, the Death Merchant amused himself by listening to the various noises on the central station of the S.E.A. system; that is, he "watched" the lights of the station. The size of each light was in proportion to the life-form closest to it. Insects were hardly visible. Snakes, rabbits, and other small animals made a red flashing glow the size of the head of a pin. A human being would have four times that size. Two or more human beings would fill in the half-inch circle.

Now and then aircraft passed over, usually commercial airliners, or U.S. Air Force fighters, the latter so high that only their contrails were visible. Occasionally a low flying private plane cut across the sky, but it was obvious that none were searching for anything or anyone.

Used to danger, uncomfortable without it, the Death Merchant enjoyed his surroundings. The cottonwoods on the plateau were bursts of yellow, while the Aspens moved in the wind in all their golden splendor. For hours, he would study the countryside through binoculars. The face of the past peered over each sun-washed peak. A craggy land with mind-stretching beauty, these mountains were once the hunting grounds of native Indian tribes, then stained with blood from their clashes with the Spanish conquerors. Many said this was the true origin of the name of the mountains.

The Blood of Christ Mountains were not exactly giant hills, such as the Superstition Mountains in Arizona. They weren't the Alps either. The Blood of Christ range rose at its highest at Wheeler Peak, a height of 13,161 feet. The highest eminence in New Mexico, Wheeler Peak embraces three of the seven life zones found in Western North America, from the ponderosa pine of the Transition Zone to the tundra of the Arctic-Alpine. The Hand of God was at 4,147 feet.

On the 18th day, the Death Merchant had two visitors, a young man and his wife, both of whom were studying anthropology at the University of Southern California and had come to New Mexico to study the customs of the Spanish of the area. The Morrisons might as well have remained in California, complained Mrs. Morrison. The people they had met in Cundiyo, Espanola, Chimayo, Cordova, and in other villages not only had not cooperated, they had regarded the Morrisons with open hostility.

"Little wonder," laughed Camellion. "They thought you were *rico*—rich—and had designs on what little property they have. You can't blame them for being suspicious. Their memories of the Spanish are long and bitter."

Not for a moment had Camellion trusted Fred and Sandra Morrison, although he didn't feel that they were part of any operation dreamed up by Silvestter. Duplicity was not in their eyes or their manner. However, he had to get rid of them quickly, and give them some sort of explanation for being in the mountains.

"I am here to make contact with intelligent beings from another world," he said seriously. "They have contacted me in my dreams. They will land here this evening in their spaceship."

The Morrisons had left ten minutes later, climbing back down the south slope of the *Mano de Dios,* much to the amusement of Camellion.

That same afternoon, blue-black thunderheads reared over the rim to the west and obscured the bowl of sky. Tongues of lightning stabbed every which way, and the rains came, a torrential downpour that had no preliminary of scattered droplets. Standing in the mouth of the cave, Camellion watched the storm. All that had been dazzlingly bright was now gray and dreary, the green peaks of the *Sangre de Cristo* clutched by clouds and forbidding. The mountains knew only sunlight or shadow, and now the shadows had taken over. Camellion thought of how increased mobility and television were beginning to dissolve the Spanish dialect traceable to Castile of the 1600s. Eventually the dialect would die out. Yes . . . but the *Sangre de Cristo* would go on forever, in lonely magnificence.

The rain stopped. The skies began to clear. Dressed in Marine camouflage, shirts and pants, Camellion left the cave, to check the Hand, to see how the storm had affected the terrain, and to collect rainwater from pockets in the larger rocks. He also had to check to see if the wind and rain had exposed any of the Little Johns or the S.E.A. units.

He moved out across the plateau, an Auto Mag on his hip, the Mannlicher .308 strapped to his back. His speed depended on the route over which he travelled. Some sections of the huge rock were flat and bare, or covered only with liga moss or short razor grass. Other parts were chopped up into grasslands and small hills. Technically, many of these hills were *roches moutonnees,* that is, rounded "bosses" of rock. Scattered around were boulders, and boulders perched on boulders, some carved into weird shapes by wind and water erosion. There were larger hills of the conventional kind, and, between them, small, twisting hollows.

Camellion filled four canteens with water, took them back to the cave, picked up a shoulder bag full of clips, and picked up the Ingram M11. The S.E.A. units and the Little Johns had to be inspected, not only at the north, south, and east edges, but on the west ridge. In case of trouble, he couldn't afford to be caught without the sub-machine gun. He supposed it really didn't matter all that much. Should he be trapped on the long slope or on the ridge, he wouldn't have any chances of survival. With the M11, he would be able to take more of the attackers with him into eternity.

Going up the west slope would not be any cakewalk. The rains had turned some of the slope into muddy mush and had loosened any number of rocks of all sizes. Nonetheless, Camellion did not dare wait until the next day, until the sun had dried the ground and had cemented the rocks in place. All any enemy had to do was find just one S.E.A. unit or a Little John. The secret of his major line of defense would then no longer be a secret.

It took the Death Merchant, slipping and sliding, two hours to climb the slope; another three and a half hours to inspect the entire curved ridge and to climb back down to the Hand. Only two S.E.A.s and one Little John had been exposed.

By now it was dusk. Darkness was slowly dropping over the mountains, the long shadows deepening. Time to settle down for the long night. Patiently, Camellion hung the black plastic sheet over the entrance of the cave. Over the outside of the sheet, he placed the overlaying covering of camouflage. He pulled aside the two sheets of plastic, went inside the cave, and went about "triggering" the trap. In the center of the mouth of the cave, he had wedged two canisters of TH3 between three large rocks. Six fishline cords were attached to the ring-pin of each canister, six stretched to the left, six to the right. Camellion tied the lines of the canisters to the lines of the two sheets. The extra foot lengths he secured to the eyes of medium sized pitons he had driven into the rock walls. Should the sheets be pulled, any one of the taut lines would dislodge the pins in the grenades. Six seconds later, the mouth of the cave would be a roaring hell of burning blue-white thermite.

Going farther back into the cave, Camellion lit the lantern, cleaned the mud from his boots and ate supper—a tin of sardines, two packets of C-rations and a vitamin pill washed down with rainwater.

He made sure his weapons were in order and within reach. As was his daily custom, he sat down and polished the two Auto Mags. The two Internationals were not twins. One .41 retained its stainless steel finish. The other .41 AMP had a flat-black finish and was equipped with a foot-long noise suppressor, a 7-power Vemko scope and a metal shoulder stock. Silencer, scope, and stock—all were dull black. The weapon had been designed for night operations, though the black surface would prevent the sun's rays from glistening off the surfaces.

Time for dreamland. Camellion first made sure the S.E.A. and the Little John control stations were in place. He then proceeded to use self-hypnosis[1] to put himself to sleep, in such a manner that, as he rested with his back against a rock, his eyes would remain half-open. Combined with a self-induced posthypnotic suggestion, this method would awaken him instantly should any of the S.E.A. lights indicate a human sized life form in the area.

He awoke the next morning at dawn, spent an hour doing his Yoga and Kung Fu exercises and ate breakfast—more C-rations and a cup of powdered milk mixed with

---

[1] This is not fiction. The technique is simple, but requires a lot of patience and persistence.

rainwater. Today was a special day. Carlos and his brother were due with supplies.

Just as Camellion wsa about to turn off the Primus lantern, he heard the familiar sound. At first, he was not certain. He tilted his head and listened. There it was. There was no mistaking the *duddle-duddle-duddle-duddle* of a helicopter—and the sound was getting louder. This could be it, the strike he had been waiting for. *And just maybe it isn't!*

He buckled on the gun belt. In one holster was the Varga .45 auto. The regular .41 AMP was in the right holster. He slipped the canvas straps of the shoulder bags over his head and buckled the bags to his hips. Next came the Mannlicher rifle and the black AMP with stock and silencer. The AMP went over his right shoulder; the Mannlicher over his left. He looked at lights of the S.E.A. station; all was normal. He picked up the M11 Ingram, hurried to the mouth of the cave, untied the lines from the pitons, moved through the two plastic curtains and went outside into the early morning sunlight.

The sound of the whirlybird was much louder. The bird was coming in from the southeast. His cobalt blue eyes glittering, he looked around. The west slope started a hundred feet to the west, but no one on the ridge could see the mouth of the cave. Intervening rock rubble, that had tumbled from the slope over the years, acted as a barrier. East of the cave were tall, pinnacle-like boulders, all in a row, as if stuck there by giant hands. The boulders prevented him from seeing the helicoptor.

Keeping to the side of the boulders, Camellion moved south. He came to the last boulder and looked up, shielding his eyes with one hand. There it was—a big helicopter, flying at about 1,000 feet.

The Death Merchant opened the case attached to the back of his gun-belt and took out the rubber armored binoculars, although the craft was low enough for him to recognize it as a Curtis LB-16, a big deal that could carry twenty-three passengers besides the pilot and co-pilot. The LB-16 had a spaced out tricycle landing gear and two large rotors, one directly in back of the control cabin, the second protruding from the tail stabilizer.

By the time Camellion had focused the binoculars, the chopper was halfway across the plateau and in a line of approach that placed it several hundred feet east of his position. With its airfoils chopping the air like blades of a windmill, only a hundred times faster, the big bird roared by and continued toward the northwest. Soon it had disappeared over the ridge, the racket of its rotors fading. But not for long!

The chopper turned, and the sound of its eight rotor blades again increased until the racket was an intense, ear-pounding roar. On this return run, the chopper bore in straight from the north, two to three hundred feet lower. Catching the front of the craft through the binocs, Camellion could see the pilot and co-pilot. The craft then passed directly overhead and roared off to the south.

The Death Merchant now had the answer to a question that had puzzled him for some weeks. Yes, the aura device could track a target across the United States. Regardless, the helicopter didn't make sense. It was logical that Silvestter would use a helicopter to fly to the general area. A chopper would enable him to sit down almost anywhere, on any flat surface. But why would he deliberately advertise his presence, as if he wanted Camellion to know that he was about to attack.

Camellion didn't have to scratch his head for the answer. Cleveland Winston Silvestter Number Two wasn't in the helicopter. The chopper was a ploy, a deception, a detraction to force him to open fire and reveal his exact position. Evidently the tracking device could place a target only within a certain radius. Now, it was up to the copter to lure him into the open.

Silvestter? He had to be waiting on the high west ridge or on the north or the south slope leading to the top of the Hand. Camellion's battle with Silvestter had proved that while the young multimillionaire had tremendous nerve and was amazingly resourceful, he was not a fool. And he had to remain alive in order to look down at a dead Richard Camellion and spit in his face. . . .

The helicopter flew out across the valley to the south, so far it was almost invisible in the mists. With a low chuckle, Camellion unslung the black Auto Mag from his shoulder. *Let them try to hear the death whispers of this baby!*

He thumbed off the safety and waited for the chopper to return.

It did. The blue and white craft made a wide circle,

dipped down to within 200 feet of the ground and came in like an avenging eagle. This time it meant business. On each side of the fuselage, behind the control cabin, was a Dutch door. The bottom halves of the doors were closed, the top sections open to accommodate light machine guns mounted on bar-swivel mounts. Both machine guns began chattering the second the chopper was over the plateau.

Streams of 5.56mm slugs poured out of the Colt CMGs, two streams of fire that chopped leaves, jumped off granite, and sent up spurts of dust and rock from the ground. Camellion smiled. The damn fools in the chopper thought they were waving a red flag at a bull. *Only this bull is not going to bellow when he charges!*

He felt safe enough for the moment. Silvestter and the cruds with him wouldn't make their move until the chopper flushed out the target—*which happens to be me!*

The helicopter passed too far to the east for Camellion to fire at it. He could have triggered off a clip; yet he didn't want to waste ammunition. When he did fire, he wanted to be positive of a strike. Ricochets rang all around him, some of the projectiles coming in so close, on a slant, that bits of chopped leaves fluttered down in his face.

The Curtis LB-16 turned short three-fourths of the way across the Hand and reversed course, making an approach from the northeast, its CMGs snarling. Damn it to hell backward! This time the spitting big bird was too far to the west and on a route that would enable the portside gunner to place slugs in a line that would cut across the Death Merchant's position. Camellion scooted to a pile of rocks and snuggled down underneath a slab of jutting overhang. *Zing! Zing! Zing!* Projectiles ricocheted off the rock above him. Then the helicopter was gone. A few miles to the southwest, it turned and headed back.

Looking out from underneath the slab, Camellion saw that unless the pilot took the craft to the left or the right, it would pass directly over him, with the two streams of slugs missing him by a wide margin. The gunners could depress their weapons only so far on the mounts. It was as though Camellion would be at the center, at the point, of an upside down V. Each line of slugs would be at the end of each side.

Good enough. The Death Merchant crawled out from

underneath the overhang and took a new position in the center of some black alder bushes. Should the pilot change course, Camellion knew he would have time to dart back underneath the slab.

The pilot did not deviate from his straight line approach. The Death Merchant extended the metal stock of the Auto Mag when the helicopter was 500 feet ahead of him; he raised the weapon, put the stock against his shoulder and sighted through the scope, lining up the crosshairs on the front of the control compartment.

A .41 JMP cartridge pushes a 170 grain JHP projectile at 1,900 f.p.s. Careful! Allow for drift. There's a lot of downdraft from the rotor blades. Easy. Not too fast. Not yet. A few seconds more!

NOW!

Camellion gently squeezed the trigger. The Auto Mag jumped slightly, the butt-plate of the stock pushing against his shoulder. There was only a soft hissing sound from the noise suppressor. The Death Merchant was not surprised at the performance of the new-type "silencer." It had been designed by Lee E. Jurras, who pursued research and development with ten times the intensity of a wino looking for his next drink. Excellent was never good enough for Jurras. It was perfection—or back to the drawing board.

The Death Merchant pulled the trigger again, noticing how the eggbeater had begun to wobble. The roaring of the rotors increased, and then the chopper was directly overhead, the 5.56-millimeter slugs chopping the land a hundred feet on each side of Camellion, who spun around and put four .41 projectiles into the belly of the craft.

"En el nombre de la Cruz y del humanado verbo— suceder!"[2] he said softly to himself and watched the helicopter which was now skidding all over the sky, from left to right, as if the pilot had lost control.

The pilot had. Camellion's first bullet had pierced the plexiglass and had sliced upward through the right nostril of the man, into his brain, and out through the top of his skull, the impact lifting him up against the seatbelt. He had been alive one second and dead the next.

The Death Merchant's second bullet had missed its

---

[2] "In the name of the Cross and the word incarnate—success!"

target, the co-pilot; had missed because the pilot had jerked on the handle of the collective and throttle when the bullet had hit him. Instead of the second bullet hitting Ardel Rigdon, the co-pilot, it missed him and shot out the roof. Horrified by the sudden death of Mercer, the pilot, and by the bullet hole that suddenly appeared over his head, Rigdon quickly took over the controls. But his experience in flying helicopters was limited. His confusion increased to sheer panic when Clymer, the machine gunner to the left, let out a bloodcurdling scream. One of Camellion's slugs had torn his right foot off.

The helicopter started to go down. Try as he might, Rigdon could not correct the trim or pull in the pitch. He didn't know it and never would, but the main source of the trouble was in the turboshaft engine, in a gearshaft that had received one of Camellion's slugs. One small link-gear was locked. The rotor could not spin.

"I can't hold it!" Rigdon screamed at the gunner. "We're going to hit!"

A satisfied Richard Camellion watched the doomed helicopter.

Rotor decay. He hasn't a chance. He'll be in hell in a few minutes. . . .

He knew what had happened and what was taking place. The pitch had increased to an angle that was too great for the power available, and the smaller rotor in the tail could not do the job of lift alone.

Like some giant, drunken bug, its front blades spinning only by air pressure, the craft veered crazily to the west, losing altitude with each second. Its tricycle landing gear skimmed the tree tops as the craft headed for the rocky west slope. Ten seconds more and it hit, 75 feet up. There was a loud explosion, a beautiful ball of red and orange flame. Then nothing but falling and burning wreckage clanking down the mountainside.

The Death Merchant did not linger to admire his work. Keeping low and staying as much as possible to high rocks and trees, he ran for the cave.

He had a lot of buttons to press. . . .

Chapter Fifteen

The Death Merchant was halfway to the cave when bullets began clipping the leaves around him and ricocheting off the rocks—the shots, from automatic rifles, coming from the top ridge on the west slope. Independently of the helicopter shoot-down, searchers on the ridge had spotted him. Now, they would come in force, now that they were positive he was on the plateau—come not only from the ridge but from the north and the south slopes of the Hand. How many? Silvestter, with all his money and contacts, could have moved a small army to the region. No doubt he had. This explained why it had taken him so long to arrive at the Hand of God. Arrangements had required meticulous planning. The problem of transportation had to be solved, had to be synchronized to throw off the FBI. Not much of a problem there. The CIA was another matter. Whether Silvestter and Boden and Meunier had foiled Grojean's Qs was a vital question that had yet to be answered.

Camellion didn't have the time to speculate. He had to slow the gunsels on the ridge, long enough for him to get to the cave. He *had* to. Darting like a roadrunner awakened from a bad dream, he finally found what he needed: a jumbled mess of rocks shaped like *tufa* domes.

He dashed into the rocks, got down behind one of the larger sandstones and unlimbered the Mannlicher. He couldn't see any of the enemy, but he had to let them know he was alive, in good health and able to kill. He aimed at the ridge and rapidly fired off a full clip, spacing each round so that the 20 projectiles covered the length of the ridge. He pulled back the empty rifle, slung it over his shoulder and resumed his wild dash to the cave. He didn't stop until he came to another stretch of rock that offered protection from enemy bullets.

146

He snuggled down behind a box-like boulder surrounded by common juniper and sprouts of Nootka cypress, looked at the ridge ahead and pushed the M11 Ingram into place. Taking another magazine from his ammo bag, he could see two or three heads popping up, looking for him.

Grinning, he raised the deadly little M11 and squeezed the trigger. There was no roaring, only a loud hissing as he fired off the entire magazine in short four-round bursts, each .380 projectile six to ten feet from its predecessor; and after he had fired off the entire magazine, he pulled out the empty magazine, thrust in the full magazine and did it all over again.

If that doesn't keep them back for a time—I've had it!

The day was heating up. His back was wet with sweat. He reloaded the M11, scooted back from the rock and moved as fast as he could, his booted feet pounding the rock and grass. In a short while, he had the rock rubble between him and the west slope. He hurried to the entrance of the cave, slid past the two curtains at the opening, and hurried to the panels of the two central stations. Three-fourths of the light board of the Model-9 S.E.A. system was flashing, including the three units on the south side. The lights of the four units on the north side were blank.

He thought of Norberto and Carlos Martinez, relieved that Silvestter had not found out about them. Camellion, by listening to the bugs he had planted in the Ford pickup and had tied in with his walkie-talkie, had found out plenty about Carlos. He was using the truck for a lot of extra-marital activity. OK. That's his business.

Camellion did some thinking along other lines. He had placed five S.E.A. units on the south side. But only three were flashing. Ah-ha! Either the party on the south side was very small, or else only a part of the force was within range of the transmitting sensors. *If some of the men on that side are hanging back, why? Because Silvestter must be among them!*

Camellion could detonate all the Little Johns at once. The big blast would certainly blow some of the mountain's "purple majesty" all over kingdom come. Better though to worry the attackers. Better to keep them rattled and on edge and give them the business bit by bit, blast by blast.

He pressed No. 4 button on the panel.

The result was seismic—the concussion of the explosion gentle music to his ears.

His fingers began pushing buttons. . . .

Chapter Sixteen

Perched by the side of a large rock, one hundred feet below the rim, on the south slope of the Hand, Cleveland Silvestter was beginning to doubt the wisdom of his actions the previous weeks. Boden and Meunier had argued against the scheme, never for a moment deviating from their insistence that the Death Merchant would never have gone to New Mexico without some master plan maturing within the fertile garden of his mind.

"He's coming after us while we think we're chasing him!" Boden had said. "I'm telling you! That's the way he operates."

Laban Denbow had agreed with Boden and Meunier.

As the time had drawn closer to go to California, Boden and Meunier had flatly refused to have any part of the plan, calling the scheme suicidal. They had changed their minds when Silvestter told them that he had taped numerous conversations and, should he be killed, his attorneys, without knowing the contents of the tapes, would mail them to the United States Department of Justice. Silvestter had threatened Denbow with the same kind of exposure. So the three "cowards" had better put their experience at dirty tricks to work and do all in their power to make sure the strike against Camellion succeeded.

It had. Through Laban Denbow's contacts in the underworld, eighty-two thugs had been hired in the Los Angeles area, given an initial payment of $1,000 each, and told that they were being employed to go to a certain place and kill one man. They were further told that, after the mission was completed, each man would be given an additional $2,000.

Through the Continental Import & Export Shipping Corporation, the Curtis LB-16 had been purchased. Denbow had found a pilot and co-pilot.

The problem of transportation had presented a more difficult problem. The thugs had left Los Angeles in cars, in groups of two and three, an hour's difference between the departure of each group. The schedule had been carefully worked out, in that the last group would arrived in Trinidad, Colorado, three days before the dawn attack on the *Mano de Dios*. The Auraic Transfinder had confirmed that the Death Merchant was in the southwest section of the *Sangre de Cristo* Mountains. An intense study of topographical maps of the mountains closed tight the vise of doubt. Camellion was on a large plateau known as the Hand of God. Where else—although the Transfinder showed he might be anywhere within a 4.06 mile area.

The entire project hinged on timing. The Curtis LB-16, carrying Silvestter and his highly nervous aides, arrived in Trinidad two days before the morning of the scheduled attack. A surplus Curtiss-Wright C-46 Commando transport had left Los Angeles the day before the attack. It had flown to Trinidad, picked up the men, then had flown to an unused WW II airstrip six miles north of Ojo Caliente, where arrangements had been made to have three buses waiting. On the sides of each bus had been painted *Colorado Research Society for the Investigation of Unidentified Flying Objects & Other Related Phenomena*. The LB-16, flying much slower than the C-46 Commando, had left Trinidad hours ahead of the transport, both flights synchronized to permit the transport to catch up with the helicopter and for the two crafts to land at the same time.

The flight plan had worked like the mechanism of a fine Swiss watch.

The helicopter—pilot, co-pilot, and two gunners—had remained at the airstrip.

The buses had driven Silvestter, his aides, and the rest of the men to the same area where Camellion, much earlier, had parked the Ford pickup and where Carlos was still parking it before he hiked up to the Hand with supplies. From this point, Silvestter and his people had proceeded on foot to the bottom of the south slope, since maps revealed this was the most ideal route to the top of the plateau.

From the bottom of the south slope, a creep named Moss G. Trinkett had led a party of forty men to the highest ridge on the west slope. Trinkett had kept in contact with Silvestter by means of a hi-band closed-circuit transceiver.

150

Thirty more men had climbed the south approach and had taken positions along the south rim.

It had taken Trinkett and his group until 3:30 A.M. to get into position at the edge of the ridge. Silvestter had then called Ardel Rigdon and had ordered the pilot to lift from the air strip and to fly to the plateau. Silvestter had ordered Rigdon to fly back and forth across the plateau, to fly low in the hope that the Death Merchant would open fire. If the Death Merchant did not, then force him to. Fly very low and rake the entire Hand with machine gun fire. Once Camellion had revealed his position and they were sure he was on the plateau, Rigdon and his crew would fly back to the air strip and wait for further instructions.

The helicopter had arrived half an hour late, Rigdon explaining by radio that he had gotten lost. That was the beginning of things going wrong, of tiny, hairline cracks in the dam. Silvestter had yet to set eyes on the plateau; so had Bogen and Meunier, and Nario Hokakawa and Laban Denbow. They and Little Beans Banta and eleven other men were with Silvestter—all hugging large boulders on the side of the slope.

None of them had seen the helicopter slam itself into the side of the west slope. They had heard the explosion, a short but loud *WERROOOOMMMMMMM,* the sound rumbling across the mountains and dissolving in echoes that stumbled into each other.

Nick Humber, one of the "advance" men on the south rim, had reported by walkie-talkie what had taken place. The helicopter had skidded all over the roadway of sky and then had crashed into the slope. That's all there was to it.

Well, damn it! Had there been any gunfire from the ground? Had they seen any flashes?

Humber didn't know. He and the other men hadn't heard any, nor had they seen any flashes.

Hugh Boden, lying next to Silvestter, had said in a rage, "The Death Merchant used a silencer, you fool. I told you we shouldn't have stuck out our necks. That smoke from the wreck will be seen for miles. Before you know, the U.S. Rangers will be flying over to investigate!"

Silvestter had not replied. He had only glared hatefully at Boden.

151

A few minutes later, Trinkett had contacted Silvestter to report that he and his group had spotted a figure running toward the west side of the Hand. Should they open fire?

"You idiot!" screamed Silvestter into the mouthpiece. "Why do you think we came to this God-forsaken place. Shoot! *Kill Him! Kill him!*"

Meunier, to one side of Silvestter, looked up at the south rim bright from the sun that by now had risen fully. Like the rest of the men, Meunier was dressed in Army surplus clothing. "We've come this far," he said resignedly. "Let's get up there and run him down. There's more than enough of us."

He glanced at Silvestter, who was making a face that would have frightened the devil. The helicopter had cost $1,218,000. Now all that remained of the craft was burning junk and thick black smoke drifting south with the wind.

The stink of burning metal thick in his nostrils, Silvestter got to his feet and, without a word, began to climb the slope. Hugh Boden caught Gerald Meunier's eyes. Meunier shrugged, indicating Nario Hokakawa by moving his eyes. Boden understood. The hulking Hokakawa was behind them on the slope, and both men suspected that if they tried to retreat, the damned Jap would kill them. It would be just like Silvestter to have given such orders to Hokakawa.

Boden and Meunier obediently began climbing the slope. So did Little Beans, Denbow, and the rest of the men, everyone of them wishing he had never set foot in New Mexico. This included the gunmen and thugs that had been hired in Los Angeles. But not one of the eleven men wanted to be the first to say, "This is a bad deal. Let's get out of here."

Silvestter and Hokakawa were of a different breed, their logic of reality operating on a different plane. Silvestter's hatred of the Death Merchant blinded him to all reason. Hokakawa was a total fatalist who was convinced that everything was preordained, that the creature called man was simply a chesspiece of the universal gods.

They were only thirty feet from the top of the Hand of God when they heard the first tetrytol explosion on the west ridge, an enormous blast, deep and rock-shaking. Before they had time to organize their thoughts and get over their surprise, there was a second and a third and a fourth explosion from the west ridge.

"He's blowing them up!" yelled Laban Denbow. "He'll kill all of us!" He looked around frantically, huge drops of sweat flowing down his fat face.

Came more blasts from the west ridge.

The first Little John exploded on the south ridge above Silvestter and his party. There were several high-pitched screams and, much to their horror, Silvestter and most of the other men saw several mangled bodies flying through the air. One corpse shot out to the south and started its drop far behind them. The second bloody lump of flesh smashed against the rocks above them. Then there were the rocks of all sizes and shapes, the rocks thrown up by the explosion.

"Get down, all of you!" Meunier shouted in a loud voice. "Even the small rocks will be like hammerheads!"

The men did the best they could, jumping to the first rock large enough to shield them, including Silvestter and Hokakawa, slipping and sliding on loose pebbles and stones and shale resting on shale.

Then—one, two, three, four crashing explosions from the edge of the plateau directly above them, an explosive benediction blessing twelve of the men on the rim with instant death and disabling six more with broken arms and legs and ribs. The huge crashing wall of sound was followed by more shrieks and a flood of crushed rock that rolled down the slope like a dirty wave. Four of the men screamed in terror and pain when chunks of granite, the size of footballs, slammed into them. There wasn't a thing the men could do, nothing but hug the slope and keep their heads down.

The thought crawled around in Gerald Meunier's mind: What they were doing was a piece of insanity! Trying to kill the Death Merchant was as ridiculous as an Archbishop trying to discuss theology with a pack of naked savages!

Gradually, to the roaring of more explosions on the west ridge, the rolling rock rumbled by and soon was tumbling down the slope behind the men. Now, only small stones continued to fall from the rim.

One by one the men raised their heads and looked around.

"Oh my God!" choked Denbow. He jerked back from a

bloody arm that had fallen across his legs and started to gag and retch.

One of the men from L.A. cried out weakly, "I think my leg is broken." Another called out, "This man next to me is dead. His skull's crushed."

The explosions had stopped. All that remained were the echoes and clouds of dust on the rim.

His hands shaking, Silvestter pushed the TALK button of the walkie-talkie. "Humber! Can you hear me?" His voice shook almost as much as his hands.

There was no reply.

Five times Silvestter called out to Nick Humber. Finally he switched off the walkie-talkie, clicked on the transceiver and tried to contact Moss Trinkett on the west ridge.

He did not receive a reply.

There was a wild, fanatical look on Silvestter's face as he turned off the transceiver, looked around at the dirty faces and said, "All of you, listen to me. We have to leave the wounded where they are. We must get to the top. We won't be safe until we do."

Silvestter didn't wait for any of them to reply. He turned and, with a burst of speed, began to claw the last thirty feet to the top.

Chapter Seventeen

Some people drink for pleasure. Some climb mountains. Others play cards. Or even skydive. Richard Camellion derived a lot of his kicks from blowing up things. Like a kid with a new toy, he pushed the buttons on the Little John panel and listened to the blasts from the south rim and the high west ridge. He didn't entertain any hope that the explosions would kill all of the enemy or frighten off those still alive and able to run. Silvestter didn't have enough sense, and he was in command.

It required only minutes to press the buttons, including the one that exploded the Little John in the cave's upward passage to the first ridge. The blast from the "chimney" crashed against his ears, and he could hear rock falling from the opening farther back in the darkness.

Exploding the Little Johns had been the easy part of his defenses. Now would come the highly dangerous task of hunting down the attackers and terminating them without getting smeared himself. As he moved to the mouth of the cave, he ran another analysis. Silvestter and his group would move north and attempt to rendezvous with the force from the west ridge, with the men who hadn't been killed by the series of explosions. Camellion would adapt his strategy accordingly. He would swing to the north, inspect the north rim, come up along the east edge, then dart around from the south. No doubt Silvestter would have a rear guard. *OK. I'll go to the northeast, then turn and bear due west.* There could be a hitch. Silvestter might have his men fan out in all directions, in which case the mop-up would be more difficult and far more dangerous.

He slipped past the two plastic curtains, although this time he stopped, reached around the plastic and tied the lines to the pitons, once more turning the grotto into a death-trap.

With great care, he moved along the wall of rock rubble. Each drifting shadow could be an enemy. Each rock could be harboring a gunman with a submachine gun, though the odds were against it. None of Silvestter's men could have moved that close in so short a time. Camellion listened. The birds had quit singing; there were no animal calls. Black smoke from the burning helicopter drifted across his face—a foreign stink that was out of place in this phantasmagoria of pre-civilization America, where the ghosts of painted tribes walked in bitter loneliness; a very modern stink that marred the fragrance of wild honeysuckle and meadowsweet.

In due time, Camellion came to that section of the rock debris that dipped, that permitted him to see the west ridge. Dust still drifted above the topmost ridge, 200 feet up. On the slope, he counted one, two, three, four, five bodies sprawled out grotesquely among the conglomeration of rubblestone, slabs of shale, and granite boulders. It was evident there would never be a resurrection for them. Nor for the six other men climbing down from the ridge, the six of them at various heights from the edge of the rim.

The Death Merchant disliked neutralizing the dumb-bells—almost. Any idiot can shoot fish in a barrel—*or morons on the side of a mountain!* Not that it was all that simple. The six gunmen were spread out all over the width of the face. Should he use the scoped Auto Mag, he might not be able to whack out all six quick enough. The ones he didn't get would drop to the safety of the rocks.

He switched the firing selector on the M11 to three second bursts, looked around again, then raised the Ingram. He kept both eyes open, his line of sight on the elevated wedge at the end of the noise suppressor. He swung the wedge to the first man and gently squeezed the trigger. *Bzzziiitttttt.* The man jumped outward, flopped back down and slid a dozen feet on the pebbles of the slope. He hit the second and third targets with equal ease. The fourth man, seeing the third man jerk and throw up his arms, guessed that they were being fired on by someone using a silencer. In a crazed panic, he made an effort to crawl down to some tub-sized boulders eight feet below him. His feet and legs were dropping between the slope and one of the boulders when a slug smacked him in the neck and knocked him into eternity.

Trinkett, the fifth man, was lucky. He happened to be very close to a large depression that was directly below him. Seeing Murdock, the fourth man killed, he dropped into the cup-shaped hollow an eye-blink ahead of three .380 projectiles that dug into the slope above him. His face cut from flying stones, he tried to claw into the pebble and hard clay. His entire body ached from the battering of small stones and his right arm was in pain from a BB embedded half an inch underneath the skin, just above the elbow.

A 42-year-old soldier of fortune, Trinkett had fought in a lot of little wars, but never had he been faced with a situation like this. It was unbelievable. There had been thirty-nine men and himself. Within several minutes, explosions had killed thirty-one, had mangled them to pulp. Four more couldn't move and might even be dying, helpless from shattered bones and internal injuries. Oh God! Now Murdock and the others had been killed. Never in his life had Trinkett felt so helpless and so all alone. Through a fog of misery, he knew he had to get down the slope and make contact with the survivors from the south side. He wondered how many of them were alive. . . .

The Death Merchant shook his head in disgust. By the time the man he missed managed to climb down—*I'll be moving on the north side. One more doesn't make all that much difference.*

He slipped a Ranger camouflage head-net over his snap-brim hat and moved out with complete confidence in his ability to nail Silvestter and the remainder of his attack force. Silvestter was special. The Death Merchant had special plans for him, provided he didn't have to blow him away with a slug.

Silvestter had made two fatal mistakes. He hadn't been patient. He had come to Camellion, to territory with which the Death Merchant was familiar, extremely so since he had had 18 long days to familiarize himself with every physical feature of the plateau. It may have been the Hand of God, but Camellion knew it like the palm of his own right hand. He had even memorized various clumps of boulders and thick bushes where he could hide and affect an ambush. The flaw was that he had no way of knowing how many men he had to terminate. Capturing one of the lice would not be all that easy.

He kept away from the high areas where the terrain rose in gentle elevation, and did his best to keep small ridges and piles of rock between him and the region toward the south. In the northwest and straight west there were several large areas big enough for a helicopter to sit down. One was a gargantuan slab of granite, the other a grassy rectangle bordered by roches moutonnees. He avoided these two landing sites by wide margins.

Eventually, drawing close to the north rim, he was able to make better time, running through a network of gullies that merged into arroyos still wet from the previous afternoon's rain; and every second he made use of his intense training in Ninjitsu[1]. Toward the north-central section, he came to a ridge of piled-up sandstone that stretched out to the very edge of the plateau. By keeping down to the west side of the ridge, he was able to make his way to the rim, crawl through the high whip-grass and look down the steep slope—hundreds and hundreds of feet of tumbled stone, a forest of rock like the surface of an alien world. Barren. Nowhere was there any sign of activity. No, none of Silvestter's force had come to this side of the plateau.

The Death Merchant moved on to the east rim. . . .

Cleveland Silvestter and the men with him found only the work of the Cosmic Lord of Death on top of the south edge of the plateau. Most of the thirty men, who had first climbed to the top, had foolishly remained grouped together. Because they had, the five Little Johns had ripped twenty-one of them apart within a few minutes. Concussion had torn arms and legs from bodies with the suddenness of a sadistic little boy pulling the wings and legs off flies. Steel BBs had torn into bodies with the force of .22 magnum projectiles, shredding clothes and flesh.

A hundred foot length of the rim had been turned into an outdoor slaughterhouse and looked it. Pieces of clothing lay scattered around the area whose rocks and grass were wet with drying blood and plastered with flesh and viscera—all glistening in the bright new-day sun.

[1] The ancient Japanese art of stealth. In the 13th and 17th centuries, the Ninjas were the medieval masterminds of espionage, arson, sabotage, and assassination. The Ninja not only mastered the techniques of moving silently but was an expert with darts, daggers, star-shaped spurs, medieval brass knuckles, caltrops, garrotes, rope ladders, guns, grenades, acid-spurting tubes, poisons, lead-weighed bamboo staves, etc.

Silvestter, both hands wrapped tightly around a Stoner assault rifle, stared down at a foot—still in its combat boot, only six feet away—and listened to the low buzzing and humming. Already the garbage brigades of Nature had gathered, the flying insects and the crawling things that come up from the ground to feed on the dead.

There were low groans and pitiful cries for help. Seven men had been badly mangled by the blasts. One had a broken back and was paralyzed from the waist down. He kept begging for someone to shoot him. Another man was on his knees, his face looking as if he had fallen into a meatgrinder. He had been blinded, his eyes punctured by BB shot. The rest of the wounded had broken arms or legs, or both.

"We'll never be able to move them down the slope," the logistic-minded Boden said to Silvestter. "Some of them would be dead anyhow by the time we got them to the buses."

Gerald Meunier faced Silvestter squarely and said sharply, "If we continue to go on, we're fools! Look around you, Silvestter! Take a good look. The Death Merchant has cut us down to almost nothing. Of all the men who came up here, only two are in fighting shape, Humber and Wilson. There are only seventeen of us, and we have no way of knowing what other surprises he might have waiting for us."

"There must be survivors from the west side," Silvestter snapped.

"Don't be an idiot!" Hugh Boden growled. "There were more explosions on the west side than here. I doubt if any of them survived."

Acting as if he had not heard Boden, Silvestter looked around at the dirty faces staring at him, the faces of men who were afraid and uncertain. He knew that he and Nario Hokakawa could not force the others to continue. He decided on another method.

He turned to the hawk-faced Nick Humber, who had been knocked out from the blast but was otherwise unhurt.

"Is that your method, Humber? To run from one man?" demanded Silvestter, his voice ringing with sincerity. He waved his hand at the dead and the wounded, then pointed with the barrel of the Stoner toward the north. "There is only one man out there. There are seventeen of us. What kind of cowards would we be if we ran from one man?"

He raised his voice. "I'm going in there after him, and I'm going to kill him. You cowards can stay here and wonder how to get the yellow streaks off your backs!"

Once more Silvestter swept the men with a savage stare. Then he started running toward some rocks to the north. Nario Hokakawa hurried after him.

"By God, he's right!" Humber said and picked up his M16 rifle. "I'm not running from one single son of a bitch."

He turned and ran after Silvestter and Hokakawa. The rest of the mercenaries glanced at each other. One by one, they followed.

Laban Denbow looked as if he had been hit in the face with a sock full of razors. "What are we going to do?" he whispered.

"We can't stay here," Little Beans croaked. "All this stink and blood and guts and stuff laying around! What the hell's to stop us from climbing back down and scramin' outta here, huh? You tell me! There ain't nobody stoppin' us."

"Yes, there is," Boden said. "Silvestter is. He's got the transceiver. We can't call the transport without it. And we can't go back and wait for the buses."

"Why in hell can't we?" Little Beans' two chins wobbled as he spoke.

It was Laban Denbow who gave him the answer. The private detective was every bit as clever as the two ex-CIA agents; the only difference was that he lacked the sophistication of Boden and Meunier.

"There's a chance that Silvestter and the others might get Camellion," he said and mopped his wide forehead. "If that happens and they come back to the buses and find us, that crazy Silvestter might kill us. I personally wish I'd never gotten involved in this business."

No one answered him.

Chapter Eighteen

Professionals are people who do the job well even when they don't feel like it, and since the Death Merchant was more than anxious to get his M11 wedge sight on Silvestter —better yet, his hands—he made very good progress. Moving through shortcuts along the east rim, he presently found himself to within 75-feet of the south lip. With the speed and the silence of a master Ninja, he sought out the length of ridge on which he had planted the five Little Johns. From concealment among tall pitcher plants intertwined with bloodroot, he inspected the carnage, satisfied that he had done his work well. The world now had less scum and trash.

He lingered only long enough to inspect the razor grass behind some rocks farther to the west and to study the numerous footprints in clay made soft by yesterday's rain. Camellion could track a rattler over an acre of pine needles. He had not the slightest bit of difficulty reading the signs. Leaves, insects or superimposed animal tracks indicate age. These footprints had been made within the hour. It was also evident that some men had remained behind for a very short time and then had hurried to catch up. There were wider spaces between their tracks, and the impressions were deeper, indicating the men had been running. He estimated that fifteen to twenty men had moved inward. It was not difficult to know the direction they had taken. Bits of dirt, leaves and other ground refuse, when disturbed, will always be pushed in the direction of travel. The force had moved due north.

His eyes glowing with a strange light, Camellion moved north and slightly to the east—*who said revenge isn't sweet?* Determined to catch up with Silvestter, he kept to the larger boulders and, when he had to cross an area that was relatively free of rock cover—or else go around and lose precious time—he got to his belly and slithered through the thick razor grass like a snake, as silent as a sunbeam. Even with his ability and training, such a course was difficult because of the equipment he carried. The only weapon he didn't carry was the Mannlicher. He had hidden it under some rocks on the north side. The Mannlicher was too expensive to lose. Should he get blown away, he wouldn't need it.

After a time, he consulted his wristwatch, certain that he had achieved his purpose. Putting all his senses on Red Alert, he crawled through grass between jumbled masses of granite in which a good deal of reddish-brown quartz showed. Had his memory blown a circuit? There had to be a long ditch-like depression at the end of the grass. But where was it? At last he came to the dip and crawled in, sighing in relief that it wasn't full of water. He duck-waddled through the ditch, came to its end, and prepared to go to the spot he wanted, a not-too-large area dotted with barrel-sized boulders surrounded by medium-length grass and sprawling bougainvillaea. Perfect! He left the ditch and began snaking through the grass and, where and when he could, underneath the canopy of bougainvillaea. Thirty feet later he came to the three rocks he wanted, the three he had marked on the map of his memory. He snuggled down between two of the rocks and waited.

Suppose he was wrong? He didn't think he was. And in kill-situations like this, one had to act on conclusions drawn from previous experience. Cleveland Silvestter didn't give a whisper in Hades about the lives of the people with him. *But he wants to get out of this in one piece. He'll fan them out. He'll send them out in twos and threes. He knows that if they can get off a shot at me, the sound of the firing will halfway pinpoint me.*

He waited. Five minutes later his logic was confirmed by the sight of two men moving through some young mountain alder trees to the northwest. Camellion didn't know the two. He didn't have to. He knew they were hired guns. *Professionals. Or would be professionals.*

The two gunsels, side by side, M16 A-Rs in their hands, moved in his direction, their heads moving from side to side. They would stop, look all around them, then move forward a few yards. They had come to the Hand of God to hunt and kill. Now, they were the hunted.

The two men advanced another twenty feet. They were only forty feet from Camellion, who was waiting to see if a third or fourth man would follow them. It was possible that they were using a diamond or "T" scouting formation. He doubted it. And they wouldn't be calm enough to make a box search or use the cross-grain method. There simply wasn't time. Silvestter might be a crackpot of the first order, but he was a born survivor who would know that the series of Little John explosions would eventually bring the police to the scene. It would be a while. Park Rangers didn't have the authority. By the time the New Mexico State Police got around to sending a helicopter, it would be high noon. The New Mexico Park Service would arrive first, probably within a few hours. The N.M.P.S. had a reputation throughout the state for efficiency.

The two men advanced another five feet, stopped, and looked around. Camellion waited to see if a third or fourth man would put in an appearance.

"Tch, tch. When the 'Roll is called up yonder,' you boys won't be there," he said softly, thrust the muzzle through the bougainvillaea and fired. *Bzzzziiittttttt!* Instant annihilation. The two men could not have felt any pain, much less realize that their lives were over.

His muscles working in unison, Camellion left the rocks, retraced his route and emerged from the granite marred with quartz. Now his danger had doubled. Should the two corpses be discovered before he could reach his next ambush point, the enemy would know he was in the general vicinity.

More careful than ever, he started to move west at only half his previous speed, halfway expecting gunfire. No matter how circumspect one is, no matter one's training, there is always risk. No man is infallible. *Except the Pope! And it isn't he who is fighting this battle!*

Camellion reached the desired point of ambush—another small grassland thick with bougainvillaea and a United Nations of wild flowers. Here and there a boulder. At one end of the field, to the north, there was a kind of ridge, a hodge-podge of rocks extending in a north and south direction. The south end of the ridge, overlooking the field, had a conglomerate of slabs and chunks of granite just right for anyone wanting to set up an ambush.

The Death Merchant bored into the grass and took a position by the side of a rounded sandstone, just within the southeast side of the field. Since he was not underneath any bougainvillaea, he had been careful not to choose a position thick with the crawling plant. The reddish-purple flowers would not blend well with his camouflaged clothing.

Several minutes passed. Five minutes became part of the past. Seven minutes later, Camellion saw a figure to the south, ducking from tree to tree, from tree to rock. Behind him came two more individuals. The first doomed man, seeing the grassland ahead, and the ridge to the north of the field, stopped and waved for the others to come forward. The Death Merchant could almost read the mind of the first man, who was trying to decide whether the object of their hunt might be hidden in the rocks of the ridge.

The last two men ran up to the first gunmen and the three held a short conference, after which they did what Camellion thought they would do. They spread out, with the intention of approaching the ridge from the east and west sides. To avoid a head-on approach, they had to advance just behind the east and west sides of the grassland, in a manner that afforded them the best cover. The joker carrying an M16 took the west route. The two mercenaries with M14 infantry rifles moved east, in the Death Merchant's direction.

The Death Merchant was not too concerned; the chances of the two gunmen spotting him were very slim. If they did, he was prepared to fire first. They didn't. They came to within twenty feet of him, but their concern was the ridge ahead, and that's where their eyes and attention were.

Camellion was patient. When the man to the west had covered half the distance to the ridge, and the other two not quite that far, Camellion put the show on the road. He first cut down the man to the west. The second two men lost several seconds by their surprise, moments they would never regain. A chain of .380 machine gun slugs smashed into them, knocked them back and pitched them to the grass. The triple extermination had taken only 4.7 seconds.

The Death Merchant moved around the grassland, cut across the front of the ridge and hurried west. He was confident that the main enemy force was to the south, behind him, but he couldn't be positive. Fifteen to twenty men had been his estimation. He had put five to sleep. The thing to do now was move to the west side, swing to the south, then move in and wipe out the main body with the M11 and grenades—*after I eliminate any scouts who might be to the west.*

Camellion knew it was foolish to pretend that he might be able to blow away Silvestter up close. Only fools took unnecessary risks. Camellion didn't mind dying, but he preferred to be elderly when it happened. Silvestter would have to die with the others.

He moved fast, calling upon experience and his Ninja training to increase his speed. At one time, he thought he heard a helicopter far to the south, then decided he had not. He crossed rocky sections, darted across areas heavy with scattered rock and bushes and came to a lot of tall, lopsided rocks known as erosional forms, soft hornblendite that had been carved by fierce wind blowing sand. These rocks were the last barrier before he would turn south, then move from the west to cut down the scouts. If there were scouts. He assumed there would be.

Most of the erosional rocks were tall and wide, and although many of the rocks were eaten through with cave-like holes, Camellion was able to move through them at a rapid rate of speed, at times even running. He doubted if there were any scouts within three hundred feet. He soon found out he was wrong.

He hurried around a long, ten-foot-high rock—and there they were! Two of the enemy, who obviously had been coming around the other side of the rock, the first man so close to the Death Merchant that he was practically eyeball to eyeball with him, so close that Camellion could see the beads of sweat on his face and congealed blood from rock cuts. The second man was right behind his partner.

"Heyyyyyyy!" The first mercenary yelled with astonishment, jerked up short and tried to bring up his Canadian C1 military rifle. Although just as surprised as the two men, Camellion was twice as fast. He reached his with his right hand, grabbed the barrel of the C1 and pushed it up, to a position that was almost perpendicular. The man couldn't twist the rifle from Camellion's hand; he wasn't fast enough. Camellion brought up the Ingram with his left hand, clipped him under the jaw with the end of the noise suppressor, and, with his left knee, shoved him back.

The man grunted, his eyes rolled back, and he sagged against the man behind him. His finger also contracted against the trigger of the rifle. BANG! The rifle roared, the loud crack causing most of the birds in nearby trees to flutter nervously and fly off.

The second man did his frantic best to get his own weapon into action, a Canadian Mark Sten II submachine gun. Unfortunately for him, he didn't have time to push the unconscious body from him. While he was trying, Camellion thrust the muzzle of the Ingram against his side and cut him open with four slugs.

The damage had been done. A shot had been fired. Silvestter was now warned. Camellion turned his attention to the man he had slammed in the jaw. He was more severely dazed than knocked out. Camellion quickly slapped him awake and shoved the muzzle of the M11 against his Adam's apple, paying no attention to the blood dripping from the cut on the goon's jaw.

Eddie Starr drew back and tilted up his chin, the muzzle of the noise suppressor icy cold against his hot skin. Thirty years old, he had red hair as long as a girl's. With eyes saucer-round with terror, he stared at the lean, hard man who was as prickly as cactus and had a voice as ominous as a cobra.

"How many are in Silvestter's group? Answer me or I'll blow your eyeballs out through the back of your head. It won't make any difference. By then I'll have cut your throat with slugs."

Starr had the IQ of a houseplant. But even if he had had the mind of an Einstein, he wouldn't have dared to lie; he was too afraid a falsehood might show on his face. He told the truth. *Seventeen in all.* The others were dead or too wounded to be of value. As the Death Merchant had surmised, Silvestter was to the south, almost a fifth of a mile back.

"Friend, you are a liar!" snarled Camellion, testing. "How come you and this other joker are up here, so far ahead. I don't see any roller skates on your feet!"

Starr's eyes darted to the dead man. "Me and Tibbits are advance scouts," he said hoarsely, knowing how the Christians must have felt in the Roman coliseum. "I dunno. I'm only guessing it's a fifth of a mile. They could be closer. But I told you the truth." His eyes rolled toward the dead Tibbits. "There were seventeen of us. I mean until you killed John."

"Wrong!" Camellion removed the muzzle of the M11 from Starr's throat, stood up and stepped back. "Only

166

eleven. I terminated five of your pals. And soon there will only be ten. You're dead, too!"

Starr's face twisted like a pretzel and he tried to cover his face with his arms. A *bzzzitttttttt* from the silencer and a burst of slugs, ripping into his chest, stopped his movement and forever erased all his terror. Blood pouring out of his mouth, he slumped against the rock.

Camellion moved west, keeping to his original plan. The rifle shot had told Silvestter and his men that there was trouble to the north. Camellion surmised that Silvestter would continue to be very suspicious and very careful until he found out what had actually happened. He would increase speed and come forward. The Death Merchant was determined to be in place by the time Silvestter realized how he'd been suckered.

In spite of his anxiousness, Camellion did not sacrifice caution for speed. Dead men never get second chances. He used previous techniques that had served him well, keeping to the trees, small hills, and larger rocks, blending himself with the foliage.

Almost panting, he finally came to the area he wanted. He turned then and raced due south, timing himself. After ten minutes, he turned again; this time he moved east, his eyes alert for the slightest movement, the slightest motion of a single blade of grass or leaf. In a sense, the rifle shot had been fortunate. He could turn it to his advantage by not having to be so choosy in deciding on his last position for an ambush. According to the map imprinted on his memory, there were masses of rock not too far distant, much of the stone on small hills as cut up and as patternless as crushed spaghetti. Twenty minutes ago, those hills were the last place in the world he would have chosen. The rifle shot had changed all that. Now that Silvestter thought the Death Merchant was to the north, he and his men would not view the rocks—which would be west of them—with undue suspicion.

Camellion came to the rocky hills and, almost panting, picked his way through boulders and over mounds to the foremost place of concealment—long slabs of sandstone held upward by huge chunks of broken granite. All around him were tables of rock, some five feet in diameter. Once these "tables" had been the base sections of tall medium-sized pinnacles, columns that time and wind and rain had weakened, until at last they had collapsed and broken into the fragments that lay strewn around.

I suppose it wouldn't be a great loss if I got whacked out today. Anyhow, most of us are too young to be as old as we are. . . .

Camellion put a full magazine into the Ingram, removed the scoped and stocked Auto Mag from his back, and gave his weary shoulders a rest by taking off the carry-all bags. He took five grenades from one bag and placed them on the ground within reach. Yes, this place was ideal. In front of him, but growing on the other side of the rock, was a wild hydrangea that shielded him from anyone beyond, to the east. Yet he could look through the fuzzy leaves and flowers and see anyone ahead. He did, only minutes later.

Cleveland Winston Silvestter and his crowd, not in any kind of formation, moved in small knots. Silvestter and Nario Hokakawa were with two men who looked like professional troublemakers. *Ahhh, there are Gerald Meunier and Hugh Boden and a big slob that looks like a retarded walrus!* Laban Denbow and two gunmen were in the rear.

Using Slivestter as the center of an imaginary circle, the Death Merchant estimated that the other nine were within 75 feet of the young millionaire—*and all of them, not more than 75 feet from me*.

With a twisted smile, Camellion pushed the firing selector on the Ingram to full automatic, all the time watching the procession through the hydrangea. As far as he was concerned, all ten men were as good as dead.

A gift from me to you, Old Bones! Let's do it!

It was the sound behind him, to his right, that stopped him from rearing up and firing at Silvestter—the sound of small rocks tumbling on rocks, rolling down a rocky hillside. Camellion didn't bother to turn and stare and yell, *Hey! Somebody up there slipping on rocks?* He used his right leg as a piston and threw himself to the left at the same instant an automatic rifle roared and a dozen projectiles hit the face of the rock where he had been crouched, the high, piercing screams of the ricochets adding to the orchestration of destruction.

A bouncing bullet cut through Camellion's shirt and raked his left side, not deeply but enough to make him feel as if he had been slashed with a lead-tipped whip. Yelling in pain and rage, he spun around and raised the Ingram as another ricochet opened a gash across his left arm. He fired automatically, by instinct, a long, raking burst directed toward the area where the A-R had roared. He would have to take out the target with the first blast or die himself. Within several seconds, the enemy would be able to adjust his aim and blow him away.

Most of the Death Merchant's projectiles missed Moss Trinkett. It was the two hits that counted—one in his left shoulder, the other in his right side, the first bullet spinning him to the left, the second tearing through his heart and lungs. Trinkett had bought the Big One. The Beretta AR70SC clattered twenty feet to the rocks below. Trinkett's corpse pitched after it.

During those eight seconds, the Death Merchant had wondered who the man was. He couldn't be a member of Silvestter's small group, or he wouldn't have been up there in the rocks. From the way Silvestter and his crowd were moving north, it was apparent there weren't any scouts sitting around in the rocks.

The fellow I missed! Camellion deduced that Trinkett had climbed down from the west side slope. *He must have been wandering around trying to make contact with Silvestter and his people. He climbed up on the hill to look around, saw Silvestter out front—and me!*

Camellion knew that now he was facing the result of catastrophe, of a plan that had dissolved like ashes being pounded by rain. He might as well have been caught between the path of a tornado and the course of a tidal wave. He didn't take time to look out and see what Silvestter and his men might be doing. He knew.

He crawled to the grenades and picked up the first one, noticing a ricochet mark only inches from another grenade. Lucky me! Hunched over, he thought for a moment, mentally measuring distance, pulled the pin and used an overhand pitch to throw the grenade. As fast as he could, he threw the other four grenades, the proximity of the explosions tearing at his ears. Between the blasts, he had thought he had heard the sound of a chopper coming in from the southeast. Now he was positive. A helicopter— *By God! Two of them!*—was coming. Another worry. All he needed was a confrontation with New Mexico State Police and park service people!

Cleveland Silvestter and his men had heard Trinkett and Camellion's firing. They had seen Trinkett's body fall

169

from the hill and realized that he had fired at the Death Merchant, who had to be behind a slab of rock to the west. Instantly, all of them had dropped to the ground. The firing had stopped.

"Spread out! Get the son of a bitch!" Silvestter jumped to his feet, his voice ringing with victory. He nudged Nario Hokakawa and the two of them began running to the northwest while the rest of the men charged forward.

The advance had covered maybe forty feet when the first grenade went off, the explosion pitching Walt Turner into the air and knocking Lincoln Williams, another tough from Los Angeles, against a small tree. Turner's body, his flesh and clothes hanging in blackened and bloody tatters, crashed back down and lay still. Williams, riddled with shrapnel, lay on his stomach, moaning.

The majority of the men realized that when one is under bombardment in an open space, one keeps moving until one reaches safety—everyone except Laban Denbow. In the first place, he could not run very fast, being short and fat. He dove to the ground and attempted to bury himself in the leaves and grass. The second grenade exploded almost on top of him. Shrapnel ripped into his skull and laid his back open. But it was the concussion that hemorrhaged his brain and killed him.

The third grenade threw up a lot of dirt and rocks and that was all. The fourth caught Big Murf Phelan, a San Francisco gunman, who had been unlucky enough to be in L.A. the day Silvestter was recruiting hoods. Phelan's hand went flying, and so did a half a pound of flesh from his stomach and chest and face. His bloody corpse came back to the ground, hit, bounced and lay still.

The fifth explosion did little damage, other than rearrange part of the landscape, although a dozen pieces of shrapnel stabbed into Gerald Meunier's left side. Meunier screamed with pain and fear and fell to the ground, thinking that he had been mortally wounded. He wasn't. The shrapnel had broken several ribs and was otherwise painful, but they hadn't pierced any veins or arteries.

Hugh Boden dropped to the ground ten feet from Meunier. He had not even been scratched. So what? How could the others know that he hadn't been killed. What others? Only Silvestter and his damned Jap bodyguard were a threat. They were far to the northwest, almost to

170

the north end of the slab. Banta and Humber—those idiots!—were about to storm around the south side of the slab. Let them! Let them get their stupid heads blown off!

Boden, listening to the helicopters, started crawling toward Gerald Meunier. Glancing up, he saw one of the choppers was visible in the southeast sky.

"How bad is it?" he asked, reaching Meunier.

"I don't know." Meunier was in such pain he could speak only with difficulty. "What's the difference? We're finished, all of us. You heard those helicopters."

"No we're not," Boden said hoarsely. "We'll hide out until it's over with and the choppers are gone. Somehow, we'll get down the slope and out of this mess."

Meunier moaned again. "We'll never do it."

"We can try," insisted Boden. "It's our only chance. Now crawl. Or I'll leave you here."

With short, agonized groans, Meunier started to move.

After throwing the grenades, the Death Merchant scampered to the low rocks to the west. With a hill between him and the slab, he crawled upward, went through a small gully and pulled himself up to a long monolith that had fallen and was lying horizontally. On his stomach, he squirmed to the front to some boulders and looked around one.

From this elevated position, he could see over the slab below. Bodies lay twisted on the grass in front of the slab. Except six! To the southwest, two men were crawling away. He couldn't see their faces. Two more were about to race around the south end of the slab. Camellion had only a quick look at Silvestter and Hokakawa, both of whom were running in a northwest direction. Then they disappeared behind a tumbled mass of granite.

The Death Merchant swung the Ingram to the other two men, concerned now because he felt that Silvestter and the Japanese karate expert were attempting to get behind him.

The Ingram jerked in his hand as the noise suppressor emitted a long *bzzzittttttttt*. Stabbed across his chest with .380 projectiles, Nick Humber threw up his arms and died, dropping into hell a few moments ahead of Little Beans Banta, who tried to throw his tonnage to the ground.

171

Half a dozen .380 slugs helped him succeed. With his left cheek shot off and blood gushing out of his throat, Little Beans fell backward and lay still.

Camellion scampered back from the front of the mono-lith, dropped into the small gully and tried to analyze the situation. Impossible. There was no way to predict with any certainty where Silvestter and Hokakawa might be. He could either sit tight and wait or try to catch them with their pants down by going after them.

He moved out of the gully, got down behind a table-rock and looked around. He saw that he was on the top of a flat hill filled with rocks of various sizes. No, on top of a long mound. The formation was too low to be rightly called a hill. He started moving west, darting from rock to rock, all the while straining to listen—a rather difficult job because of the noise of approaching helicop-ters.

Very soon Camellion knew that he had guessed cor-rectly. He saw Silvestter and Hokakawa at the same time they saw him and Silvestter, jumping to one side, got off a short burst with a Stoner A-R. A waste of 5.56mm slugs. Camellion, the instant he saw the two men, jerked quickly to his left, to the protection of a wall of rock that had a section jutting outward at its west end.

To give himself time, and to force the two to take cover, Camellion thrust out the M11 to the right, as far as he could, and triggered off a long burst, then darted along the wall to the end and took a position behind the four-foot long section of foliated granite protruding from the main section. He had seen Silvestter and Hokakawa only briefly, but long enough to know that the two targets were about 25 feet in front of him. No doubt they were now down behind one of several large rocks.

Camellion bent slightly and slowly looked around the edge of the foliated granite. He jerked back just in time to avoid a tornado of 5.56mm projectiles from Silvestter, who was behind a rounded boulder slightly to the north-west. Steel-sheathed lead stung the side of the granite, zinged off with loud whines and threw out a cloud of stone fragments.

Old Friend! Are you going to make ME the victim? Camellion dropped the Ingram and pulled the Vega .45 and the Auto Mag from their holsters. It wasn't Silvestter but Nario Hokakawa who worried him at the moment.

Just before he had pulled back, he had seen Hokakawa starting to run from a rock. There was only one place that Hokakawa could be, one place he would want to be—on the other side of the short, protruding wall.

He's less than five feet away!

The Death Merchant had been in similar fixes, but he still wasn't happy about this one. A grenade would have solved the problem beautifully, if he had had one, which he didn't.

If? If I had any sense, I wouldn't be here!

An exuberant Silvestter was positive that the long chase was over. He had the Death Merchant where he wanted him. Camellion could not climb the sheer wall and he couldn't retreat along the side of the granite. To further bottle him up, Nario Hokakawa had succeeded in reaching the outside section of the small wall. Even now he was preparing to disable Camellion and jerk him out into the open. That's when Silvestter would deliver the killing blow. He wanted Camellion to know it, to see Death coming, to know that he had lost.

Hokakawa had reached into his pocket and had taken out a Ninja's *Nuzashi,* an eight foot steel chain whose links were the size of a bicycle chain and whose fighting end was equipped with a steel ball. Any chain can be deadly, especially a *Nuzashi* when in the hands of an expert who knew how to use it.

On the other side of the granite, Camellion decided that the best chance he had was to dart out, slam slugs into Hokakawa and, until he could get to Silvestter, trigger off shots to keep him down.

Camellion was preparing to jump when Hokakawa tossed the *Nuzashi.* With a loud swishing sound, the chain curved around the end of the wall and began doing its deadly work. The Death Merchant was unprepared for the attack and totally astonished when part of the chain slashed across his right hand and forced him to drop the Auto Mag. In an instant, the *Nuzashi* wrapped itself around his waist, the last three inches and the steel ball spinning over and twisting around the other links, so that he was imprisoned in a loop of steel.

The next thing he knew, he was being jerked violently sideways against the granite, hitting the wall with his left forearm, the sudden pain forcing his left hand open. The

Vega .45 autoloader dropped to the ground. He had only time to realize that he'd been trapped by a *Nuzashi;* then he was being pulled outward, to crash against the chest of a flat-faced Nario Hokakawa, a brutal-faced Hokakawa, who was grinning sadistically. Hokakawa stopped being over-confident when he saw that the *Nuzashi*, while it had closed around the Death Merchant's waist, had failed to enclose his arms. He had more doubts when Camellion's arms came up, the fingers of the right hand formed into a killing *Herabasami,* a Tiger's Mouth, the left hand slicing in for a *Shuto* sword-hand chop.

Hokakawa jerked his head to one side and dodged the Tiger Mouth strike, but the Shuto blow, landing on the side of his neck, made him gasp and almost lose his hold on the links of *Nuzashi.* He didn't want to fight Camellion. Knowing that Silvestter wanted the pleasure of killing the Death Merchant, Hokakawa let go of the chain and wrapped his thick arms around Camellion, locking his fingers in the small of the Death Merchant's back. As strong as two bulls, he lifted the Death Merchant off his feet and walked outward with him.

Camellion, the length of chain dangling from his waist, could hardly stand the pain in his spine. There were other complications for the Death Merchant, the first being that Hokakawa was holding him in such a way that his body was bent slightly backward, making it impossible to rain any kind of effective blows against the man's temples or the back of his neck.

Camellion liked the second part of the entanglement even less. Silvestter, now standing, had drawn a Puma woodsman knife and was holding it by the tip of the blade. Camellion, in agony, realized that Hokakawa was either going to lug him over to Silvestter, to be carved up, or spin him around so that Silvestter could toss the knife into his back. Either way—dead is dead!

Camellion began to strain and exert every bit of his strength and will power. Hokakawa tightened his hold and took several more steps. Camellion strained again.

"He kill you now pretty damn quick!" Hokakawa taunted and turned around.

With his back facing Silvestter, Camellion didn't have time to say any Our Fathers. With one last effort, he exerted himself, his eyes on Silvestter, who had raised the knife, preparatory to throwing it. Camellion succeeded in moving the upper half of his body forward and down. His teeth clamped on Hokakawa's left ear lobe, and he bit down with all his might, tasting blood. At the same time, Silvestter's arm drew back, the big steel blade glittering in the sun.

Hokakawa screamed in pain and his arms relaxed around the Death Merchant's waist. Camellion dropped and pulled his head down. He was pulling himself farther down when he heard the *swooosshhhhh* above his head and the loud *UHH!* jump from Hokakawa's mouth. He glanced up and saw that the knife had buried itself in Hokakawa's chest.

The dying Japanese stood there on wobbly legs, an expression of great surprise on his ugly face. He blinked several times and worked his mouth as if he disliked the taste of blood bubbling up in the hollow of his throat. His eyes closed, his arms jerked and he fell forward.

The Death Merchant saw none of this. He was propelling himself at a stunned Silvestter, the length of chain clanking on the stony surface of the ground. Silvestter seemed unable to comprehend what had happened. By the time he put it altogether and started to draw a Smith & Wesson autoloader, Camellion was on him, slamming a savage *Shuto* chop to his right wrist and aiming a deadly *Hon Nukite* spear hand at his solar plexus. His right wrist throbbing with pain, Silvestter spun on his left heel, ducked Camellion's spear hand and lashed out with a lightning quick right-legged *Mawashi Geri*, aimed at Camellion's face. He prepared to follow through with a *Fumikomi* front stamp kick to the stomach.

Silvestter received another shock—the speed with which the Death Merchant used his right arm to execute a *Ude uke* block to wreck his right-legged roundhouse kick and countered with a left-legged *Chungdan ap chagi*.

Nario Hokakawa had trained Silvestter well. Silvestter twisted his body, avoided Camellion's middle front snap kick, came in low and attacked with a left *Hira ken* knuckle blow to Camellion's chest and a *Seiken* forefist blow to the pit of Camellion's stomach. The Death Merchant bowed his body and turned slightly. Both of Silvestter's strikes missed.

Camellion was chain-lightning with a right *Seiryu Toh* palm edge aimed at the bridge of Silvestter's nose and a *Shuto* sword-hand geared to snap the collar bone and shove the jagged ends backward into the subclavian artery.

Silvestter bent his head and took the palm edge strike on the top of his head while he blocked the Shuto slice with a *Kake uke* hooking block. With his right hand he grabbed the chain around Camellion's waist and jerked him off balance. When Camellion fell toward him, Silvestter grabbed his shirt front with both hands, jumped, placed both feet on Camellion's stomach, fell backward, taking Camellion with him, and pushed out violently with both legs. Camellion went flying over his head.

It was Camellion's presence of mind that saved him from falling on, and breaking, his back. He twisted in midair and broke his fall with his hands and feet, thinking that he might have cracked his left knee in the process. He scrambled to his feet at the same time a now frightened Silvestter got to his and once more tried to grab the length of chain dangling from Camellion's waist. This time he missed. And so did the Death Merchant who had aimed a *Haishu* open backhand at the left side of Silvestter's neck. Silvestter ducked and tried a double handed *Nukite*. Camellion ducked and countered with a *Mawashi geri* inside roundhouse kick. Again Silvestter ducked. But he failed to see the *Ken tsui* bottom fist that slammed into his chest and staggered him; yet he managed not only to duck the Death Merchant's next strike, a terrific left *Haito* ridge-hand, but to grab Richard's left wrist with both hands.

Silvestter thought of trying a high *Mae geri* forward kick—*Oh no!* Camellion was too good, too dangerous, too deadly. Instead, before Camellion could regear his reflexes, Silvestter spun him around and sent him flying toward the short granite wall, so that he would slam against it with his back.

Unable to stop his momentum, Camellion hit the wall like a freight train, the smash knocking the wind out of him. Other than bruised, Camellion wasn't hurt. But he pretended to be, moaning and acting as if he were in great pain and could hardly move. The desperate and over-anxious Silvestter fell for the act. With a cry of victory, he came at Camellion with the speed of a meteor, both hands raised to deliver a series of *Nukite* chops.

At the last possible second, as both of Silvestter's hands were descending, Camellion dropped down, crawled between Silvestter's legs and reared up at the same instant that Silvestter's hands were coming down. Off balance, Silvestter yelled in panic and fell against the wall, his face hitting the rough granite. Before he had time to pull back, Camellion had crawled out behind him and was rearing up to smash him with a closed fist blow to the back of the head. Silvestter's already cut face crashed again into the stone, this time breaking his nose.

The Death Merchant jumped in and his arms shot out to apply a rear strangle hold. He placed his left hand on the back of Silvestter's head and, at the same time, crossed his right forearm under his neck from the right. He put his left elbow over Silvestter's left shoulder and locked it in place with his right hand.

I've got him!

In this position, all Camellion had to do was push with his left hand on the back of Silvestter's head and lean forward as he tightened his right forearm. When he did, Silvestter's neck would snap.

Camellion tightened his hold slightly, forced Silvestter to his knees, and got down on his own knees behind him.

"How do you like it, Silvestter?" he ground out. "How does it feel to know you have one foot in hell and the other one about to be chopped off?"

Silvestter did his best to get at Camellion's head and neck with his hands. His efforts were futile. Every time he tried, Camellion tightened his hold, cutting off his air and forcing him to drop his arms.

Spittle flecked Silvestter's mouth. He tried to talk. The Death Merchant wouldn't let him, snarling, "I'm not interested in anything you have to say. But you can do me a favor. After you drop into hell, give your father my regards. You'll find him sitting on Satan's lap."

Camellion pushed with his left hand on the back of Silvestter's head, tightened his right forearm and leaned forward. There was a dry-twig snapping sound and Silvestter's arms and legs jerked. Just as fast, he went limp. The Death Merchant released his hold, got up and looked down at the corpse. Cleveland Winston Silvestter was not a pretty sight. His head lay at an odd angle. There was a fixed snarl on his face, his lips drawn back over his teeth. His eyes were wide open and staring at the wide blue bowl of the sky, seeing nothing.

Camellion looked toward the south. A large helicopter

was landing a quarter of a mile away—*It's unmarked! It can't be the New Mexico police!* A second chopper was hovering in the vicinity, waiting for the larger craft to sit down. . . .

Aftermath

Camellion leaned against the helicopter and sipped hot coffee that Gregory Lammwillow had poured from a stainless steel thermos. A sad-faced man, who gave the impression that he was perpetually in mourning, Lammwillow was the President of Simco Industries, which meant that he was the CIA Station Chief in Santa Fe. He didn't seem to mind when Courtland Grojean walked over from the larger helicopter and told him to take a walk.

"It's been an hour since you've landed," Camellion said, "and you haven't asked about 'The Box.' I trust you know something I don't."

Grojean smiled and pulled a cigar from his shirt pocket. "Boden and Meunier are alive. I just received the report. Some of our people found those two worthies trying to hide out in the rocks. They'll be only too happy to tell us all about the tracing device. We'll get it."

Camellion took another sip of coffee, his cold blue eyes on Grojean. *By God, I think he went out and bought new clothes for this occasion!*

The CIA boss wore dark brown gabardine pants with deep cargo pockets, a shirt to match, and jodhpurs so new they didn't have a crease anywhere, the brown leather as slick as glass. A brown continental corduroy hat sat just so on his head.

"And all this time, you knew what Silvestter and his crowd were up to?" Camellion said, his tone skirting on the edge of angry. Not too far away, he saw CIA men carrying wounded gunmen and setting the stretchers none too gently on the ground.

Grojean carefully bit off the end of his cigar, cleared his throat and looked directly at the Death Merchant.

"Silvestter managed to give the FBI the slip. We're a lot more efficient than the ordinary Feds. When our contacts in the L.A. underworld gave us the word that Den-

179

bow was hiring hoodlums, it was a simple matter to figure out what he had in mind. All we had to do was sit back and wait."

"While I did the dirty work!"

Grojean was not a man to deny anything that was glaringly obvious.

"Why not? You're the expert, and we couldn't move in on Silvestter below. It would have drawn too much attention. And to be honest about it, it took a lot of wire-pulling and some tall stories to keep the New Mexico police out of it. By the way, we stopped Carlos Martinez from coming up here today."

Camellion took another sip of coffee. "You knew about him, then. It figures. I assumed that Lammwillow put a tail on me."

"Well, you're done here," Grojean said, satisfied. "The boys are collecting your weapons." He lit his cigar and puffed mightily.

"They won't find one. I hid a Mannlicher rifle. I'll have to get it."

"I suppose you're going back to Texas from here?" Grojean said, a curious gleam in his eyes.

A warning bell rang in the Death Merchant's mind. He played it straight. "For a couple of weeks."

"Uh huh. Damon and Pythias, your pet pigs."

Camellion smiled. "That's right. I have to pick them and my cattle and horses up from a good neighbor. I must also find a dependable man to look after my ranch. But you're not asking just to make conversation. What's really on your mind?"

"Alaska!"

**He'll fight anyone—on either side of the law—
who seeks to destroy the American way of life.**

SPECIAL PREVIEW

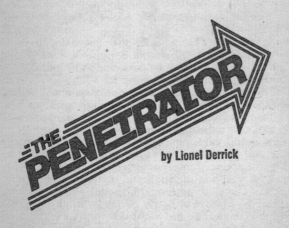

by Lionel Derrick

*In Pinnacle's explosive action/adventure series, The Pene-
trator, tough, hard-hitting hero Mark Hardin, is a warrior
without uniform or rank, dedicated to protecting the American way of life and pledged to eradicating the criminal elements in our country. His reason for living and dying is the
same—to stamp out crime and corruption wherever he finds
it. Follow the Penetrator as he travels from place to place,
leaving his personal symbol of retribution, a chipped blue
flint arrowhead, on the bodies of society's deadliest enemies.*

Mark Hardin started out as an angry, bitter young man,
striking at forces a little bit bigger than himself. Since 1973 he

has become a swift hand of justice, delivering retribution to those who see themselves above the law.

The Penetrator is, of course, an action-adventure saga. Violence and crime are all around us. After a few slashes at some of the evil tentacles, Mark realized this. *The Penetrator* series chronicles one man's answer to the pervasive wickedness that seems to infect every level of our society.

"So what? It didn't happen to me," and "I don't want to get involved," have become the watchwords of the day. Mark Hardin didn't want to get involved either. *But he did.* After the bloody hacking and smashing at Don Pietro Scarelli's Mafia kingdom in Los Angeles, the nefarious and sinister regime of the Fraulein in Las Vegas, and the unholy alliance of SIE in the nation's capital, Mark's cooler reflections began to take hold.

Mark still doesn't like what he often has to do. He takes no pride in his exploits, other than a job well done. Yet it is something he believes must be done, and as he puts it, "I happen to be the best there is at doing it."

The Penetrator asks no quarter and gives none; he tackles the toughest jobs with the most awesome odds, and, after more than five years of battling, he has managed to stay alive, although sometimes only barely.

Mark Hardin came out of the Vietnam War an expert line crosser and headhunter, a master with every hand weapon used by the army. After exposing a huge black market that siphoned off vital war materials and supplies needed by front-line troops—implicating several high-ranking army officers in the process—Mark was nearly beaten to death by those involved who thought he had violated the service code.

He survived with an intense desire to live. After his discharge he found a retired college professor who had a hideaway in the Calico Mountains. At the Stronghold, a cleverly concealed underground in an old borax mine, Mark began his recuperation, under the supervision of the professor and an ancient Indian, David Red Eagle, who discovered Mark's Indian heritage and soon made Mark aware of his Cheyenne ancestry. As Mark regained his strength, he absorbed all of the Indian lore, skills, and an understanding of the ancient religion and ceremonies.

Soon Mark met the professor's niece, Donna, and they fell in love. Donna helped Mark track down his family's records in the Los Angeles county courthouse. Without meaning to, they touched on a sensitive nerve—a project the Los Angeles

Mafia was working on—and the Mob decided to eliminate both Mark and Donna. A spinning, tumbling car crash down a steep canyon followed. Mark was thrown clear, but Donna, trapped inside the twisted steel, was burned to death and Mark couldn't help her.

Mark, Professor Haskins, and David Red Eagle formed a crime-fighting trio and swore undying vengeance against the Mafia and every other type of crime. They would battle evil, corruption, murder, arson, graft, and white-collar crime everywhere.

Mark's first fight was with the Mafia in Los Angeles, where he wiped out a huge heroin ring and scooped up hundreds of thousands of dollars from the criminals to stock the crime-fighting treasury. He's been in battle ever since, delivering retribution to those who see themselves above the law.

For the Penetrator, the future seems unlimited. Evil, ambitious, scheming people continue to plague mankind. As long as Mark has the skills and the strength necessary, he will endeavor to fight them. He also knows that someday he may be a fraction of a second too slow, or in the wrong place at the wrong time, and his own private war against crime will be over. But until that time the Penetrator will continue to take on all comers, keep seeking out the enemy who tramples on the little people of the world, and with deadly efficiency destroy the evil and push the scales a little further toward justice.

Beginning with the twenty-seventh episode of *The Penetrator,* readers will be able to familiarize themselves with the firearms, edged weapons, support equipment, and vehicles used by Mark Hardin. Each illustrated entry in "The Penetrator's Combat Catalog" will include performance data, evaluations, availability, and price, providing an informative and indispensable guide for fans.

Finally, through contacts in the media, the armed forces of several countries, government and law-enforcement agencies, a broad base of intelligence has been laid down so that the Penetrator will remain a step ahead of everyone else in locating trouble spots around the world.

There'll be plenty of surprises along the way, as the Penetrator continues his relentless battle against any and all—on either side of the law—who seek to destroy the American way of life.

* * *

Lionel Derrick is the pen name of an ex-crime reporter and former Air Force pilot with flying time in both Korea and Vietnam. Currently unmarried, he is enjoying a slice of *la dolce vita* while restoring an antique hotel in central Kansas, and spends part of his time in California with his two children.